Praise for

THE QUEEN'S MUSICIAN

"The protagonist is a real historical figure, though little is known about him, which makes him a perfect point of departure for a dramatic and engrossing reimagining of history. It's an era that both historians and novelists have extensively covered, but Johnson's work remains an original and worthwhile effort. A thoughtful, dramatically gripping work of historical fiction."

—*KIRKUS REVIEWS*

"Johnson pays attention to historical detail without allowing it to turn encyclopedic, and even though we know how it all ends, the author makes us want to carry on reading regardless. Overall, this is a heartfelt and thoughtful tale of the fragility of love. Very highly recommended."

—*READERS' FAVORITE*, FIVE STARS

"A gripping, unforgettable story of the gentle Tudor musician Mark Smeaton . . . In the terrifying free fall of Queen Anne Boleyn . . . innocent men will be condemned. Will Mark escape? Beautifully written and impossible to put down. I had tears in my eyes."

—STEPHANIE COWELL, American Book Award winner and author of *Claude & Camille* and *The Boy in the Rain*

"A captivating and deeply moving retelling of Anne Boleyn's dramatic fall, told through a fresh and compelling perspective. This beautifully written novel brings history to life with such emotional depth that it brought me to tears."

—CLAIRE RIDGWAY, author of *The Fall of Anne Boleyn: A Countdown*

The
QUEEN'S MUSICIAN

The

QUEEN'S
MUSICIAN

A Novel

MARTHA JEAN JOHNSON

Published by SparkPress, a BookSparks imprint,
A division of SparkPoint Studio, LLC
Phoenix, Arizona, USA, 85007
www.gosparkpress.com

Published 2025
Printed in the United States of America
Print ISBN: 978-1-68463-310-4
E-ISBN: 978-1-68463-311-1
Library of Congress Control Number: 2025900998

Book design by Stacey Aaronson

For musicians, one and all

A time thou hadst above thy poor degree.

SIR THOMAS WYATT, 1536
on the life of Mark Smeaton

CONTENTS

PART ONE

The Cardinal

1

THE ARC OF THE PLOT

May 1, 1536

Mark Smeaton, Tower of London

I can hear the boatmen rowing on the Thames. Their oars swish the water, and their voices float up to my cell. They greet each other and talk of the weather and the changing of the tides. Their bodies must ache from their menial labor, but I would trade places with them. They aren't shackled inside the Tower. They can look up and see the sky.

Up until yesterday, I considered myself fortunate, more fortunate than most. I was the king's favorite musician and lived comfortably in his palaces. Making music never seemed like work. But Thomas Cromwell sent for me. I rode to his house and played for his guests. Afterward, I took a cup of wine with him, and the conversation turned to Anne Boleyn. That's when my luck ran out.

Today, guards led me through a maze of halls, opened a cell, and shoved me in. They forced me to sit on the floor while they readied their jangling chains—this is a sound you don't forget. They locked my wrists in the metal cuffs and hooked the chains to the wall. One of them said, "You're as good as dead, my friend. No one can help you now." I held my head erect and met his gaze. "Rot in hell" was his response.

In my cell, a mere thread of light slips in through a narrow window. My clothes smell of the sweat of fear. Images from last night haunt me, and I try to erase them—the airless room, Cromwell's thugs, one of them pulling the poker from the fire. It's over, I think, or maybe I dreamed it. More than once, I have shaken myself: *Wake up. Open your eyes. This cannot be real.* I pray to be back in my palace rooms and feel smooth white linens against my cheek. Yet hours have passed since my ordeal began. I have to accept what my senses tell me.

The arc of the plot is clearer now. I can see its value to the king. We all noticed his pent-up fury and desire to be rid of her. Their quarreling rarely ceased. Doors slammed; goblets thrown—the venom spewed between them. So, Cromwell devised a plan to remove her, one that's certain to succeed. He claims she has taken lovers, including His Majesty's closest friends. For reasons I can only guess at, he added my name: Mark Smeaton, player of instruments and composer of song, admired as a singer and lutenist.

Is the guard right? Am I as good as dead? Sometimes I barely care. Most stays in the Tower end in execution or madness. I've heard of prisoners who lose all reason listening to the screams of men on the rack. But I push these terrors aside and concentrate on a few pitiful seeds of hope: I haven't been tried and convicted. I did what Cromwell wanted, and he promised I would live.

He told me the queen will be sent away and the others charged with treason. He said that if I confessed, I could leave England in secret. His "persuasion" was persuasive, and I signed his evil paper. He didn't say how long I would have to wait. It could be days or weeks or months. Meanwhile I will pass the time in wretchedness, hating myself for what I've done.

And it could all be a lie anyway. Cromwell isn't known as a truthful man.

Only one pursuit distracts me from my darkest thoughts—I remember the life I lost. Last week, I took a ride in the countryside and stopped my horse to take in the view. I lazily daydreamed of a luminous young woman, the one who owns my heart and inspires my music. I thought of a joke I had shared with my dearest friend, a man I trust without reservation. The hills and trees were barely green, the new color ousting the old. High in the sky, the sun sparkled cleanly, as it does in the early spring. I picture myself that April morning, free to think commonplace thoughts, free to make plans for next week.

But I am trapped within this cell, my prospects bleak at best. I will have ample time to contemplate all I did when Anne Boleyn was queen. Perhaps then I'll understand. The existence I knew is over—whether I face exile or death at twenty-four. Now, my only wish is to see the two people I have cherished above all others . . . just once more . . . for a few minutes. I doubt Cromwell will allow it.

2

UNHEEDED WARNINGS

Seven Years Earlier, October 1529
Mark Smeaton, Hampton Court Palace

My lantern offered little light as I took the steps two at a time. But I had climbed these winding stairs since I was seven years old. I knew every stone and curve. Summoned in the dead of night, I wasn't sure what I would find.

Only minutes before, Old John had pounded on my door.

"Get up. Master Peter wants you. You're to go to the chapel now."

The elderly servant held a beeswax candle and spoke sharply, which was rare for him. *There must be a flood or a fire,* I thought, as I jolted out of bed. The choirmaster must need my help to save the valuable instruments and musical manuscripts. Why else would he send for me before dawn? But I heard no clanging bells or men shouting—nothing to suggest danger to the church. Old John offered no explanation, saying only, "I'll get you a lantern. Look for him upstairs."

"What's the matter?"

"You'll find out soon enough."

After splashing cold water on my face, I pulled on my clothes and boots. Racing through the palace, I scarcely noticed the cardinal's imposing Flemish tapestries and his fine Italian bronzes. I encountered no one, apart from a few sleepy servants and the household watchmen, some leaning their heads against the wall and dozing since no one was awake to reprimand them. Outside, I crossed the gardens, normally bursting with red and gold flowers planted in circles and squares. But the blooms were gray in the moonlight, and cold air chilled the nape of my neck. I wished I had worn my cloak.

Inside the chapel, I rushed through the warren of upstairs spaces where the church musicians worked. Master Peter waited in the narrow chamber that led to the organ, the area brightly lit with torches. I had sung for him there years before, on the day I came to Hampton Court to join the boys' choir. Later, as his apprentice, I sat in this room copying manuscripts and tuning instruments, whatever the choirmaster required.

Master Peter balanced a lute on his lap, an extraordinary instrument, its amber wood gleaming, the body decorated with dark patterns and swirls. "This is for you," he said, "from Cardinal Wolsey." He handed it to me.

"It's wonderful." I touched the strings and listened as honeyed notes filled the room. With a lute like this, a player could enchant his audience. I guessed it was worth a substantial sum.

The cardinal was often generous, but I had never received such a costly gift. I assumed it was a reward for my performance for the king the week before. The royal visit had absorbed the entire household for days, from musicians to servants to cooks. By most accounts, His Majesty had enjoyed the grand feast the cardinal had planned for him, but only one moment mattered for me. I had played and sung for the king of England and won his compliments. I was seventeen. This was the most notable event of my life.

As I recalled my triumph, I noticed the dullness in Master Peter's face. He seemed exhausted—he was my teacher, always kind, but exacting. I owed my skill and love of music to him.

"It's a farewell gift," he said, his voice taut. "The cardinal is leaving for York."

"For York? For how long?"

"He won't return. He wants you to have the lute and asks that you pray for him."

"But why? Is he ill?"

Master Peter looked down, seeming to weigh his words before he began his slow reply.

"The cardinal is disgraced," he said, "and dismissed from his royal offices. He has given this palace and all within it to His Majesty, in the hope of finding forgiveness."

"But what has he done wrong?"

"Some say he has failed the king. Some claim he is corrupt."

"Is it because of Anne Boleyn and the annulment?"

Another pause, but this time Master Peter looked at me directly. "Probably."

Like all of England, Hampton Court swarmed with rumors about the king's "Great Matter"—whether the pope would annul his marriage to Queen Katherine so he could wed Anne Boleyn. His Majesty wanted a younger wife who could bear him princes. The queen's only son had died as a babe, and by this time, she was unlikely to have more children. As lord chancellor, Cardinal Wolsey's task was to persuade the Church of Rome to grant the annulment. He had already pursued this mission for several years.

"But the cardinal has done all he can," I said. "It's the pope who won't agree."

In truth, His Majesty's case seemed weak to me, but who was I to say? The argument was that the king's union with Queen Katherine was sinful because she had married his older brother first—Prince Arthur who died at fifteen. Some clerics said the Bible forbids a widow from marrying her husband's brother although the passages seemed open to interpretation. But I understood why so many people opposed the annulment. The king and queen had been man and wife for decades, and I never heard anyone complain about it until Anne Boleyn came along.

"I don't think this is the cardinal's fault," I added for good measure. My own view was that if the cardinal, with all his skills and connections, couldn't produce the annulment for the king, no one else could either.

"You shouldn't talk about His Majesty's dealings," the choirmaster said, speaking quietly but with authority. "This topic is not for you."

I nodded, accepting his judgment. I always listened to him. Until this night, I had never worried about the king's Great Matter. People gossiped about it, but none of it affected me. I viewed His Majesty's marital predicament the way you might think of a fairy tale about an imaginary ruler in a far-off land. I didn't care who the king divorced or married or what the pope decreed.

"But you must prepare yourself to live differently," Master Peter continued. "Hampton Court is now the king's."

My stomach tightened when I heard these words—as the reality of my situation became clear. If Cardinal Wolsey no longer owned Hampton Court, what would happen to me? Would Master Peter still be choirmaster? Would I be sent away? Naturally, I pitied the cardinal. He had never spoken a harsh word to me—not that he had spoken to me much at all. But I had entered his service as a ragged child and thrived because of his charity. I had no idea how I would earn my keep if I no longer lived at Hampton Court. I had no family to take me in.

Master Peter took the lute from me and set it in its case. "There's a letter for you." He held it up. The red wax seal depicted the Cornish crows in Cardinal Wolsey's coat of arms. "You can read it later," he said, placing it beside the lute before fastening the case's leather bindings.

"Maybe the king will change his mind," I suggested. "The cardinal has served him for many years."

"I doubt it. The gift of Hampton Court may ease the king's fury, but the cardinal has powerful enemies." I thought I heard a trace of anger in the choirmaster's response, but he spoke in a gentler tone when he looked at me. He must have noticed my fear.

"His Eminence has given you more than a lute, Mark. He has given you an education and an honorable skill. You did well when you performed for His Majesty. There may be a place for you among the court musicians or at another noble house. I will try to arrange it."

"Thank you, sir." I was reassured. Master Peter was a man of his word.

"Your years at Hampton Court have given you all you need to make your way in the world. Come, I want you to see."

He motioned for me to follow, and we climbed the narrow stairs to the roof. From there we looked down at the courtyard where servants held torches near a door. Two workers heaved a heavy trunk onto a horse-drawn cart and began securing it for the journey. A richly dressed nobleman walked out of the building and mounted his charger, calling to the workers to hurry. The cardinal's steward, George Cavendish, and his clerk, Thomas Cromwell, emerged and waited silently, standing near the wall.

When the cardinal appeared, I was shocked by the change in him: a robust, rosy man suddenly stooped and frail. He wore a simple brown cloak, an everyday garment. His sumptuous silks and gold chains were gone. Cavendish and Cromwell helped him climb onto the cart, but he faltered and had to try again. I could see the effort he used to pull himself up to sit next to the driver. Somewhere a cock crowed, and Cavendish and Cromwell stepped back, their faces emotionless. Evidently, they would stay at Hampton Court rather than travel with the cardinal.

As the cart pulled away, more riders gathered—a royal "escort" for the journey. Some sported the ornate fashions of courtiers while others wore the king's colors—they seemed to be guards or soldiers. All the horses were magnificent, outfitted with bridles, saddles, and barding. Several mounted gentlemen mocked the cardinal's plain clothing. One called him a "cur." A young nobleman spat at him and claimed he buggered the choir boys. The others whooped and laughed. This was a lie. The cardinal had never harmed children, though I knew of priests who did. Yet now that he was powerless, his enemies took joy in slandering him.

A week before, the cardinal had been the most formidable man in England. Some grumbled he was a second king. But his opponents had destroyed him with little warning. I could barely take it in.

Master Peter and I weren't the only ones who came out at dawn to watch the cardinal leave, our true thoughts hidden in our hearts. Dozens of others had gathered along the roadside. A few jeered and shouted the king's name, but most prayed for a man who was respectful and decent in his bearing. For all his preening and politicking, he had been good to us.

In those days, I barely knew Thomas Cromwell, though many talked of his cleverness. Since he was older and clerked in the law, I seldom ran into him. He paid no attention to me. Most expected Cromwell's fortunes to fade after the cardinal gave up Hampton Court—being tied to a fallen man is no way to succeed. But that's not what happened, not at all. In the years to come, Cromwell and I would meet many times and in varied circumstances.

3

METICULOUS PREPARATIONS

One Month Later, November 1529

Madge Shelton, Hampton Court Palace

"Make sure the wardrobe is in order," my mother told me as she closed the door. I relished my moment in charge. For nearly an hour, I watched the serving boys haul my cousin's belongings into her rooms—some twenty wooden boxes of varied sizes, each carved with a flowery "AB." They stacked the cases wherever I directed, and I thanked them when they had finished. This was my mother's rule. "God has given you a privileged life," she would say to me. "You have a duty to be kind."

The housekeeper had carefully prepared the rooms, and I walked through them admiring the thick carpets and expensive furniture—every chest, table, and chair was a work of art. I had heard people describe Cardinal Wolsey's extravagant dwellings. Many had envied him, and more than a few questioned the source of his wealth. He wasn't wellborn—his father was a cook or a butcher or a baker, some kind of laboring man. Yet however the cardinal came by his wonderful possessions, he must have regretted having to leave them behind for a harsh exile in the North.

When my mother returned, the housekeeper appeared to assure us that whatever we wanted would be provided. She curtsied to my mother. "At your service, Lady Shelton." Then she smiled and turned to me. "Mistress Shelton," she said, taking care to bow again.

She was still a young woman and must have served the cardinal since she was a girl. I wasn't sure what happened to the household when a disgraced man surrendered his palace to the king, but I hoped she would fare well.

"And we are grateful," my mother said, always correct and polite. "My daughter will unpack the traveling cases and organize the wardrobe. Will you send a woman to assist her?"

"With certainty, ma'am. May I show you the other rooms?"

My mother instructed me: "Madge, see that all is arranged before your cousin arrives. Check that everything is in its place." I had joined my mother as lady-in-waiting to Anne Boleyn a year earlier. My work included making sure her numerous garments were ready and waiting for her when she traveled from place to place.

Minutes later, Betty peeked around the door, and she would prove herself an efficient and helpful girl. We spent several hours hanging pomanders in wardrobes and tucking bundles of lavender in drawers. We unpacked and stored my cousin's nightdresses, chemises, underskirts, overskirts, bodices, gowns, and capes. I memorized the location of dozens of garments so I would be ready if she asked for "the chemise embroidered with rosebuds" or "the bodice with the green velvet ties."

Betty ran her fingers over the silver threading in the brocade skirts and touched the pearls adorning the French hoods. She marveled at the beaded silken boots, taffeta shoes, and fur-lined velvet cloaks. My cousin carried her ever-expanding collection of necklaces, brooches, and earrings with her when she traveled—the padlocked box stayed at her side. The king gave her some new jewel every few weeks as his passion for her grew.

Anne Boleyn's father was my mother's brother, so our family was part of the Boleyn clan. My mother reminded me daily of our good fortune. "If she becomes queen, you and your sister will marry very well. All the Boleyns will gain." That's the business of mothers, I suppose—finding landed, titled husbands for their daughters. My mother was devoted to this cause. "Your day will come soon," she would say, and I would immediately think, "Not too soon, I hope." At that point in my life, knights and princes in legends intrigued me more than the toadying men at court.

Although Anne Boleyn was my cousin, I had barely known her growing up. She was a decade older than me and had lived in France when I was a child. When I turned sixteen, I became one of her ladies, and by this time, everyone in England knew the king wanted to marry her, if only Pope Clement would allow it. In my new position, I saw her cast her spell on His Majesty and many others as well. She was openly flirtatious and quick to speak her mind, unlike the other ladies at court. She sprinkled her conversations with French phrases, which she spoke in a whispery, teasing tone. These traits seemed to arouse most men.

She had long resented Wolsey, complaining that he was dawdling in getting the annulment and busy enriching himself. When she finally convinced the king to dismiss him, she viewed Hampton Court as her personal prize. In this setting, she could present herself as King Henry's queen, whether the pope approved or not.

Occasionally, I saw the private woman, as much as anyone was allowed to see. When she rested or readied herself to be with His Majesty, she was quiet, as if she were memorizing a line of poetry or thinking through a strategy. She must have understood the long odds she faced and the obstacles that stood in her way: the pope, the people's love for Queen Katherine, even His Majesty's well-known fickleness and procrastination.

Over the years, the king had pursued and discarded many women while Queen Katherine looked away. Anne Boleyn's older sister was one of them, although this affair had taken place before I understood such things. I asked my mother what had happened, but she said, "We never speak of this. It's better for everyone." Since Mary Boleyn lived in Hertfordshire with her husband's people, I had only met her several times. She was buxom and agreeable, and I could see why the king might like her. Her very dull husband had prospered far beyond anyone's expectations for him. I only recently realized why.

My cousin Anne was subtler and more determined—always several steps ahead of everyone else. As her lady-in-waiting, I watched her flatter the king and accept his lengthy gazes and splendid gifts. She enticed him but never admitted him to her bed. Instead, she slipped the idea of marriage into nearly every exchange. Whenever His Majesty worried that he had no sons, she would kiss her forefinger and delicately apply it to his lips. Softly and ever-so-sweetly, she would mention that Queen Katherine was more than forty: "*Elle ne peut pas vous donner ce que vous voulez.*" According to my cousin George, her younger brother, getting the annulment was her idea.

But ending a royal marriage to a Spanish princess was complicated, and several privy counselors warned it could lead to a war. Every now and then, my cousin fretted about the delay and the pope's intransigence, fearing the king's passion for her would fade. "His Majesty is known to be changeable in his romantic preferences," she would say lightly. "Today, he is ardent, but how long will his fervor last?"

Those nearby would reassure her, and she would laugh as she glanced in the mirror. There she saw, as I did, an elegant, intelligent woman who had just turned twenty-eight.

꩜

Around three o'clock, the boys returned to remove the empty cases, and I let Betty go back to her other chores. I wanted to explore Wolsey's fabled palace while I still had the time. Once my cousin arrived, I would be far too busy serving her. For a while, I wandered the halls and galleries, as servants continually bowed and scurried away. Most rooms were unoccupied, and I wondered what had happened to all the people. I saw men in the king's livery emptying cupboards and counting silver goblets, bowls, and plates. They stood in front of tapestries and paintings, discussing their subject and estimated value while a clerk made notes. Clearly, His Majesty wanted an inventory of his new property.

I crossed a courtyard and headed to the chapel, the most beautiful in England, some said. The entry was, indeed, impressive, but I stopped short when I stepped inside. Columns and arches stretched high to the ceiling, and statues lined the walls. Sunlight filtered in through tall windows where jewel-colored glass illustrated the lives of saints. My favorite was the portly Saint Francis who sat surrounded by a bunch of rabbits and was feeding lambs and donkeys from his hands. Candles flickered on the altar, and the smell of incense lingered after the midday Mass.

I had hoped for a peaceful interlude, but I heard angry voices booming from the front. Three men were quarreling, and I recognized two of them: Charles Brandon, the Duke of Suffolk and the king's brother-in-law; and Sir Henry Norris, His Majesty's favorite groom. The duke's voice ricocheted in the empty chapel:

"And now it is the king's."

They stood next to a large, open Bible displayed on a chest. The third man wore sober but expensive clothing, seemingly one of Wolsey's men. "My lord, this is his only request. His Majesty gave this Bible to the cardinal to commemorate the Field of the Cloth of Gold."

My father and uncles still told stories about this lavish summit that took place when I was a child. King Henry met the king of France in the Pale of Calais, and each ruler displayed his fabulous wealth during the ceremonies and games. The opulence was unrivaled—even the tents and banners were tinted with gold. Many claimed the event was His Majesty's greatest diplomatic achievement, but my father said Wolsey had planned it all.

"Cavendish, you have no say in this." The duke's chest puffed out as his anger grew.

This man, Cavendish, bowed deeply to him and Sir Henry. "It would be a compassionate gesture, my lords, toward a man of God who served the king for many years."

Suffolk spat out a series of vulgar oaths aimed at both Cavendish and the cardinal. He finished with, "Better to throw the bloody thing in the Thames rather than let Wolsey have it."

Cavendish stood his ground but addressed Norris rather than Suffolk. "Sir Henry, holding this Bible would give the cardinal a small measure of comfort. He is ill and in despair."

Norris considered for a moment and then lifted and closed the Bible and handed it to Wolsey's man. Suffolk continued to fume. "You're giving it to Wolsey? That sniveling, buggering traitor? The king will be furious."

"No, I think not," Norris responded. "His Majesty is not vindictive. He is a kind and forgiving sovereign."

Compared to others close to the king, Sir Henry Norris was quieter and more discreet. He was a family man whose wife and children lived on his estates in the countryside. He and the king had been friends since their younger days.

Cavendish put the Bible under his arm, and I noticed the binding's sparkling gemstones as he left the chapel. Suffolk strode out, following some feet behind. Only Sir Henry acknowledged me, saying, "Mistress Shelton." I bowed, and then I had this glorious space to myself at last.

I began my tour of the chapel by walking up the center aisle, delighting in my leisure and basking in the marvelous light. I made sure to pray for my family's safety and thank God for His many gifts to us. Then, I sat in a pew, my mind turning to the changes of the past few years—my cousin's rise, the Boleyns' sudden prominence, my own arrival at court. Compared to my earlier life in Norfolk, I wore prettier dresses and danced with clever, ambitious men. I had even danced with the king.

At the same time, I couldn't help but notice His Majesty's tendency to turn against those he once favored, including Queen Katherine, his wife of twenty years. He had moved her to a moldy castle in the hills and refused to let her daughter visit. He paid her ladies to spy on her and seized her jewels. These he grandly presented to my cousin, one glistening gift at a time: a sapphire ring, a garnet necklace, a diamond bangle for the wrist. He had banished Wolsey, who had served him for decades, and sent the ailing old churchman to York.

Still at home in Norfolk, my little sister Mary imagined being in my cousin's shoes. "I wish I could marry the king," she would say, "and become queen of England." She made crowns for herself out of fabric twisted with ribbons and gave orders to her dolls and pets. But I never envied my cousin or her gowns or jewels or all the people flocking to see her. In many ways, I found her thinking inconceivable. In my view, King Henry was too unreliable, besides being grumpy and as old as my father. There wasn't enough gold in England to make me want to be his queen.

As I turned to leave the chapel, a young man my own age entered from a side door, the handsomest being I had seen in months. He wore the cardinal's livery, and I asked his name.

"Mark Smeaton, ma'am, one of the cardinal's musicians. I hope to play for you."

He bowed, and I introduced myself even though I didn't have to, given his lower station. "Margaret Shelton . . . I serve the Lady Anne Boleyn. She arrives with His Majesty tomorrow."

He smiled and bowed more deeply. "Then it would indeed be my honor to play for you." *What a shame he isn't a gentleman*, I remember thinking. He certainly looked like a prince. Master Smeaton was an agreeable change from the chattering peacocks I met at court, but he needed to learn to use the past tense when speaking of Wolsey. His patron was out of favor. My cousin had won the day.

4

THE CARDINAL'S LAST FEAST

November 1529

Mark Smeaton, Hampton Court Palace

I repeatedly told myself I had nothing to fear while I waited for news about my future. I spent my time practicing and helping Master Peter at the church. Almost every day, I read the cardinal's letter: "Your gifts are rare, my boy. You may not know how rare. When you play and sing, I hear the angels whispering. I pray you will prosper and find joy in life. May Our Merciful Lord protect you." A few words he didn't have to write. His belief in me cheered me.

Soon the king would arrive at Hampton Court with the notorious Anne Boleyn. In the household, many whispered that she was the one who hated the cardinal and coveted his palace. Some called her "the French whore" or "the concubine." Others went further, providing vivid descriptions of her hands, breasts, and private parts, said to be those of a witch. Much of it was farfetched, and I was secretly curious to see the woman who was considered so alluring and yet so dangerous and malicious.

With my own prospects uncertain, I walked through the palace's galleries and staterooms, remembering the past and wondering what tomorrow would bring. The king's agents had already ousted many who served the cardinal. In this case, loyalty to one man made you suspect to another.

In the Great Hall, men were removing the Flemish tapestries, and I watched as the workers took them down and rolled them up on the floor. I asked what would replace them.

"His Majesty's banners. The king's colors will cover the walls."

"What will happen to the tapestries?"

"Greenwich," the man said. "We're taking them to Greenwich— they're worth a fortune. Your cardinal was rich for a churchman."

Knights on white chargers, fire-breathing dragons, fair ladies with flowers in their hair. When I was a child, I used to go to the Great Hall when it was empty so I could gaze at the tapestries at length. Then I would stand in the center of the room, twirling in its warming light. I imagined myself a knight defending a maiden or a troubadour roving exotic lands.

I suppose it's natural to dwell on the past during times of up- heaval—a device to hold onto what will disappear. Standing where I had dreamed of such adventures, I thought of my boyhood and the decision I made when I was seven years old, when I decided to leave my family.

⚜

Cardinal Wolsey's father was a butcher, and his enemies mocked his humble birth. But his rise from such low beginnings gave hope to people like me. I admired him, and I wasn't alone.

My own father was a carpenter—he died shortly after I left home. He brought our family to England from Flanders when I was still an infant. I have no memory of the journey. But I could draw a picture of our shed on the River Aire and the tools my father used. I can still see his rough hands and the tawny dust that covered his apron and seeped into his clothes. Yet what I recall most is the hunger and my father giving me his bread. He had hoped his life would be easier in England, but that was not to be. He had little business, and his customers often cheated him and mocked his accent. Most of the English hated the "filthy Flemings."

My mother taught me lullabies and folksongs as she cooked and scrubbed, trying to make our dingy shed a home. When I was five or six, I began collecting coins by singing along the road to the village green. One day the parish priest heard me and asked me to sing at the Mass on Christmas market day. This was how my new life began.

At dusk, the country people filled the small candlelit church, and bayberry scented the air. I sang a traditional carol describing trumpeting angels and lowly beasts rejoicing at Christ's birth. After I finished, a fat man in a red robe and hat spoke to me and raised his fingers over my head. I never forgot his words: "Your song gives glory to God, my boy, and joy to those who hear it."

He was a very important visitor, they told me later—a cardinal who advised the king.

The next morning, a well-dressed man came to our shed to talk to my father. Their conversation ended when the visitor said, "I'll wait for your answer outside."

My father knelt beside me. "Would you like to live in a great man's palace and sing in a magnificent church?" He touched my cheek with his calloused fingers. "You will be in the choir and study music. Would you like to do this?"

My mother stood behind me, her hand touching the side of my head. I felt her body shudder, but she never spoke. I told my father yes.

The next morning, I watched my mother wrap my belongings in an old cloth sack—a threadbare shirt, mended socks, and a small toy horse with a saddle and stirrups cleverly carved into the wood. My father had worked most of the night to finish it, his parting gift to me.

"Your family is proud of you," my mother told me. "You will go to school. Your father dreams that you will become a famous Flemish musician like those who serve the kings of Spain." My baby brother sat on his pallet on the floor and giggled while my mother kissed my forehead and then my fingers. When the man came to take me, she held me close and whispered, "We will pray for you every day of our lives. You will always be our child." My father had walked into the town early that morning. He couldn't bear to watch me go.

I didn't want to leave them, but even then, I knew the rules. The cardinal had offered me a way out of poverty, and my family could not refuse. During the journey to Hampton Court, the cardinal's man told me he had given my father a bag of money, enough for my family to eat for two years. That day, I was afraid and fought off tears of separation and loneliness, but knowing this comforted me.

⚜

The last time I spoke to Cardinal Wolsey was the night I played for the king. For me, the evening was thrilling, but the cardinal must have felt like a man teetering on a wall, his footing unsteady. He hadn't produced the annulment, and negotiations with the church had stretched into years. I believe he hoped to save himself by reminding the king of his many accomplishments, feats such as the Field of the Cloth of Gold. To do this, the cardinal invited the king to visit Hampton Court and ordered an extravagant banquet, providing every delicacy His Majesty was known to enjoy.

Although the cardinal lived splendidly, a royal stay demanded weeks of planning involving everyone. Cooks ordered game and vegetables, while farmers fattened geese. Servants scrubbed every corner and washed every window, and the gardeners trimmed and clipped. The older servants taught the younger how to greet the visiting nobles and officials—what to say and what not to say. Kitchen maids practiced their curtsies to the kitchen boys, who sat at long tables polishing silver.

As for the musicians, we practiced fanfares for the king's entrances and exits and hymns and canticles for special Masses. We learned new arrangements—mainly Italian madrigals and new Venetian consort music written for a blend of instruments. Master Peter told me I would perform at the banquet for His Majesty, saying, "I am confident you are ready."

Some days later, the cardinal asked to hear the songs I might sing, something he had never done before. I sat with him and Master Peter, lute in hand, performing some two dozen possibilities. They selected the ones they thought would please the king most. Then the cardinal asked me to sing each one again to make sure no words or phrases could accidentally offend. By this time, he must have sensed his precarious position. The slightest miscalculation would be used against him.

"Can you sing in French, Mark?" he asked.

"Yes, Your Eminence." I had sung in Latin as a choirboy and, at Master Peter's insistence, learned to sing in Spanish, Italian, and French, the languages of courtly music.

The cardinal explained: "I would like to include a love song in French, as a tribute to the Lady Anne Boleyn." Everyone knew she had been educated in France before returning to beguile our English king. I sang several favorites, and the cardinal selected the most youthful and romantic, a wonderful composition. Even a cynic would recall his days of love on hearing its melody and lyrics.

"Will she be there, sir?" I asked. Maybe this was my chance to see the woman everyone gossiped about.

"No, but we will honor her in her absence. Sing this one at the end."

After the cardinal left, Master Peter told me the king played the lute and sometimes composed songs. "His Majesty is known to take an interest in promising young players and compliment them. But don't be disappointed if he says nothing. He may be preoccupied with other matters."

During these weeks of preparation, a special tailor arrived from London with a group of seamstresses, cloth cutters, and embroiderers. Master Lucas and his workers took over several rooms on the ground floor where they created new garments for the musicians, fashions devised to honor the king. We visited these rooms to be measured and fitted, three or four of us at a time.

"Is this what we're going to wear?" I frowned at the coarse fabric a young woman was wrapping around my arm. It was cloth for a sack of potatoes, not for clothing for a royal performance.

"No, silly, this is for the pattern, to make sure we cut the fabric to fit." She laughed, a husky laugh for a woman. "You'll be gorgeous when we finish with you."

She was perhaps twenty-five and from somewhere in the west, based on her speech. I could see red curls slipping out from her kerchief. One slithered down her neck.

"This is what we're using for you," she said. She showed me a bolt of forest green cloth, more luxurious than anything I had ever worn. The cardinal had always dressed his musicians well, but this was something closer to what a courtier would wear. Andrew, a trumpeter being fitted across the room, asked if he could sell his outfit after the king left and live in comfort ever after.

"You're Mark, is that right?" The woman glanced at a sketch of men's clothing with small bits of fabric sewn to the paper. "You must be quite the main player. You're to have a new hat, as well as a doublet and cape. You'll be the most beautiful of the lot."

"I am singing for the king during the feast in the Great Hall." I briefly wondered whether the question I was about to ask was proper, but I couldn't see the harm. "Please, mistress," I said, "would you tell me your name?"

"I am Nan, at your service, sir." She laughed again, this time teasing and affectionate.

I returned a few days later for my next fitting, standing stock-still as Nan fussed and fretted, adjusting fastenings and pinning the cuffs. The king's initials and red and white Tudor roses decorated my doublet and flowing green cape. Since the royal colors were red, green, and white, the design was a sign of respect.

Master Lucas appeared to inspect Nan's handiwork. She fiddled with the doublet's neckline while the tailor examined every seam. A small, rabbit-faced man, Master Lucas was as meticulous about his tailoring as Master Peter was about music. He asked me to turn in a circle and then asked me to do it again.

"Raise and lower your arms," he said. "Yes, it fits him well." When he judged Nan's work to be "excellent," her face relaxed, and she smiled.

After the tailor stepped away, I felt her fingers touch my neck when she checked her stitching again. As I lay in bed that evening, I found myself reliving the sensation of being touched by her and began imagining what it would be like to slip her dress off her shoulders and press my lips against her breasts. Although boys younger than me visited the brothels, I was still innocent of sex. I had been thinking of going—after all, I had just turned seventeen. But up to that point, I had only daydreamed about the act and pleasured myself in secret. Luckily, I had been given my own small room when I became Master Peter's apprentice, so I no longer slept with the choirboys. I found myself returning to visions of sex with Nan every night and sometimes during the day. In my mind, she acquiesced readily to my overtures, and this became an intoxicating fantasy. I saw her naked and golden, reclining on my bed.

"Mark," she said during my next visit. "I've forgotten your hat. Could you wait while I bring it out?"

It was late, and the other workers were hanging up their aprons and neatening their tables. Soon I was waiting alone. I glanced around the room: scissors, pins, spools of thread, some of it silver and gold. Bolts of lush red silk lay on a table next to me—new finery for the cardinal, I supposed.

Nan was laughing when she came up behind me and put my new hat on my head. "Do you like it?" She came round to look at me directly. "Do you like me as well?"

I don't remember what I said in reply. I was completely unschooled in the art of flirtatious banter. But I didn't need words. Nan took me to a storage room in the back and carefully secured the latch. She pulled a soft brown blanket from a shelf and spread it on the floor. We made love next to boxes and baskets of sewing supplies, but our humble surroundings vanished when Nan slipped off her kerchief and her curling red hair fell to her breasts. In my mind, we were the only two people at Hampton Court.

She helped me out of my clothing, and then I helped her. She guided my hands and whispered instructions; her body responded readily to mine. She didn't seem to mind teaching me the skills of sexual pleasure, and she delighted in my progress during the following days. She teased and praised me as I advanced from surprised fumbling that first night to more confident lovemaking as time went on.

Once the affair started, I made excuses to go to the tailor's shop at the close of day when I knew she would be alone. Another musician asked me about it: "What are they doing down there? Dressing you up like the Earl of Surrey?" I shrugged and said nothing, but I pictured Nan's soft, rounded body and her fingers stroking my skin. Sex was a new realm for me, as seductive and artful as music. And like music, I found that it had many themes and variations that benefited from practice.

Yet as the days passed, my assignations with the amiable seamstress began to trouble me. The sex was exciting, but I wondered what was on her mind. Did she think we would marry? Suppose she became pregnant? Nan was tempting but not the woman I envisioned when I thought of "being in love." I really knew nothing about her, and I was far from ready to support a family.

"Nan, you're not married, are you?" I asked the next time we were together, after an agreeable hour of sex. I propped myself up on my elbows and looked at my clothes draped over my boots set down in the corner. I usually try to weigh my words before speaking, but on this night, I blurted out my thoughts: "Have you ever been married? How old are you?"

"Pet, you'll never win a lady's heart by asking questions like that. Let's just say I'm older than you, but younger than the cardinal. And I have my plans, don't you worry. They don't involve you."

"What do you mean?"

"I expect to marry soon . . . to a respected man with means."

"But suppose something were to happen with us . . . I mean, suppose you got pregnant." Getting a woman with child was the kind of scandal that would displease the cardinal and disappoint Master Peter. Nan's future husband, whoever he was, would be angry and might want vengeance against one or both of us.

"Nothing to trouble yourself about," she replied with mischievous grin.

"But what would you say if you were with child? It would be obvious to everyone."

"No one will suspect you, my dear. I'll just say it's the tailor's baby."

"But. . . ."

"But what? You're a nice lad, but my future is with Master Lucas."

It took me a moment to figure out what she meant.

"Yes, my dear . . . you're not the only one, as pretty as you are. The master's wife died some months ago, and we are lovers. We'll be married before the year is out."

I was mildly disappointed to learn I was sharing Nan with another man, but mainly I was relieved. She explained her reasoning between kisses: "The tailor will take care of me and give me a home. Are you able to do that? This is the way of things."

After that, our liaisons were freer and more passionate—I had no fears of disgrace or a sudden forced marriage or some furious man coming after me with a whip or a knife. These were carefree days. But as the king's visit grew closer, I pulled away from Nan. It was time to return to my music.

I had seen the king from afar on several occasions when I was a boy chorister—when he had visited Hampton Court. But at the banquet, I would be the soloist in a concert planned especially for him. I had to perform at my best. Each day, I rose at dawn and practiced my songs, and I repeated the process in the afternoon. I performed them for Master Peter, who helped me improve my fingering, phrasing, and the control of my breath. I even played the lute notes on the coverlet before I fell asleep at night and again when I woke up. The day of the banquet, I practiced the entire concert from beginning to end with no stopping—and then I did it multiple times. I imagined walking into the Great Hall and bowing to the king of England. I rehearsed what I would say if he happened to speak to me. The lovely Nan never crossed my mind.

That night, I watched the cardinal greet the king and his party— sturdy men wearing gold chains of office, their hands heavy with signet rings. The Duke of Norfolk complained about mud on the road. Sir Thomas Boleyn, Anne Boleyn's father, talked with every-one, seemingly without taking a breath. His son, George, was there too, a handsome man who was quieter than the others.

Once the banquet began, I moved to an anteroom so I could check the tuning on my lute and wriggle my fingers to keep them loose. Servants filed by with silver pitchers of wine and quickly returned for more. A parade of platters laden with bread and cheese followed the pitchers. Two men carried a roasted swan sitting on a bed of apples and pears. The four men who brought in the boar marched to a fanfare that accompanied the presentation. Finally came a gigantic cake shaped like the Crown of Saint Edward—it was nearly two feet high. Cherries and blackberries stood in for the crown's rubies and amethysts; gold-colored spun sugar adorned its points and curves. Cheers from the Great Hall spilled outward, hurrahs for the king and the pastry cook.

Cavendish told me to get ready, and I rose, carrying my lute at my side. A page opened the door, and I walked in and stood by my place, a cushioned, crimson-colored stool positioned at the center of the hall. At the back wall, beneath the windows, heralds brandished the king's banners, the colors creating a striking display. His Majesty sat at a long table in front of me, the cardinal next to him. More nobles and officials occupied tables on each side of the royal dais. I was surrounded by the most powerful men in England, the king just twenty feet away.

Even if he hadn't been a king, His Majesty would have been a commanding figure. He was vigorous, with masculine features, draped in white and gold. The rotund, graying cardinal hovered near him like a honeybee buzzing a flower. Recalling the scene later, I could see the rupture between them. More than once, the cardinal leaned close to His Majesty to begin a conversation, but the king turned his head away.

The room was still noisy, the diners talking among themselves. I waited for someone to call for quiet so the concert could begin. Several minutes passed, and I stood beside the stool uncertain what to do. I bowed to His Majesty and the others, but they took no notice. I began to worry that my great opportunity would turn out to be a humiliating disappointment. Then the king brought his goblet to his lips, drank slowly, paused, and raised his hand for silence. He said nothing, but his command was clear: *I am ready now. You may begin.*

Dressed like a prince and given this chance to entertain the king, I was pleased with my performance that night. I played six pieces, mostly English, before ending with the French love song.

The king stood at his place and applauded. "Excellent, my boy, wonderful. Your songs bring me back to my younger days."

I stood and bowed deeply. "Thank you, Your Majesty." I glanced at the cardinal who looked only at the king.

"What is your name?"

"I am Mark Smeaton, Your Majesty." I bowed again, elated by even this brief attention.

"The French song—it was perfection. I might want to sing it. Send me the music and the words."

"With great pleasure, Your Majesty. I would be most honored to prepare a copy."

"Be sure to get it from him." The king motioned to one of his grooms who, like me, kept bowing his head.

The cardinal edged closer to the king and said, "It will be done before you leave, Your Majesty." The king acted like he didn't hear.

After my performance, I joined several other musicians playing light music to enhance what seemed like a festive mood. The cardinal approached and said, "Thank you, Mark—your songs have lifted His Majesty's spirits. Please prepare the manuscript tomorrow morning."

"You will have it before ten o'clock, Your Eminence." In this moment, my excitement at playing for the king blended with my concern for the cardinal's enterprise. "I hope I have helped you, sir," I added. The old man's nod of the head signaled his gratitude.

The next day after breakfast, I ran to the chapel to make the copy and tell Master Peter that the king had complimented my playing.

"The king has already left," he said, "much sooner than planned. We will send the copy to the Lord Chamberlain at Greenwich. His Majesty may forget about it by the time he returns, but it is an honor for you, nonetheless." Master Peter placed his hand on my shoulder. "It was a superb performance, Mark. I stood at the back to listen. You played and sang exceptionally well."

Nothing the king or the cardinal said meant as much to me as Master Peter's approval. The choirmaster wasn't given to flattery.

The king's unannounced departure surprised everyone—exhibitions of archery and falconry canceled; elaborate foods prepared for the king served to the household instead. I stopped by the tailor's shop early that evening to say goodbye to Nan. She had waited for me as I knew she would. Unsure what words to use, I presented a bouquet of flowers from the gardens. I had asked the gardener to choose the best.

She seemed delighted by them, curtsying by way of thanks. "You're a sweet one. You've made me feel beautiful." She smiled and squeezed my hand. After she was gone, she became a happy memory: the woman who introduced me to the delights of sex. I never saw her again.

Not long afterward, the cardinal, too, became a memory, but a sadder, more troubling one. Those of us who had served him missed him. No one said so aloud. Those backing the Boleyns called him a traitor, and the charges grew fouler as time went on. Whispers about "the witch" still dominated the kitchens, larders, and servants' halls. But with Anne Boleyn's arrival imminent, we measured our words when we spoke with strangers. What choice did we have?

Still, I rejoiced in one unforeseen development: I met a girl in the chapel, a fair maid if ever there was one, her face and manner serene. Her voice was musical, with a lilt, as if she were easily amused. I had glimpsed her gleaming light brown hair at the edge of her hood and imagined the silken feel of it. That night, I asked Old John if he knew anything about her. As a palace worker, he would have heard more about the newcomers than I had. He said she was Anne Boleyn's niece or cousin or second cousin—he wasn't exactly sure. Yet the distinction hardly mattered. She was a Boleyn and a person of rank. I was a common player.

At the time, I had little knowledge of society outside Hampton Court, but I understood what was allowed and what was not. I could only admire Mistress Shelton in my imagination, and even that was fanciful and unwise.

5

FIND THE BOY

November 1529

Madge Shelton, Hampton Court Palace

veryone was in a dither about my cousin's arrival, all of them nattering about Anne Boleyn. Hundreds of people gathered along the road to watch for the king's carriage. My mother and I waited at the main gate, ready to greet and assist her.

"He is bringing her openly to Hampton Court," my mother told me. "This confirms it . . . he intends to make her his queen."

My immediate task was to collect my cousin's jewel box from the carriage and take it to her chambers, along with her cloak and gloves if she left them behind. Earlier in the day, I had checked her rooms to make certain all was arranged as she preferred. She was very exact about what she wanted.

That morning, the king's men filed through the palace handing out small cloth pennants in the royal colors and instructing the household to gather to greet the king. They told everyone to cheer loudly as soon as the royal carriage appeared on the road. These men knew from experience that His Majesty's mood improved whenever a noisy crowd greeted him. Some of the cooks grumbled because their spit boys and kitchen maids would disappear for an hour to be part of the welcoming throng. But for the boys who turned the roasting meats and the girls who chopped onions, the day was a holiday without the saints and prayers—you didn't even have to go to Mass.

By this time in November, the trees were bare, so I caught sight of the carriage as soon as it came around the bend. A dozen horsemen rode ahead of it, and a long string of carts and riders followed. As the procession neared the palace, the crowd's roar rolled in our direction, gradually becoming louder and more sustained. The king's subjects applauded and waved their pennants, which created a fluttering sea of white, red, and green. At one point, the cheering stopped, and several people yelled, but whatever happened was quickly resolved. Perhaps someone had fainted or startled one of the horses, I thought at the time. Maybe a mother had lost sight of her child.

When the carriage pulled into the gate, the heralds sounded their trumpets and flourished Tudor flags. My cousin sat beside the king and delicately waved her gloved hand to acknowledge the excited crowd. People fell to their knees, and men and boys took off their hats. Anne Boleyn was radiant as she surveyed Hampton Court's stately buildings. I knew she had pursued this dream for many months, and I wondered how she felt.

The hubbub seemed to please His Majesty. He raised his arms to recognize his subjects, his sleeves and gloves glittering with golden threads. Pages scrambled to open the carriage doors and escort the royal couple across thick carpets laid on top of the paving stones. A few raindrops fell, so I quickly collected my cousin's jewel box, which she had tucked under the seat, along with her Genoese velvet cloak. She spoke quietly to my mother, and I followed them into her rooms.

Servants had set aromatic fires beforehand, and the refreshments she liked most were near at hand. I had organized the adjoining room for her to bathe and rest if she wished. The atmosphere was thrilling, and my mother beamed. "How could anyone doubt that our kinswoman will soon be queen of England?" she asked. But once my cousin stepped inside, she pulled off her hood and threw it down, its gold beads skimming along the floor. She turned away from us and wrapped her arms around her stomach as if she were in pain.

As she did this, the king entered, followed by Suffolk, Norris, the Duke of Norfolk, and Sir William Brereton, a soldier and Cheshire landowner. My mother and I dropped surprised curtsies, and my cousin turned round and stood before them, slender and strangely immobilized. Only her dark eyes suggested her distress.

"We will find him," the king assured her, "and punish him. Norris, see that it is done."

She nodded but said nothing.

It took me several minutes to work out what had happened. A young boy had thrown a dead rat at the carriage and yelled, "All your male babes will die," or perhaps it was "All your babes will die," or it could have been "You will die," before he ran away. Several voices in the crowd had joined him, screaming insults such as "Witches have no children." Apparently, the rat had landed inches from my cousin's feet, but someone must have removed it instantly because I saw nothing when I stepped into the carriage to collect her belongings. As I thought about it later, I had to admire her self-control. When she arrived, she smiled and waved to the crowd as if nothing was wrong.

"Question all the riders. Someone must have seen him as he ran away. Round up the people who stood along that section of the road," the king said. "Arrest anyone who spoke treacherous words."

Norris bowed and turned to my cousin. "Ma'am, were you able to see what happened? Did you see the boy? Or perhaps you would prefer to rest and speak with me later."

"I will rest shortly. Yes, I saw his face. He was small . . . *crasseux* . . . very dirty and rough."

"Perhaps around eight years old, ma'am?"

"*Oui, c'est ça.* He had dark hair."

Norris bowed. "He likely works in the palace or lives nearby. We will search for him."

The king embraced my cousin, telling her the boy would be publicly whipped. My always practical mother brought her a goblet of spirits and tended her like a nursemaid. Norris ushered the men out and asked me to accompany them.

Outside and out of the king's hearing, the men discussed what to do. Suffolk proposed questioning the palace workers individually. "They all know who it is. Bring them into a room and show them the lash. Tell them they'll feel its sting if they don't give us the name."

"There's no need to frighten everyone," Norris countered. "Just find out if a boy is missing from his post." He suggested starting in the kitchens and stables.

"The description is useless," Suffolk complained. "A dark-haired urchin? What are we supposed to do with that?"

The Duke of Norfolk approached the problem differently. "Well, there are plenty of dark-haired boys to choose from if we can't find the guilty one. No one would know the difference."

I had always considered Norfolk a mean, tricky sort of man.

Brereton spoke up. "And there are plenty who would agree to a whipping for a couple of coins. A quick show may be enough to satisfy His Majesty."

I tried to hide my horror at the idea. I knew almost nothing about how poor people lived. I had heard that some sold their teeth to barber surgeons for use in dentures, enduring what must be terrible pain for money. Perhaps Brereton was right. Maybe some random boy would volunteer to suffer if offered a sufficient payment.

Norfolk, Suffolk, and Brereton left, talking among themselves, no doubt preparing to bully the palace workers into revealing the wanted boy. Norris spoke to me. "Mistress Shelton, it would be well if you could comfort your cousin and distract her with happier thoughts. This boy will hide, and others will protect him. Finding him will not be easy. He may have fled into the countryside."

"Would you punish another boy in his place?"

"No, it is only talk. I wouldn't allow that to happen."

"And what will be done to the boy if he is found?"

"He is quite young, but there must be punishment for an act like this one. We cannot allow such deeds."

"Sir, I hope he is gone—all children can be foolish."

"I hope that too. The best solution would be for His Majesty and Lady Anne to turn their attention to other matters. Whipping a small child will not help your cousin win the people's hearts. His Majesty will see that in time."

I returned to my cousin's rooms where the king still consoled her, his fur-lined cape covering her legs. Servants presented plates of dainties, and the king indulged himself while describing his plans to renovate Hampton Court. My cousin ate nothing at all. By this time, though, she seemed to have recovered from the shock of having a dead rat at her feet. She gazed into the king's eyes and thanked him for his tender words. She had paid a small price for obtaining the king's complete attention. I had no doubt she would make good use of it.

6

QUEEN OR WITCH?

November 1529

Mark Smeaton, Hampton Court Palace

I didn't hear about the rat until supper when it was the sole topic of conversation. A small boy had traitorously insulted our king or bravely defended Queen Katherine of Aragon, depending on the storyteller. A few maintained that the rat had landed in Anne Boleyn's lap. Someone swore it hit her in the face. A boy threw it, everyone agreed on that, though no one admitted to knowing him. Maybe he was from another town. He might even be Irish or Welsh.

Since I was inside the courtyard when the king arrived, I was nowhere near the incident on the road. I had looked for a place where I could watch Anne Boleyn step out of her carriage—after hearing so much gossip, I wanted to have a good view. She was thinner than I expected but elegant, wearing a green gown and a hood rimmed with gold beads. She balanced one gloved hand on the king's arm as she descended the carriage steps and kept it there as they walked toward the entrance. Anyone who didn't know otherwise would have presumed they were man and wife. Trumpets blared, and we all cheered and waved our pennants. And it was in this moment that I understood that Cardinal Wolsey would never return to Hampton Court. The king of England had claimed it as a stage to display his future bride.

At the chapel the following day, I asked Master Peter what he thought about the boy throwing the rat. He said musicians should keep their opinions to themselves. He seemed tired, with much on his mind, but assured me he had written to the king's master of musicians, describing my skill with the lute and other instruments and my knowledge of courtly music. He said he was optimistic: "I may get word today."

That morning, we rehearsed for the Sunday Mass, when I would play the organ. I sat high up in an enclosure at the back of the chapel while Master Peter conducted the choir below. The men occupied pews on one side of the gleaming wooden choir stall while the boys sat across from them on the other side. As we rehearsed, layers of sound rose into the ceiling, the men's voices alternating with the bell-like singing of the boys. The music often started simply before the notes multiplied into chains of melody that merged and then split apart. My favorite was a motet by John Taverner, an astonishing work for six singers, a mixture of the men and boys.

To honor the king, I played the "Agincourt Hymn" by John Dunstaple, a magnificent organ work celebrating England's great victory over the French. The music flowed from my fingertips into the keys and then traveled into every corner of the church. To me, playing the organ was exhilarating—I felt powerful, at least for a while. From my first days at Hampton Court, music had been my refuge. It was the one domain on Earth where I was more than an impoverished immigrant's child.

That morning, Master Peter reviewed each piece many times, drawing attention to needed improvements. He was demanding, but his respect and love for the music was contagious: the words must be clear and the notes exact. The timing must be flawless.

We ended around twelve o'clock, and the men and boys left to eat their midday meal. Master Peter went up to his work room, and I practiced the "Agincourt Hymn" several times more before going downstairs to collect the musical manuscripts. Since I was alone, I took the chance to sit in the choir stall—in my old place in the boys' section. I recalled my youthful fascination with the fantastical birds and beasts carved into the stall's polished wood. I remembered my awe the first time I saw the multicolored windows. I assumed I would soon leave Hampton Court, no matter what my future path. There were other churches just as beautiful—this is what I told myself.

I heard some scuffling in the empty pews where the congregation sat, followed by breathing and some thumps. I stood up to see a thin dark-haired boy crawling out from a row near the back. My mind moved quickly to a single explanation—the rat-thrower was in the church. I knew this immediately, even without evidence, because I knew this boy.

"Jacob, what are you doing here?"

This was the first of many questions I wanted to ask. Why had he thrown a rat at the royal procession? Had he been hiding in the church all night? Did he think this was a game—that he could insult the king and future queen and escape the dreadful consequences? I silently cursed his childishness.

Jacob was an orphan chosen for the choir, another beneficiary of the cardinal's grace. He had a beautiful voice, but he couldn't follow the music or remember the words. During services, he squirmed and put his fingers in his nose and mouth. He often looked up at the ceiling rather than paying attention to the choirmaster and the priests. Master Peter had tried to teach him, and I tutored him as well, but the choir was not for him. After some months, he was sent to work in the stables, and I don't think he minded. He quickly learned how to care for the horses and keep them clean and calm.

He stood up slowly and made his way to the aisle. There he

wrapped his arms around his midsection and began shifting his weight from leg to leg. When I walked in his direction, he started rubbing his hands over his face and hair.

"Did you throw the rat at the king's carriage?" I thought I should confirm my guess.

He looked down and said, "The woman is a witch."

I took this answer as a "yes."

"No, she's not. Why do you say that?"

"She has six fingers on one hand."

"Do you know this for a fact?"

"Everyone says it, and she has warts on her chin."

"No, she doesn't. I saw her yesterday. Do you really believe the king would choose a woman with warts and extra fingers to be queen of England? He can take any woman he wants."

During this pathetic exchange, I weighed my dilemma, as awful as it was. If I revealed Jacob's whereabouts, he would be brutally punished. If I didn't, I could be accused of hiding him and aiding His Majesty's enemies. The king's men might blame Master Peter and all of us who worked in the church.

I heard the creak of the main doors opening—someone was entering, maybe the king's men searching for their prey. I grabbed Jacob's shirt and dragged him away from the pews while I silently bemoaned our bad luck. I pulled the boy into an alcove with a large statue of King David, Goliath's severed head at the feet. I blew out the tapers on the wall before we crawled into the gap behind the pedestal. Jacob squeezed my hand as we crouched down together.

Two women walked down the center aisle and stopped near the altar to pray. I recognized Mistress Shelton immediately and assumed the older woman was her mother. As they prayed, I prayed too—that Jacob wouldn't cry or move or cough. The women were Boleyns and would naturally want the boy punished. Jacob grasped the need for silence. We waited as the women bowed their heads, light from the windows falling on them as they knelt.

Again, I observed the younger woman's quiet beauty and the grace with which she held herself. After some minutes, the mother touched her daughter's arm, indicating that it was time for them to leave. I wondered what it must be like to feel a mother's love every day. My own mother and little brother had returned to Flanders after my father died. At Hampton Court, many people had been kind to me, but it wasn't the same as having a family.

If I had been alone, I might have greeted them—this would have been more courteous than hiding in the dark. But protecting Jacob had to be my main concern, and I welcomed the sound of the heavy chapel doors closing when the women left.

When Jacob and I emerged from behind the statue, he was still holding my hand, his breathing faster than before. I looked around, considering places where I could hide him while I came up with a plan. Upstairs would be safer for Jacob but more incriminating for the rest of us if the king's men found him there. I thought about returning to my room to get the few coins I had saved—at least the boy could buy food if he got to another town. Since he worked at the stables and knew its routines, he could probably steal a horse without being discovered. But if he were caught, he would be branded or put to death. Every idea that occurred to me was unworkable or dangerous.

Then I recalled that felons sometimes took refuge inside churches—I had heard tales of highwaymen who escaped execution this way. If there were any way to save Jacob, this might be it. Perhaps the church would give him sanctuary.

"We must talk to Master Peter," I said. Jacob's face showed his desperation and loss of hope. My own stomach convulsed as I looked at him. "The choirmaster will help you if he is able to. I don't see any other choice."

I tugged at his hand to guide him—he didn't resist at all. We snaked through the chapel's darkest aisle to the staircase off the nave. I told Jacob to go first so he couldn't turn and run away. Even then, I kept asking myself whether it would be better to let him go. I mentally practiced lies I could tell the king's men if they questioned me: *The boy fled before I could catch him . . . no, I didn't see where he went.*

Then Jacob tripped and lay down on the steps, shaking and crying. "I am afraid they will hang me from a tree."

"They can't hang someone as young as you," I said, although I wasn't sure. Suppose they killed him—he didn't deserve it. I would never forgive myself.

I had expected to find Master Peter alone, but he was talking with Father Bryce, one of the priests who performed the Sunday Mass. When I saw the good father, I feared I had made a terrible error. I knew Master Peter would protect Jacob if he could. I didn't know what Father Bryce would say.

The two men were sitting at a table, reviewing papers and conferring. Both looked up when we entered, and I saw that Master Peter recognized Jacob right away.

"Master Peter . . . Father Bryce, pardon me. I am sorry to disturb your work."

Neither spoke, so I continued with my explanation. "I found the boy in the chapel. He has admitted that he threw the rat at the royal carriage. He has come here seeking holy forgiveness and blessed sanctuary." I tried to speak with confidence and choose words that might satisfy a priest. In truth, I had no idea what I was talking about.

"Jacob, why did you do this?" Master Peter asked.

The boy said nothing. I knew he was too afraid to answer.

"Jacob has come to the church for protection," I said.

Master Peter gazed at the boy and then spoke to Father Bryce. "Can we help him, Father? He's barely more than a child."

The priest stood up—he suddenly seemed larger and more menacing. He clasped the rosary he wore at his waist and walked over to stand directly in front of Jacob. Some churchmen were known for bending the rules in difficult circumstances, but Father Bryce wasn't one of them. He had a reputation for hewing to the letter of church law. I felt Jacob's body shaking beside me, and I was frightened for him. The king's men could be merciless.

The priest gripped his rosary in his palm. His voice was sharp and precise. "If you seek sanctuary, boy, you must ask for it. You must declare yourself."

My own relief washed over me, and I gently pushed Jacob's shoulder. "You have to say that you want 'sanctuary.' You have to use that word."

Father Bryce continued speaking, pronouncing the words as if he were reading them. "Church law allows forty days of sanctuary, followed by banishment." He turned and looked back toward Master Peter. "We must arrange for him to leave."

After that, it was all done quickly. After several failed attempts, Jacob mumbled the required phrase: "I seek sanctuary from the Holy Mother Church." Father Bryce said he would write to the church authorities summarizing the facts. He added that the boy would probably go to Ireland.

"Jacob, this is the only solution," Master Peter said, his low-toned voice reassuring. "We must get you some food and clean clothing. You will have to stay inside the chapel for several days."

Both Master Peter and Father Bryce seemed confident of their decision and unafraid of any repercussions. Father Bryce led Jacob away, and as I watched the boy go, I noticed he had soiled himself in his terror. Dramas like this one, I suspected, would be the story of his life. He would pursue some reckless, meaningless scheme and then worry about being caught. I was thankful he wouldn't suffer some cruel punishment for his foolish prank, but I asked myself how he would survive in a foreign land. He wasn't a boy who learned quickly, and he couldn't restrain his own behavior.

After Father Bryce left with Jacob, I, too, turned to go. But Master Peter said, "Stay. . . there is news. I have received word that you will join the royal court musicians. This is an important advance for you."

"Thank you, sir—this is good news indeed."

It took me a moment to absorb the information, and I should have been overjoyed. Any musician would be proud to serve the king. Yet even as I expressed my gratitude, I realized that I would soon be living and working among strangers in places unknown to me. I remembered when I left my family to serve the cardinal, that sudden harsh loss of affection and warmth. I thought of my father, wishing that he was still alive so I could send word to him of my new position. This was his dream for me when he touched my face with his rough carpenter's hand. It was the last time I ever saw him.

But it was Master Peter's other news that devastated me. He, too, was leaving Hampton Court—time to retire and see his grand-children, he said. He claimed he was looking forward to spending his days reading and resting, with no worries about music for the Sunday Mass.

The cardinal was gone. Master Peter was moving to Cornwall. I had recently learned that Old John was heading north, returning to the village where he grew up. Hampton Court had become a shell, emptied of those I knew as friends and protectors. Once again, my life was breaking apart, as it had that day on the River Aire.

Later that week, I said goodbye to Master Peter.

"You will do well at court, Mark," he said. "You have a gift, and they will see it. You are nearly a man now—it is time."

I didn't feel like a man. I had come to love Master Peter as I had loved my own father. It was hard to imagine my life without his guidance.

He clasped me by the arms, his voice barely a whisper. "I wish you every good fortune, my boy." He pulled me closer, putting his arms around my shoulders, holding me near him a short time before stepping back to look at me. "If you wish to pay tribute to your old teacher, you must be strong. Make the music your life's work. If you do that, my effort will be rewarded."

I left him and began walking down the stairs, round and round, descending from the chapel's heights to the ground floor. I stopped as I approached the last few steps, placing my hands behind me and leaning my back against the wall. I tried to hold back tears and quell my fear of being alone. I had to be resolute. I had done it before, I told myself. I had built a new life among strangers. Surely, I could do it once more.

In the coming years, I would meet many brilliant, accomplished men, but none would measure up to Master Peter. He was quiet and sober and loved music more than wealth or rank. He was the wisest man I ever met.

PART TWO

The Court
of Whispers

7

THE KING'S NEW PLAYER

1529 to 1530

Mark Smeaton, The Court of King Henry

A redheaded boy brought the message the week after Master Peter left.

"Silas Bray summons you to the music room at nine o'clock tomorrow." The handwriting was striking: "His Royal Majesty's Master of Musicians," it read, with a trio of swirling *M*'s. I had heard that Simon Bray was coming to Hampton Court, along with a large group of players.

That night I brushed my clothes and shined my boots. I rose early to practice and tune the cardinal's lute. I went down to the music room, walking quickly at first and then slowing my pace as I neared the doorway. I paused and took a slow breath to prepare myself. I stepped inside just before the hour.

Bray was large and angular, with a handsome but sunken face. He was alone and remained seated when I entered and bowed to him, saying "Master Bray, I am Mark Smeaton. It is a privilege to meet you."

He indicated a chair across from him. "Play something."

I began with an Italian piece, one of my favorites, both subtle and complex. Bray sat forward listening. When I finished, I expected him to test me by asking me to play a different piece or perhaps a different style of music. Instead, he gazed across the room at the impressive array of instruments the cardinal had collected. I cradled my lute and waited.

He got up and walked away toward the windows. I twisted my shoulders sideways to see where he had gone. He stood silently, with his back to me, while I ran through silent questions: Should I play something else? Should I speak to him? How long should I wait before saying something?

"We'll see," he said, finally turning to face me. "Maybe you can measure up."

I stood and bowed again, somewhat confused. I had assumed I had a place among the royal musicians, but the arrangement seemed provisional. I would have to prove myself.

"I will do my best, sir. I am honored to have this chance."

"Where did you get the lute?"

He must have recognized its value—the darker decorative swirls on its shining gold-brown wood showed that it was costly and rare. For a moment, I considered hiding the truth, but I couldn't think of a credible lie.

"It is my own, sir . . . a gift to me. Cardinal Wolsey left it for me."

"Did he?" Bray lifted his chin. "With us, you'll play the lute we give you—one of the instruments in the king's collection."

"Of course, sir. As you wish."

I tightened my fingers on my lute's neck, fearing he might take it away. But he only said, "That's probably expensive—I'd keep it hidden if I were you."

He sent me to be outfitted in the king's livery. Evidently, my skill ensured that much. I vowed to work hard and be respectful. I was certain I could show my worth.

⸙

The king employed some sixty musicians, an astonishing group of players including Germans, Italians, Flemings, Portuguese, and a trumpeter from Africa. Drummers and horn players announced His Majesty's arrivals and departures. A large group of lutenists provided background music while the courtiers and ladies talked, played cards, or danced. The most favored musicians devised programs and performed for the king and his illustrious visitors. [1]

King Henry's court—meaning His Majesty, the Lady Anne Boleyn, and a large group of grooms, family members, friends, advisers, and attendants—moved continually from palace to palace, from Greenwich to Whitehall to Eltham to Hampton Court. He often took much of the court to stay at a great nobleman's estate, but on these occasions, I was generally left behind. For these visits, he brought only a few favored players with him.

The winter passed and then the spring, and my lack of progress began to gnaw at me. My main work was collecting and storing instruments after the other musicians rehearsed or performed. When the court moved to a different location, I helped the boys who loaded the carts. Since instruments require gentle handling, I began to load them myself. The boys were sometimes careless, and I feared being blamed for any damage.

Bray also ordered me to tune the lutes of the other players, a time-consuming daily task. I rose before dawn to prepare several dozen instruments while the others slept and ate breakfast. "You must get up with the kitchen boys," one joked when I handed him his lute. Some of the others laughed—I had found no friends among them. The worst of it was that I was seldom allowed to play. From time to time, I joined a few lutenists supplying background music, but only if no one else was available and never when the king was there. This music wasn't challenging—no intricate passages, no solos, no vocals. At best, I was an unseen minor player, strumming a lute in the corner.

I couldn't help comparing this demoralizing situation with my life when the cardinal was at Hampton Court. Master Peter gave me solo parts shortly after I became a boy chorister. I mastered the lute and organ and other instruments and entertained at the cardinal's feasts. I helped the choirmaster select the most beautiful works for Sunday Masses and sometimes rehearsed the choir myself. Every day, I had learned something new.

⚜

One morning, I was in the music room distributing lutes to a line of players. One thanked me and asked if I needed help tuning the instruments. I said no, but Paul Markham appeared the following day anyway.

He was slightly older, about twenty at the time, and a very accomplished player. During the hours when we tuned the lutes, we began to talk. He came from a family of court musicians—his father had played during the reign of King Henry VII, His Majesty's father and the first of the Tudors to rule. Even so, Paul was relegated to playing background music as I was, although for different reasons. His left foot turned inward, and he walked with a noticeable limp. It was a handicap from birth. While his limp didn't affect his playing, he couldn't join in the dancing as the other musicians did. When he first came to court, he said, Bray had told him, "Watching you stumble around would disgust people." Paul never forgot it.

One day I mustered the courage to ask him why the other players avoided me.

"They suspect you're loyal to Wolsey. Some say you're a spy."

"A spy? That's ridiculous."

"Is it? You were in Wolsey's household. You know him and the people close to him."

"But what would I report on? I'm never near anyone of rank."

Paul shrugged. "There are other stories . . . about what went on at Hampton Court when Wolsey was there." His voice died away.

"What do you mean?"

"People say things . . . that you were the cardinal's 'special boy.'" He inhaled and then eliminated all doubt about the rumor's nature. "They say you were his bugger boy."

This is vile gossip, I thought, *maybe the vilest of all*. I remembered the young nobleman who abused the cardinal the morning he left— the one who spat on him and claimed he buggered boys. Just random viciousness, I had thought then. I had certainly known of priests who satisfied their sexual needs with choirboys, altar boys, stable boys, pupils, any child within their reach. A friend in school was the priest's "favorite," and he told me what being the favorite meant. Some priests were cruel, beating boys for little reason and appearing to relish it. But the cardinal never did these things.

"This isn't true," I said. "The cardinal keeps a woman . . . or he used to. It was common knowledge at Hampton Court."

"Some men pursue all kinds of lusts."

"Well, yes. But the cardinal never lusted after children. I am sure of that."

"Maybe not, but he is out of favor now, and among his enemies, any accusation will do. Many are betting he'll lose his head."

For a second, I saw the image—the old man kneeling on the scaffold, trembling as the executioner raised the axe.

"But this is an outright lie. The cardinal wasn't like that."

"Truth doesn't count for much in politics. People will say whatever they think will damage their opponents. But you don't want to be dragged down with the cardinal. You have to pick a side."

"I don't have a side."

"Everyone at court has a side . . . everyone has to choose."

"But I've never spoken out in favor of the cardinal or criticized His Majesty. I only want to play."

"You need to show your loyalty to the king and the Boleyns.

You've been here several months." Paul smiled at me—a crooked smile. "Of course, you would do better with Bray if you didn't play so well. Your skill makes him nervous. I'm sure he'd like you out."

Paul wasn't handsome or witty, but he was observant and understood the ways of the court. The next day he asked, "Do you know Lord Sandys? The new Lord Chamberlain?"

I had heard the name.

"My father knew him years ago," Paul went on. "He's fair and respects ability. You need to show him how accomplished you are."

The following week, Lord Sandys met with the entire corps of musicians to introduce himself. But in that setting, there was nothing I could do. Not all the court's customs were clear to me, but I understood that low-ranking musicians don't walk up to Lord Chamberlains to present themselves. The rule is, "Stay in your place."

Even so, Thomas Cromwell was apparently inching his way into royal favor after serving Cardinal Wolsey, much to everyone's surprise. If he could do it, so could I.

⚜

I couldn't deny the court's splendor: elegant clothes in vivid colors, topped by luxurious furs. Every neck, ear, wrist, and finger sparkled with jewels and precious metals. An opulent wardrobe revealed a person's rank, either actual or hoped for.

The king's life was an unending parade of ceremonies, royal showmanship for every season, month, and week. King Henry reveled in these events—the more elaborate the better—and he rewarded his favored musicians well. Sometimes he paid for their weddings and funerals, as he had done when the African trumpeter John Blanke married an English widow and when the Italian musician Pietro de Casa Nova died. [2]

Often, on Lady Anne's instructions, a celebrated performer

arrived from abroad to entertain the court. The list included vir-
tuosos of the flute, rebec, lute, and organ, along with eminent
singers and composers. I heard music performed by the most
skilled players from a dozen countries—men who overwhelmed
me with their talent but motivated me as well.

Apollo Minetti, the organist at Saint Mark's in Venice, was one
such player. I was assigned to carry his cases and music and do
anything else he might need. At first, I was angry about my lowly
task, but he was a pleasant man, liberal with *grazies* and *per favores*
which he mixed in with his limited English. Serving him gave me a
unique vantage point.

Minetti's concert was unforgettable. I sat near him high in the
Chapel Royal, watching closely as he performed. His hands were
smaller than I expected, with strong, curved fingers that flew across
the keys. Sometimes he applied the full power of his body to the
organ, creating a resonance that entered your flesh and bones. At
other times, he paused, giving his listeners time to absorb the
notes. His gift was more than skill—he took the music into his soul.
During his recital, I resolved to learn all I could from him. Could I
ever make my own playing that magical?

Afterward, I gathered Minetti's music and cloak and accompanied him into the nave. Lady Anne praised him, as did the king and
several others. His Majesty presented the organist with a small
black velvet bag, no doubt containing his reward. The king didn't
notice me—he had probably forgotten my performance at Hampton
Court. Holding the organist's belongings, I faded into the background, another nameless servant. But the young woman from the
chapel was there, Mistress Shelton, a member of the royal party. She
glanced at me with a smile of recognition, or at least I thought so.
Perhaps I had imagined it.

Minetti's concert changed me—I practiced more, not only the
lute, but also the viol and the virginals. I volunteered to make
copies of musical manuscripts arriving weekly from across the

continent. I began composing songs, at first to fill my lonely hours and then because the challenge absorbed me. I still looked for ways to improve my station, but my goal altered the day I heard Minetti play. I wanted to be more than a prosperous musician. I wanted to be exceptional.

Near the end of my first year at court, Cardinal Wolsey was arrested in Yorkshire, never having recovered the king's regard. Word was that Lady Anne had persuaded the king he was a traitor—she and the other Boleyns. The cardinal died before his trial, which was probably a blessing. If frail health hadn't taken him, he would have been executed on Tower Hill.

I hid my sorrow while the others cheered. Alone in my room, I held my wondrous lute and played some of the Irish music he loved. The cardinal was no humble man of God—he craved wealth and power like the others did. But he was generous, and he loved beauty.

"Their fathers are poor," he would say when he presented the boys' choir to his famous visitors—Sir Thomas More, Bishop John Fisher, and others. "They were unwashed and unschooled when they came here, and now they sing like angels." He treated us to honey cakes and gingerbread on these occasions, our days of hunger gone.

When I became Master Peter's apprentice, the cardinal heard of my eagerness to play music from abroad. After his trips, he would often seek me out, open his satchel, and pull out a sheaf of French rondeaux or Italian madrigals.

"These are for you, Mark," he would say, his small eyes twinkling above his fleshy cheeks. "I have been carrying them for days."

"Thank you, Your Eminence." I would bow. "You are more kind to me than I deserve."

"Nonsense, my boy. Learn to play them, and you can impress our guests."

After the cardinal left Hampton Court, I wanted to thank him for the lute, but Master Peter advised me not to write. "They read his letters," the choirmaster warned. "You don't want your name on someone's list."

This was the world I lived in—politics seeped into every act.

PROPHECIES

1530
Madge Shelton, Greenwich and Whitehall

My father was often away on diplomatic missions, but he kept half a dozen horses at Greenwich. One was a brown palfrey he bought when I was eight years old because the animal was so gentle and calm. "The horse is yours now," my father had said. "What name should he have?"

I pointed to the white splash on the palfrey's forehead and replied "Starlight." To me, the answer was obvious.

Being a beast, Starlight kept my secret—that I sometimes stole away from the palace to ride into the countryside alone. I never had a particular reason or destination—just a desire to escape the mincing chatter at court. When I rode through the soft hills and fields around Greenwich, I was never bored. I liked having an hour or two when I didn't have to please anyone except Starlight and myself. My ruse was to tell my mother I was going to the market and walk down to the stables instead. Since the boys would never question a lady, I could take Starlight's reins and lead him away from the palace boundaries. Then I mounted and rode astride, just as I had as a girl. Starlight and I galloped and trotted through leafy valleys and glades, and I let my hair go free. When I returned, I gave the boys some coins to care for Starlight. Like him, they happily kept my secret.

One day, I got caught in a sudden rain and came home with dripping hair and sodden skirts. My mother helped me dry off and change into clean clothing while I described the downpour at the market, inventing details to sound more convincing. "The troughs were overflowing, and the water was gushing down the street. It was so sudden everyone got wet. I went into one of the shops and waited until the rain stopped."

She smiled at me as she handed my wet clothes to a serving woman who rolled them into a bundle and left. When my mother resumed our conversation, her voice was affectionate. "I used to love riding as a girl," she said, "sitting astride a horse and feeling the wind against my skin. I remember getting caught in a summer rain—I didn't mind at all."

My body stiffened while my mind weighed the possibilities. I had been so careful—was this really a motherly recollection, or had she found out about my scheme? "Sometimes I miss Norfolk," I said, "and our life in the countryside. Now I seldom have the chance to ride."

"To sit astride a horse that is galloping across a field," she continued, "this is a country pleasure. It is not a sin." But then she gently placed her forefinger at the side of my chin so I couldn't look away. Her voice sharpened. "But it is not suitable for an attendant to Lady Anne, my dear. Here at court, we ride as noblewomen, always sitting sideways. And we don't wander off to the countryside alone without telling anyone. We ride with chaperones."

I was angry and disappointed. My minor offense had been discovered, and I assumed my riding days were done. To my surprise, my mother spoke dryly, as if she were sharing an amusing secret.

"So, when you go out, Madge, don't dawdle. And don't stay outside if it begins to rain. Be sure you leave time to change and present yourself properly at the hour when your duties begin."

I smiled at her, elated at her rare benevolence. She almost never bent the rules.

"It is an innocent liberty that you may enjoy for now," she said. "Soon enough, you'll be married, and I doubt your future husband will approve."

⚜

From everything I saw, the king loved my cousin, but Katherine of Aragon was still his wife. Months went by, and Wolsey was gone, but the pope still refused to grant the annulment.

My cousin waited, swathed in silks and jewels. She danced with the king and stood by him at church. At supper, she gazed at him and lowered her eyes before suggesting names for the princes she would bear. Within the king's hearing, she spoke to foreign dignitaries: "*Le roi d'Angleterre est brillant et viril, n'êtes-vous pas d'accord?*" Then she glanced back at His Majesty, who pretended he wasn't listening.

When she was with the king, she was confident, but in private she fretted and complained. "He doesn't have to wait for the pope," she would say. "Why doesn't he just divorce her? *De quoi a-t-il peur?*"

Meanwhile, strange incidents unnerved her. The rat was only the first. One morning, my mother and I entered her chambers to help her dress. She was sitting on the bed with a crimson shawl draped over her nightgown and velvet slippers on her feet. She held an open book on her lap, but had covered the pages with her fingers in a way that seemed intentional rather than accidental.

"Keep the servants out," she said to us as she snapped the book closed. Her voice was brittle—no *"Bonjour, ma chèrie"* today. I couldn't see the book's title, but astronomical patterns decorated the dark leather binding—celestial bodies and phases of the moon.

"Perhaps we're too early, my lady. Do you wish to be alone?" My mother sensed her restless mood.

"Do you believe in the ancients' prophecies?"

"I believe in the word of God, ma'am," my mother answered.

"Very wise of you."

My cousin smiled in that superior, detached manner she had and handed the book to me. "So, Madge, what do you think of this? Look at the page with the title. Do we have a great artist in the making?"

I opened the book and glanced at the page. A chill entered my flesh. Someone had drawn three figures in the blank space below the title [3]: A king, presumably King Henry, held a scepter and sported an enormous, bulging codpiece. Queen Katherine stood beside him, easily identifiable because Her Majesty's motto, "humble and loyal," was printed on the skirt. The third figure was headless, blood spurting from its neck in a star-shaped pattern. The severed head lay on the ground and featured a beaded French hood, a fashion favored by my cousin. Anyone who saw it would immediately think, *Anne Boleyn.*

The drawing was crude, almost comical, but clear enough to make its point. I wasn't sure whether it was a prediction or a threat, but neither idea was comforting. I immediately passed the book to my mother, glad to be rid of it.

My mother gazed at the page for a moment and quietly closed the book's cover. "Do you know where this came from, my lady?"

"I found it on my table next to my Bible. It wasn't there when I went to bed."

Someone had entered her quarters in the middle of the night —a disturbing thought in and of itself. It had to be a servant or one of her ladies. Very few people could enter that part of the palace without being stopped and questioned. My mother suggested sending for the king.

"No, not now . . . . this is nothing. *C'est ridicule. Je n'ai pas peur.*"

"It is a nasty joke, ma'am," my mother said. "And someone came into your rooms while you were sleeping. I do not think it is nothing."

"Then, we'll talk to my brother. I don't want to upset the king."

"But shouldn't His Majesty see this? Whoever drew it is an enemy."

"No, I think not. His Majesty is prone to superstition, and this might distract him."

My cousin was always like that, weighing risks and possibilities.

We began the process of dressing her, and she took her morning meal. As far as I knew, she never spoke with her brother. On her orders, my mother and I never mentioned the incident again. No one was accused or punished, and I don't know what happened to the book. Yet whispers about the drawing made their way through the court—"It showed Anne Boleyn without her head, and her neck was gushing blood."

After that day, my cousin was more vigilant, sometimes saying to George and others close to her: "*Les gens ne m'aiment pas, et cela m'inquiète.*" She began sleeping with the torches lit and armed guards posted outside her doors. Many nights my mother and I stayed nearby in her other rooms to give her peace of mind. Yet, whatever her private thoughts and anxieties, she hid them the moment she stepped outside her chambers. To all appearances, she was a woman who had never known a hint of fear. This was an oddity of her personality: confidence and daring in public but doubt and dread behind closed doors.

King Henry made his unhappiness over the stalled annulment known to all his privy counselors, regularly blaming the pope and the Catholic Church. Sometimes his tirades even reached back to the boy who had thrown the rat and received sanctuary. "Why should he get away with it? These priests shelter traitors and criminals. Why is the church above the law?"

At first, his counselors advised conciliation. They still hoped to persuade the pope. But over time, a new set of men entered the scene, and they proposed a different solution.

"The Roman Church is a stew of corruption," Archdeacon Thomas Cranmer argued. "England needs a cleansed religion." Cranmer was one of the king's diplomats in addition to being a churchman. He was well traveled and articulate.

Thomas Cromwell said, "Crawling to the pope is useless. The only question is how to break with Rome without risk to the realm." Cromwell had tiptoed from Cardinal Wolsey's inner circle into the king's inner circle almost imperceptibly. Though many complained about his common birth and service to Wolsey, he was universally judged as "clever." Whenever he spoke, people listened, His Majesty most of all.

My well-read cousin plotted with Cranmer and Cromwell, and she easily matched them in her grasp of European politics. Whenever the men's arguments failed to move the king, she stepped in to try to sway him.

"England needs a prince, Your Majesty." She spoke softly and gazed into his eyes while her fingers strayed onto his knee. "I promise you the prize will be worth the price."

The king straightened his shoulders and lengthened his back as he boasted to the others in the room. "See, she is magnificent. She will birth me a batch of sons."

Sir Thomas More, who had become lord chancellor after Wolsey, was the naysayer—he opposed a split with Rome. My parents knew him and considered him a great writer and humanist. He believed in educating girls as well as boys. When I was twelve or so, he had asked me, "Do you read, Mistress Shelton?"

"Yes, Sir Thomas. I love stories and poems."

"Then you shall have a new book—the myths of the Greeks and Romans. After you read it, you can write to me and tell me what you think."

The book arrived within days, and I began a correspondence with him. Some months later, he introduced me to his daughter, Meg, and we continued to be friends.

Compared to the king's other counselors, Sir Thomas was more devout and less conniving. "To marry without the annulment is bigamy," he would say. "It would be a mortal sin, and I would fear for Your Majesty's soul." Cranmer and Cromwell argued that the Roman Church was merely favoring the Spanish and Katherine of Aragon over the English. The pope was playing politics, they said.

His Majesty seemed ambivalent, which was perhaps under-standable. He was the one who would burn in hell. My cousin took on the delicate task of bringing him along. During their intimate suppers, she would say, "You should lead the church in England. Why should it be the pope?" She prodded him with silky words and unanswerable questions such as, "Why should England live by Rome's rules?"

As fall approached, the king was still undecided, and my cousin's patience began to fray. "This is taking too long," she whispered to me and my mother. On her twenty-ninth birthday, she stayed within her rooms until the king persuaded her to come out to dance.

❧

More than once, my cousin asked me whether the common people loved her or whether Queen Katherine ruled their hearts. I didn't know—I sometimes wondered myself. So, when the court was in London, I walked the city and asked those I met what they thought of Anne Boleyn. Naturally, I never mentioned my family connections or my position at court.

"England is not safe without a prince," a shopkeeper told me. "This Anne Boleyn looks like a woman who can birth a boy." He paused while those around him nodded in agreement, one man adding, "His Majesty knows best."

A baker offered his own extended theological explanation for Queen Katherine's fall from favor. "First, she married the king's brother—that was Prince Arthur that died so young. Then she married her dead husband's brother who is now our glorious Majesty." The baker apparently placed the blame for this sinful act entirely on the queen, and he shook his head at her folly. "Holy scripture forbids such a union, so God took the male babes to punish her."

But many others defended Queen Katherine and used words like "witch" and "concubine" to insult my cousin. A laundress on the Thames showed her outrage by vigorously wringing wet clothing. "Is it the queen's fault the king has no sons? It's a poor excuse to cast Her Majesty aside and put this French whore on the throne."

Women often viewed the matter stoically. "It is a terrible shame," the haberdasher's wife whispered, "when a man wants to leave his faithful wife after so many years. But this must be God's will." She turned her eyes upward. "Who are we to question it?"

My spying provided little reassurance about the English people's views, although I told my cousin that all would come to love her once they knew her better. Even as I spoke, I had my doubts about my cousin's potential appeal. Those who resented her seemed to hate her.

My own life proceeded as it was—I laid out my cousin's clothing and jewels, read to her, cheered her, and ensured that the servants did what she desired. From time to time, my mother mentioned names she kept in a mental ledger—wellborn men, their property and titles, their ages and availability for marriage. One day she would latch onto a name—a man who met her ambitious criteria—and then my life would change. But until then I was free to daydream and imagine my own future. I could picture any handsome suitor I pleased.

9

SEIGNEUR DU BELLAY'S BALL

January 1531

Mark Smeaton, Greenwich Palace

*T*he tailors, lacemakers, and embroiderers set up shop at Greenwich, just as they had at Hampton Court. For the musicians, they stitched doublets of black velvet slashed with crimson, a sophisticated design unlike anything I had ever worn. I only hoped that my fitting meant Silas Bray planned for me to play something in public at some point. This was expensive clothing for tuning lutes.

The occasion was a visit by Seigneur Guillaume du Bellay, a French diplomat arriving to discuss the king's still unresolved "Great Matter." According to His Majesty's men, a grand ball, an event of unparalleled luxury, would ease negotiations and persuade the French to support King Henry's aims.

When I went downstairs to be measured, I looked around for Nan, remembering her coppery hair and curving breasts. I assumed she had married the tailor as planned but hoped she might be open to a diversion. Unfortunately, I met only French-speaking strangers.

Lady Anne had selected the tailors, judging them the most capable on the continent.

In King Henry's court, finery for the men easily matched that for the ladies, and clothing for the highest-ranking courtiers hung from life-sized wooden figures arranged in a semicircle. Each bore a name: Sir Henry Norris, a dark blue doublet and cloak; Sir Francis Weston, green and gold; Sir William Brereton, brown with touches of ocher. The most lavish garments were a shirt, doublet, and cape—crimson and glistening with silver threading—for George Boleyn, now known as Lord Rochford. He had been collecting titles deemed fit for a queen's brother.

Plans for the king's robes were secret. He would appear at the ball, uniquely radiant, encased in priceless fabrics and furs. Anne Boleyn would wear rubies ordered by the king especially for this occasion. They were worth a king's ransom, some jested.

Nearly all royal musicians played the lute, as did many courtiers and ladies. But some of us were professional lutenists, more skilled, practiced, and versatile than an amateur would be. A few days after Twelfth Night, Lord Sandys summoned the most accomplished lutenists to meet with him, and I was surprised to see my name on the list. Bray must have added it, but I wasn't sure why. I prayed that my tedious initiation had finally ended. Paul should have been chosen but wasn't. He accepted the insult more readily than I did.

"Doesn't it make you angry? You play better than almost all of them."

"It's not Bray's fault. People are either nervous or pitying or disgusted when they see me. I don't think he has a choice." Paul blinked, and then he laughed, probably to avoid sounding sentimental. "But what you said . . . that I play well. It matters more to me than what Bray thinks."

"It is true." I wondered if Paul understood how much I admired him, as a musician and my friend. "Someday, we'll play for the king together," I added, "at some grand event, maybe when a new prince is born."

"It's a fine idea," Paul answered, "but I doubt we'll do it together." His eyes crinkled as he smiled. "But you'll perform for His Majesty again—and very soon. This meeting with Sandys is your chance."

"Do you know why Bray put my name on the list?"

"Maybe someone suggested it."

"But who would suggest me?"

Neither Paul nor I had any idea.

⚜

The group waited for Lord Sandys in the music room, some players in conversation while others seemed lost in thought. I brought the cardinal's lute despite Bray's order to hide it. If this was my opportunity to attract the Lord Chamberlain's notice, I was prepared to take a risk. I touched the strings, careful to make no sound, just to feel their power in my fingertips. Master Peter had believed in me, and so had Cardinal Wolsey. I was confident of my skill.

Bray sat to the side, talking to another player named Humphrey. Over the year, I had observed that Bray was an expert lutenist, adept at the traditional Spanish pieces favored by Queen Katherine. But he disliked the new music from the continent—"mere frippery," he called it. He seemed aggrieved at having to learn the French chansons favored by Lady Anne and often complained about rehearsing the new consort music: "All the instruments jangling together? I doubt most people even like it."

At the stroke of nine, Sandys entered, accompanied by George

Boleyn. Bray and Humphrey quickly rejoined the group, and we all stood, bowing to the Lord Chamberlain.

"I present Lord Rochford," he said. We bowed more deeply this second time, and Sandys told us to sit down. An attendant arranged a large stack of musical manuscripts on a table while the Lord Chamberlain explained the purpose of the meeting.

"These are compositions we may ask you to perform at the ball for Seigneur du Bellay. We will play music from France to honor him and include new works from across the continent to demonstrate the refinement of His Majesty's court."

No musician would dare show discontent in the Lord Chamberlain's presence, but I was sure Bray wanted to roll his eyes. He said nothing, but I read his displeasure in the way he twirled the neck of his lute in his hands.

"We will ask you to play these pieces today so Lord Rochford and I can choose the most suitable and decide who will perform." Sandys distributed several copies of a manuscript so we could review it before playing, asking us to look at it quickly and then pass it along. The piece was Italian and difficult to read on sight. Different musicians in different countries used different markings to indicate tempo and repeating themes. Even musicians within a single country used a variety of symbols to show whether the music should be played powerfully or tenderly. Many composers wrote down only what they themselves needed to recall a piece, so chords and tempos were often missing. This meant the musician had to add whatever was needed to give the music shape. This selection was a work for three lutes.

"Master Bray, could you play?" he said. "And Humphrey?" He looked around for a third lutenist, and I lifted my hand to indicate my willingness. "Yes, young man. I am sorry. I do not know your name." Sandys was unfailingly polite in all my dealings with him.

"I am Mark Smeaton, my lord."

"Yes, very well . . . Silas, Humphrey, and Mark, could you play for us?"

Lutes in hand, we sat nearer each other. Bray placed the music sheets on a pedestal in front of us and assigned the parts. This was my moment—my service copying manuscripts for Master Peter and later at court was about to bear fruit. I may have been the lowest ranking musician in the room, but I had more experience deciphering foreign musical manuscripts than any of them. The piece was a fantasia by the great lutenist, Francesco Canova da Milano. I could see that it required each player to improvise at specific points, and I suspected my companions could not.

We started off playing together before the music called for Humphrey to improvise. Not realizing what was intended, he held a chord for several seconds but then stopped playing. I picked up to avoid an awkward silence. Bray learned from Humphrey's mistake, but his improvisation showed little imagination. He filled the time with a bland series of chords. When my turn came, I played a variation based on the previous musical phrases. Although the piece was new to me, I already knew something of the composer's style.

When Sandys asked us to play the piece again, Humphrey bumbled through his section using a jumble of notes unsuited to the music's spirit. Bray repeated the chords he had played before, but my second improvisation was better—more intricate and demanding. I glanced up at Sandys and Rochford. Both liked what they were hearing.

Sandys selected a new manuscript from the table and called for several other players to come forward. Bray, Humphrey, and I stepped away to make room for them.

"Please remain here, Mark," Sandys said before nodding to the others. "Thank you, masters, both of you."

The work of the morning resumed. In various combinations, we played chansons by Sandrin, de Sermisy, Janequin, and others. Most had originally been written for voice but adapted for the lute, so they required considerable improvisation and even guesswork. Then came collections of Italian madrigals and Burgundian court music.

Shortly before noon, the players rested while Sandys and Rochford conferred. They lined up the manuscripts and spoke quietly. At one point, I heard Rochford refer to "the younger one. He's the better player by far." Sandys turned and called me forward.

"Mark, this piece is for lute and voice. We would like you to perform it for us."

It was French and quite well-known, so I had played it before. As I sat down, I thought back to Apollo Minetti, remembering how he varied the touch of his fingers to give the music sentiment and voluptuousness. For this piece, I decided to emphasize the melody's joyous arcs and to soften its gentle descents. I gave it a stamp of my own.

After I finished, I saw Bray sitting at the back of the room, his eyes closed, his lute leaning against his leg. I doubted he had fallen asleep in such company—this was a gesture of disrespect. I rejoined the others while Sandys and Rochford whispered among themselves.

Sandys spoke to me again. "Have you performed at court before, Mark? As a solo player?"

"I have not done so yet, my lord. But I have had the honor of performing as a solo player for His Majesty."

"Have you indeed? When was that?"

There was no going back. I had to answer truthfully. "During the time when I was in service to Cardinal Wolsey. The king visited Hampton Court, and I performed in a concert prepared for His Majesty. It was the greatest privilege of my life."

"I see. Very good."

Rochford looked at me with an easy smile. Only nobles were that relaxed. "So, you're the player from Hampton Court. His Majesty mentioned your performance but didn't recall your name. I asked Master Bray to include any of Wolsey's players in our audition this morning."

I briefly worried that I might be expected to condemn the cardinal publicly and proclaim my devotion to the Boleyns. But Rochford was good-humored. "We're glad you play for us now." He emphasized the "now."

"Thank you, my lord. I am pleased and grateful to be here."

"Then all is well."

I couldn't see Bray from where I stood, but I could easily imagine his bitter thoughts. Basically, he had been ordered to include me—the upstart, the cardinal's special boy, someone with the skill to take his place.

The Lord Chamberlain ended the meeting. "Thank you, masters. Lord Rochford and I will consult with His Majesty and meet with you again. The ball is three weeks away, so we have much to do."

We collected our lutes, and Bray stood stiffly by the door.

"A promising day for you, Smeaton," he said as I approached and bowed to him. His voice was thin, as if he were choking. Was he furious? Did he fear me as a rival? Was it a mixture of the two? I had no doubt he resented Rochford's interference. He must have worried that I had impressed the king. But these were minor concerns compared to what had happened that very morning. I had performed better than he had with Sandys and Rochford listening. The noblemen had said as much.

But surely, I told myself, competition among musicians is commonplace, a customary part of the profession. Besides, what choice did I have? Was I supposed to sit there and pretend to be less skilled than I was? That was no way to get ahead.

The ball was in early February on the coldest day of the year. Outside, ice glistened on fountains and hedgerows. Within the palace, dozens of torches lit the hall.

Dressed in our black velvet, the musicians played easy melodies while the nobles feasted and talked among themselves. King Henry sat at the front in the center of the table. As predicted, his golden robes were magnificent, studded with sapphires and pearls. His billowing sleeves made him appear twice the size of a normal man. Lady Anne also wore gold, the celebrated rubies gleaming at her neck. She sparkled from head to toe. Seigneur du Bellay, his wife, the Dukes of Suffolk and Norfolk, Lord Rochford, and Sir Thomas Boleyn, the father, now the Earl of Wiltshire, took other places on the dais.

Behind the king stood Thomas Cromwell, occasionally leaning over to whisper to His Majesty and the Lady Anne. Cromwell was famous for leaving diplomatic feasts once the music and dancing started. I wasn't sure whether he disliked the entertainments or was sending a signal that he had more important matters on his mind. Mistress Shelton was there, too, sitting at another table next to Sir Henry Norris. She wore a gown of the palest green. I judged her the most beautiful woman in a room of beautiful women. I tried not to look at her.

The torchlight glinted on silver plates and goblets, and atten-dants rushed to ensure every cup was filled. Waiters presented trays of meats and delicacies, ending with a chess board and pieces made of sugar and ground almonds. It was astonishing in its detail. The seigneur asked to have it wrapped and sent home for presentation to King Francis. He proposed a toast to King Henry and the pastry chef. [4]

As the audience nibbled sweetmeats, Bray played the first chanson. His voice was strong, and his playing flawless, but some in the audience spoke softly while he performed. When my turn came, I sat in the center of the room and waited, giving the audience time to notice me. As I began, I saw the seigneur put his goblet down and listen more intently. Lady Anne turned her head. I had volunteered to perform the most difficult pieces and had practiced until the music permeated the muscles of my fingers and hands. That evening I played the most intricate passages without error or hesitation. Sound flowed from my mind and body as each listener slipped into his own private thoughts and recollections. This was a gift I could give.

When the dancing began, I switched to the virginals, one of four musicians taking turns. Our task was to accompany the dancers late into the night—no single musician would have had the strength to do it alone. The king danced with Lady Anne, their eyes locked on each other as they paraded across the floor. Together, they embodied every tale I had ever heard about royalty and romance. He was masterful and charismatic. She was glamorous and raven-haired. That night, they must have believed their future was pre-destined, that history and nature would bend to their desires. Sir Francis Weston danced with the seigneur's wife and then with the other ladies, one by one. All seemed delighted to be his partner, and this surprised me at the time. He wasn't as wealthy or powerful as many others.

When some men turned their attention to politics, musicians took their places for the dances so all the ladies would have partners. For an instant, I danced the pavane with Mistress Shelton, our fingers touching and her shimmering pale green skirt swirling near my legs. I remember my thought when I took her hand: *This is as close to her as I will ever be.*

The ball ended in the early morning, the king and his court departing while servants and musicians cleared away chairs, benches, and instruments. Lord Rochford stayed behind, and he approached me and thanked me for my performance. He gave me a small bag of coins, the first gift of money I had ever received from a nobleman.

I didn't open it in his presence—no musician would do that. I returned to my room, stored my lute in its case and put my wonderful doublet away. I sat on the bed holding the bag in my hands, preparing to be disappointed. Sometimes even the wealthiest patrons filled the pouches with small copper coins that didn't add up to much. But when I looked inside, I saw the flash of silver. George Boleyn, Lord Rochford, had given me an exceptionally large sum of money.

10

LA VOLTA

Winter 1531

Madge Shelton, The Court of King Henry

I had never heard of a woman teacher, but as the months went by, I became one myself. I was continually explaining the rules at court to the newest ladies-in-waiting, a growing number of them. The king rewarded his allies by inviting their daughters to attend the woman he planned to marry. My sister, Mary, was among the most recent arrivals. She was just thirteen at the time.

These younger women copied my cousin's fashions and speech and fumbled through the French phrases she used. They aimed to catch a nobleman's eye, someone who might marry them and increase their family's wealth. For them, Seigneur du Bellay's ball was like a hunting park stocked with well-fed prey. They were more single-minded and pragmatic than I was.

I expected my cousin to become queen and reign for decades. I hoped I would eventually encounter—well, if not a prince, at least a dashing young nobleman. For me, marriage was the price women paid for the romance that precedes it. I dreamed of a long courtship spent exchanging poems, walking in gardens, and whispering amorously while dancing.

For the seigneur's ball, my gown was the most exquisite I had ever worn—a lustrous pale green silk with embroidered sleeves and pearls stitched around the neck. The dressmaker told me the fabric was the color of an exotic gemstone found only in Byzantium. My cousin had given all her ladies new dresses for this special occasion. In that respect, she was generous.

Since the younger girls had never attended a court ball, I schooled them in the dancing. In some dances, the men and women start off in lines across from each other, approaching and touching palms. In others, they dance in circles and occasionally stop to clap. The nearest man holds his hand above the woman's head while she touches his fingertips and spins around. Dancing was my favorite part of court events.

⚜

Seigneur du Bellay's great ball began with extended proclamations by the king and the guest of honor. The Frenchman's jumbled English perplexed me and many others, and he lacked the gift of being concise. Some men drank liberally and grew wittier, while others drank too much and began boring everyone. Waiters brought courses of fish, game, fruits, and sweets and then whisked away the plates. The musicians performed, and when the young man from Hampton Court played and sang, I noticed I wasn't the only woman watching him. Maybe others had unsuitable thoughts, as well.

Soon the dancing began, and the musicians alternated traditional pavanes and galliards with newer dances like the saltarello. I recognized the exhilarating strains of the la volta the moment I heard them. In this Italian dance, couples draw close together in movements said to provoke desire. I was surprised and flattered when Sir Francis Weston asked me to be his partner. We began, our steps quickening as the music rushed forward. When it intensified, Sir Francis winked and put his hands around my ribs. Before I knew it, he had lifted me off the floor and turned around three times while the other dancers cheered. Apparently, this move was common in France and Italy, and my cousin laughed—I'm sure I looked astonished. But my mother frowned. For her, public displays of intimacy between men and women were vulgar. She had raised her daughters to be modest.

The king danced—regal, impressive. In these public settings, he was amusing and diplomatic. My cousin George ignored his wife, Jane, and partnered an assortment of other ladies, all thrilled to dance with "Lord Rochford." He later explained to me that this was "good politics." Sometimes I felt sorry for Jane. Sir Henry Norris also joined in. He was not an especially able dancer and seemed to regard dancing as a duty. I sat near him at supper, and his conversation was mostly predictable. He told me I reminded him of his wife when he first met her, and I wondered whether he missed her or just couldn't think of anything else to say.

After the first hour, some men left the Great Hall so they could drink and talk of sport and state affairs. With too few men remaining for the dancing, several musicians took their places. For the next pavane, I proceeded down the length of the hall with Mark Smeaton at my side. We stopped, as the dance required, and I turned round and round, his fingertips touching mine. Smiles and bows, nothing more—he quickly moved on to other ladies, including my younger sister, Mary. Within minutes, he rejoined the musicians. He was amiable but unknowable, just as those who serve are trained to be. When I was near him, I longed for another la volta, imagining that, like Weston, he would place his hands at my waist and lift me into the air. But this was a silly thought. No musician would ever touch you like that during the dancing. The limit was a brush of fingertips.

‽

I had assumed no one was watching or assessing my conduct. After all, it was only a dance. But the next morning, my ever-alert mother delivered her judgment: "Weston is married. He's not for you—nor is the pretty musician. You must watch your behavior, Madge, if we are to find you a suitable match."

"It was a dance—it was nothing. I have no power over what Sir Francis does."

"You must have encouraged him. You carry too much in your face."

"What do you mean?"

"You must avoid attracting gossip and think of your future. Whatever fantasies you have, Madge, abandon them. Marriage is why you are here."

11

THE TUDOR ROSE

1531

Mark Smeaton, The Court of King Henry

fter the ball, Lord Sandys asked me to join the small
group of musicians who traveled with the king. I began
performing regularly at court celebrations and occasionally for His Majesty and those who gathered with him in the
evenings. One day he spoke to me. "Ah, the young player from
Hampton Court. I admire those with great musical skill."

My stomach flipped with pride while my mind scurried for a
proper reply. "Your Majesty, I have heard you are a wonderful musician—a composer, player, and singer."

I inhaled and bowed. The king smiled, and his stance conveyed
a hearty good humor. Evidently, my response had met the standard.

After du Bellay's ball, Bray no longer limited my playing. If Lord
Rochford or Lord Sandys asked for me, Bray had no choice but to
comply. Eventually, he eliminated my other tasks—the only lutes I
tuned were my own—but his resentment was transparent. I tried to
show my respect for him by word, expression, and plentiful rounds

of bowing. The other musicians were noticeably friendlier now that I was no longer at the bottom of the pecking order.

⚜

Like everyone else, I watched Anne Boleyn at King Henry's side with awe and curiosity. She presided at feasts and ceremonies as if she were already queen. They traveled, rode, and dined privately together. His Majesty's eyes followed her every move.

All the women at court danced, sang, embroidered, and spoke a smattering of French. They posed near windows reading prayer books, sunlit visions of demure femininity. But Lady Anne was dramatic, like an unexpected summer storm. You could almost hear the wind swell when she entered the room. Personally, I preferred another, but it was Anne Boleyn who tempted His Majesty.

I don't recall the date—April, raining again, one of those weeks when people ask if winter's drizzle will ever end. The king had gone to Portsmouth to inspect the navy, and given the weather and dull destination, much of the court stayed behind at Whitehall. Paul and I were practicing, reworking the fingering for several difficult pieces. As we played an especially tricky Italian round, a page entered with a note on a pewter tray. Paul looked at the message. "Lady Anne's riding was canceled because of the rain," he said. "We're to play for her now."

"In her chambers, you mean?"

"Yes—they're waiting."

Despite my recent success, I still relied on Paul to explain the customs at court. Playing in Lady Anne's privy chambers was different from playing publicly or for the groups gathered around the king. We would be in a room with her and only a few others. This would be a much more intimate setting, and she might speak to us.

"What do you think we should play?" I asked.

"Duets, fantasias . . . honestly, they talk more than listen. We're just there for atmosphere."

"Should we change clothes?"

"No, let's go quickly. They'll barely notice how we're dressed."

We picked up our instruments and made our way to Lady Anne's chambers, passing through half a dozen hallways, going up and down the stairs. I intentionally walked slowly so Paul could keep up easily. Outside, I heard the heavy rain pounding on the ground. When we arrived, we presented ourselves to Lady Shelton, Mistress Shelton's mother, who showed us to benches in an alcove to the side. Mistress Shelton sat across the room with several other ladies. She was sewing and did not look up. Lady Anne was iridescent in a rose-colored gown that spilled onto the floor, a fluffy white dog asleep in its folds. Her heavy, high-backed chair resembled a throne, and four gentlemen hovered near her—sturdy green leaves bordering a Tudor rose. By then I knew them all by sight.

Lord Rochford was nearest, his head inclined toward his sister. Since he had favored me, I followed the talk about him more carefully. He was well-liked, and many chatted about how close this brother and sister were. The Boleyns always stuck together, people said. They were famous for it.

To Lady Anne's left stood Sir Henry Norris, smiling his placid smile. Norris decided who would see the king and when they could see him, so anyone who wanted something from His Majesty worked hard to stay in Sir Henry's graces. He had spoken to me several times since I had joined the king's traveling players, often complimenting me on my skill.

Sir William Brereton was a different sort—gruff, bearded, soldierly, his face darkened by the sun. A keen sportsman, he hunted and jousted with the king and had given Lady Anne his prize falcon. More than once, the king had ordered him to the North to restore order when there was unrest among the locals. I doubted Brereton would recognize me if he tripped over me.

The fourth man was the one I would have traded places with, were it within my power. Sir Francis Weston was casually handsome, stunningly well-dressed, only a year or two older than me. Witty, athletic, and a brilliant horseman, Weston greeted me and the other musicians whenever he saw us. He applauded generously when we performed.

The afternoon passed quickly. We played unobserved while the others talked and laughed. As evening grew nearer—and after several trays of wine and ale had passed among them—the conversation quieted, and they began to listen. Paul and I looked at each other, evidently with the same idea in mind. We began to play the old English country songs most had learned as children. Some started to sing. To my surprise, Brereton was the best singer, his rich voice booming out words from sea songs and country ballads. He knew some bawdy verses I had never heard. When I laughed to myself, he noticed. When the song ended, he looked in my direction. "So, you've never heard those verses before, have you?" He turned to Lady Anne. "I am pleased, my gracious lady, to educate these young players. We need to expand their musical knowledge."

She laughed and clapped for him. Then, she looked at us directly and whispered to her brother, who seemed to answer her question: "The dark-haired one is Mark. I do not know the other's name."

An hour later, Lady Anne stood, rousing her little dog from its sleep. She spoke to it: *Pourquoi, viens avec moi.* Mistress Shelton scooped him up, and he nestled happily in her arms while the other ladies gathered round. The men picked up their cloaks and hats, and George Boleyn, Lord Rochford, walked toward the alcove where we sat. Both of us rose from the bench and bowed to him.

"Your music has diverted and pleased my sister," he said before he turned to Paul. "I am sorry that I did not know your name when my sister asked."

"You are most gracious, my lord. I am Paul Markham." My friend showed no emotion, but I was pleased for him.

"I thank you, both of you," Rochford continued. "Very fine indeed."

⚜

The next day, Anne Boleyn spoke to me directly as I was walking through a downstairs gallery, headed back to my room. She approached from the opposite doorway surrounded by her ladies, Mistress Shelton among them. Exquisitely dressed and laughing lightly, Lady Anne stopped before me and looked at me steadily. I focused on her hands—perhaps to control my nervousness, perhaps because even her hands were perfect and immaculate. I remembered my mother's hands, reddened and cracked from work. In the countryside, even at the cardinal's palace, women never looked like Anne Boleyn. She was a woman of silken faultlessness.

"The musician—Mark, isn't it?" She turned to her ladies. "He's a handsome fellow, don't you think?" The women tittered and lowered their eyes.

"Ma'am." My fingertips tingled as I bowed. "May I play something special for you at supper this evening?" This was pretty much the extent of my conversation with any person of rank.

"Something special this evening? *Très agréable*. His Majesty is away, and we are bored." Her voice caressed the phrases, and she toyed with the syllables. "What do you think, Madge? Perhaps we should ask Mark to play something entirely new? Music we've never heard before?"

Mistress Shelton smiled in agreement but never looked in my direction.

"I will be happy to prepare something, my lady," I said.

In my mind, I thumbed through musical manuscripts, considering what she might like and what might be new to her. I reminded myself to steer clear of Spanish music since we had been instructed to avoid playing it in her presence. I secretly doubted she was so narrow-minded. I think everyone just assumed she loathed all things Spanish because Queen Katherine was born in Spain. Whatever the reason, a whole category of outstanding music was completely out of bounds.

"Yes?" she replied, a light edge to her voice. "And how can you be sure you are choosing music I have never heard before? In France, the most celebrated players entertained us playing every kind of instrument and presenting compositions from every land."

"If I may, my lady, I could play some pieces of my own invention, so they are sure to be new."

This was a gamble but the only answer I could summon at that moment.

"*Très bien.* We will prepare to be delighted." She turned to her ladies. "So young and talented, and a composer as well. . . ." There was a hint of challenge in her words, but an ease and kindness as well. The women buzzed appreciatively and moved away, their skirts rustling back and forth, their voices combining into a delicate hum. Mistress Shelton glanced back at me, a second only, before disappearing with the rest.

I flew to my room and rummaged through music I kept in a wooden box, pulling out the best of my songs so far. Knowing I would perform for the Lady Anne in a few hours prompted a burst of inventiveness. I concentrated as never before. For a moment, I feared my own music might not be good enough to impress the court, but, in my soul, I knew it was. As evening approached, I readied myself, washing up and brushing my best clothes. I prepared my lute, an activity that calmed me before performing. Walking through the palace, I considered my rich surroundings and remembered my family's shed on the River Aire. I had escaped poverty to become a court musician. If I did well entertaining Anne Boleyn, I might rise still higher.

The meal was interminable as I played with a group of lutenists sitting to the side. Even then, I rehearsed my own pieces in my head. Soon enough, the scene shifted. Servants cleared platters while attendants refilled goblets and laid out cakes. Mistress Shelton sat near Lady Anne, only a dozen feet away. At one point, she turned my way, her eyes shining, but then quickly looked across the room.

A French singer performed first, relying on set pieces many knew well. He had an easy, soothing voice but received only polite applause. I believed I could do better. Next, a juggler hurled crabapples and plums high into the air and caught them in various ways. Dressed head to toe in yellow and black, he never paused and never missed a catch. Occasionally he spun around and grabbed a plummeting piece of fruit seconds before it would have splattered on the floor. He closed by collecting four plums in his left hand and catching the last in his mouth. He crushed it until the juice rolled down his chin. The group laughed, and though I was preoccupied, I laughed too. He was a small, mousy man in everyday life but a marvelous performer.

Then it was my turn. The floor was cleared except for a single chair. I walked forward and took my place. When I touched my lute, its liquid sound filled the air.

Music can be an enchantment, and a sprinkling of magic dusted over me that night. Lady Anne's dark eyes deepened with pleasure. Maybe she was thinking of King Henry and the magnificent life she would share with him. When I finished, she raised her glass and motioned to the others to do the same.

"Beautiful, and superbly played," she said. "How fortunate we are to have this gifted musician with us. We drink to you, Mark, and thank you."

I bowed, listening to the murmur making its way around the room. I glanced at Mistress Shelton, who applauded and smiled like the rest. Until that precise moment, I had been invisible to most of them, one player among many, barely more than a piece of furniture. But that evening, my own modest creations had assured my future or sealed my fate—depending on how you look at it.

⚜

The more I played for Anne Boleyn, the more I saw the glowing Mistress Shelton. I often thought of the seigneur's ball when I was her partner for a twinkling of time. In my mind, I could hear the exact notes that were playing when my fingers touched hers. I remembered the flush on her cheeks and the rustle of her skirts as she danced beside me. Late one night, I imagined a song about her—a strand of melody that expressed my longing for her and the ridiculous hopelessness of my situation. Over the next few days, I refined the rhythm and added harmonies and variations. When the music was ready, I sketched out some words: A man adores a woman who is above him. She is gracious but doesn't see his love. Even if he gains fame and fortune, he will never be more than a common, base-born man. There can be nothing between them, and she will love another. No other end is possible.

When I read the verses the next morning, I burned the pages. These were prohibited thoughts. I wrote new words about a wealthy gentleman whose lover disdains him, though he gives her jewels and clothing of silk and gold. I expected my audiences would enjoy this sad tale of unrequited love among privileged people like themselves. It was much safer than the truth.

12

PERSEVERANCE

1531

Madge Shelton, Greenwich Palace

*O*ne day, while the king and my cousin were meeting with a Venetian diplomat, the youngest ladies asked me how they had fallen in love. We were stitching and embroidering, enjoying the pause in our duties. Four lutenists played, Mark Smeaton among them. Over the past months, he had become one of the most popular musicians at court. The girls quickly gathered around me, like small birds eager for a meal.

"The Lady Anne had just returned from France where she had learned the arts of dancing and witty conversation," I began. "One New Year's Eve, the ladies of the court performed in a holiday masque depicting the Seven Graces. Everyone watched, including the king." [5]

One of my young listeners sighed, probably picturing herself in my cousin's place.

"Lady Anne danced the role of Perseverance in a gown of amber silk. Her skirts twirled in rhythm to the music, and she curved her arms above her head, framing her flawless face. In this moment, His Majesty's heart caught fire—while she was dancing that winter night."

The girls applauded, and a few got to their feet and swirled around the room. They tried to imitate my cousin's flowing, seductive movements, but they were sticklike and slow. Among my family and acquaintances, people often told the story of this New Year's masque, although I was never sure how true it was. They typically added that Perseverance was the perfect role for my cousin: "She is a woman who never gives up."

A page brought word that the diplomatic meeting had ended, and my cousin would soon return to her rooms. Time for all of us to resume our tasks. The musicians stood to leave, and I saw no harm in speaking to them. "Thank you, masters," I said. They all bowed their heads. "I have a question, sirs. Are any of you familiar with the holiday masque I mentioned?"

Mark Smeaton knew the answer. "I believe it must be *The Triumph of Love and Beauty*, ma'am, composed by William Cornysh."

"The triumph of love, is it?" I laughed, and so did he, an infinitesimal second of spontaneity. But his unreadable gaze returned instantly.

"Perhaps," I said, "we should perform it again."

He blinked—his eyes were gray rather than blue or brown or green. But he spoke as required of those of lower station, politely and without emotion, as if he had no heart. "The music is wonderful, ma'am, and there would be parts for all the young ladies."

My sister giggled and raised her shoulders in excitement. "You're Mark," she said, stepping in front of him. "I danced with you at the ball." Her manner was too familiar. Mary had a bad habit of drawing attention to herself.

"Yes, I remember." He smiled and bowed his head to both of us.

The other musicians watched, holding their instruments, no doubt eager to be dismissed. Mary looked around the room, as if she were seeking allies. "Let's dance it again . . . I will be Perseverance. Mark, you can play while we practice."

"Mary," I said, interrupting her. "The Lady Anne makes these decisions."

"You're the one who suggested it—we could dance the masque in her honor."

"Now is not the time to talk of this. The musicians need to leave." I was afraid she might argue. "Lady Anne should not return to empty rooms. You must go there now."

I turned back to the musicians, "Masters, thank you. That will be all."

The girls scurried away, and I blamed myself for opening the conversation. I could easily predict my mother's lecture if Mary decided to describe the episode later: "Why did you speak with the players, Madge? You should set an example for your sister. You're the one at fault."

All evening, Mary and the younger ladies talked about reprising the masque—their costumes, the dances, the thrill of performing at court. In many ways, their excitement was charming. To my relief, Mary never mentioned Mark Smeaton, but I worried about her lack of restraint. It was true that I couldn't meet my mother's impossible standards of modesty, but Mary was more likely to cause a scandal.

cḃ

Some weeks later, my mother entered my room early, just as I was just getting out of bed. She asked my servant to light candles and bring fresh water before sending the woman away. Then she herself poured the water into a basin for me to wash my face; she helped me brush and pin my hair. She adjusted and tied the laces on my garments as she talked lightly about the weather and events planned for coming days. Every gesture was affectionate, but her purpose was evident. She had come to talk to me privately on a subject of some importance.

"I have news of Sir Henry Norris. His wife died yesterday." She adjusted the hood she had placed on my head. "Today, he returns to the country to see to his children."

"They have lost their mother," I replied, picturing the children in tears. But within seconds, I grasped my mother's intent—this was more than sharing sad news.

"Yes, it is unfortunate . . . but these tragedies occur in life." She looked at my reflection as she fastened a necklace, deftly tying the ribbons into a bow. "Sir Henry is the king's closest friend and companion, and he must marry again. That would be expected."

My mother isn't hardhearted. I had no doubt she regretted the family's grief. But she saw this death as a lucky circumstance for her daughter and of value to the Boleyns. I waited, mentally listing objections I couldn't utter aloud: *The poor woman isn't even in her grave yet . . . Sir Henry is as old as my father . . . Surely the man should have time to mourn before you offer me up to him.*

My mother seemed to read my thoughts. Perhaps she had been right—I carried too much in my face. "He isn't a young man, but he is gracious and powerful. And he is very wealthy, with large estates and profitable properties. If a union could be arranged, I know he would treat you well."

"But I am not drawn to him—not in the least. Have I no say in this?"

"Life isn't like your fairy tales, Madge. You must serve your family and play your role—as all of us do. Sir Henry would be an exceptional match."

I thought of going to my father, briefly entertaining a flimsy hope that he might take my side. But I suspected he would also see the arrangement's benefits and would doubtless urge me to agree.

"Just keep an open mind," my mother continued. "This is all I ask. I will consult your cousin to find out if she approves of this possibility."

My mother's use of the word "possibility" meant she planned to coax me along—she always chose her words with care. That morning, she began her long, maternal campaign like a diplomat. She was subtle but persistent. "Why don't you find Sir Henry before he leaves and offer your condolences?" she asked. "It would be a kind and Christian gesture."

I resisted, but later reconsidered. The man appeared to love his wife, or, at least, he mentioned her with some feeling—which wasn't the case with my cousin George or Sir Francis Weston and many others at court. My mother told me Sir Henry's wife had been ill and was younger than her husband, perhaps around thirty-five.

I found him in a Privy Council room, alone except for his clerk. He sat at a desk covered with papers and stood up when I entered. He wore the even expression he always wore.

"Sir Henry," I said. "I am truly sorry to hear news of your wife's passing. I will pray for her."

"Thank you, Mistress Shelton." He handed papers to the clerk who inserted them into a traveling bag. "I must go to my children this afternoon—my son is not yet five."

I immediately regretted seeking him out, fearing he would attribute my mother's blatant motives to me. But he said, "I am truly grateful for your words, ma'am," a tactful response. I was a Boleyn, after all.

Maybe Sir Henry and I shared more than I knew. We both understood the court's strange, strategic rules of life. Power, money, and politics trumped our private preferences and desires, whatever those might be.

13

PRINCE AND FLANDERS

1532

Mark Smeaton, The Court of King Henry

Once Anne Boleyn noticed me, I profited. Titled people paid me well to perform in their homes. Hiring me showed they shared the Lady Anne's tastes and preferences and demonstrated their admiration for the Boleyns.

Most days, I played at court in the afternoon, rushed to a noble house to perform at supper, and then entertained the king and his court late into the night. In what leisure I had, I composed or practiced. For me, music was like hunting or jousting is for other men. Its difficulty made it exciting.

My new visibility brought me privilege. The king named me a groom of the privy chamber, and I moved into an airy room at Greenwich. As a child, I had shivered in a shack and slept on a pallet. My new quarters had a fireplace, a featherbed, and windows facing a garden. The small wooden horse my father had carved for me sat on my table, next to books of poetry and myth. As a child, I had held it and imagined riding a magnificent steed. Thanks to Anne Boleyn, I had enough money to buy one.

I was often startled by the course my life had taken and exulted in fate's gifts. Isn't it natural to enjoy your good fortune? Wouldn't most people be proud and pleased?

Sir Francis Weston kept a pair of riding horses at Greenwich, two incredibly beautiful creatures. One was a magnificent black stallion without a spot of white. The other was a reddish-brown mare, a sorrel, with a color so unusual that people stopped in the streets to stare at her. Weston only rode them for processions. He had other horses for hunting and jousting—horses trained for those sports. But the black stallion and sorrel were the ones I dreamed of, and I often stopped by the stables to see them. I stroked their heads and gave each a slice of apple or pear. I loved the feel of their soft noses pushing into my hands. Weston's horses lived better than most people in England.

One day a stable boy told me Weston wanted to sell them, which surprised me. I asked Tom Chandler, the stable master, if this was true and if he knew Weston's price. Chandler looked at me curiously and suggested I speak to Sir Francis directly. I assumed he thought someone like me couldn't afford to buy a horse, much less a pair of this quality. But I had been saving, and by this time I had accumulated a healthy sum. I wasn't supporting a wife and didn't drink or visit the brothels to excess. I never gambled—to me, risking your money in games of chance was foolish, though many musicians did it.

But after talking with Chandler, money wasn't my main concern. Approaching Weston was. I wasn't supposed to speak to those above my station unless they first spoke to me. You wait to be addressed; you wait to be dismissed, and you never forget to bow.

But apparently, Weston wanted to sell the horses, and I was sure the purchase was within my reach.

"You can't be serious," Paul said when I described my plan. "You can't buy Weston's horses. How could you afford them?"

"I have the money saved."

"But it's more than the price of the horses. You'll have to pay the stables to feed and exercise them. It's going to be a lot."

"Yes, I've thought of that. I know what it costs."

"This is crazy—a musician owning horses. People won't like it. Bray and the others are already jealous of you."

"They'll be jealous whether I buy the horses or not. What difference could it make?"

"It's not just the musicians. People will say you're trying to rise above your station."

"People don't care as much about that as they used to. Look at Cromwell—his father was a blacksmith. The cardinal's father was a butcher. If I have the money, why shouldn't I buy the horses?"

His qualms showed in his face. "And look at what happened to Wolsey . . . the way they ganged up on him."

But Paul knew he wasn't going to change my mind. "Well, you can't just walk up to Weston and make an offer. Maybe you should write. That way, if he thought you were being disrespectful, he could ignore your letter."

Paul helped me draft my note, even as he continued to argue against the idea. I tried to write humbly, being careful to show my respect. I described how magnificent the horses were and how honored I would be if he would consider my offer. I assured him I had the means to keep the horses well—they would never be neglected. I promised to keep them together and explained that if we agreed on a price, I could give him the money that very day.

By the time I had copied the letter in my best hand and asked a page to deliver it, I was doubtful myself. Someone like Weston would never sell his horses to a commoner like me—he would want another gentleman riding them. So, I was surprised when, late that afternoon, Sir Francis appeared at my door. He looked as roguishly handsome as ever—tall, lean, richly dressed, and completely at ease. When he took off his cap, his straw-colored hair fell to his shoulders, and I noticed his blond-lashed eyes. Some ladies said his eyes were the color of sapphires, which wasn't true, but I could see why they said it. Women loved talking to Weston and listening to him. They loved dancing with him and sitting near him in church. But men liked Sir Francis too. He was mischievous and occasionally indelicate—no humdrum conversations with him.

"Excuse me, Mark, may I enter? I received your note."

"Yes, of course, sir. Please come in." I quickly stood up from my desk and bowed.

"No reason to beat around the bush," he said smiling. "My price is a hundred sovereigns for the pair."

It was far more than I expected—and far more than customary. I hoped my face hadn't conveyed my surprise. "They are beautiful horses, sir. . . ."

"Yes, I've had them since they were foals. The black is a true black—his color will never fade."

If I were buying something from a clothier or shoemaker, I would have made a counteroffer—maybe sixty sovereigns, something closer to what I had in mind. But in this case, the seller was Sir Francis Weston, the king's companion and one of Lady Anne's favorites. Bargaining might be seen as insolent.

Weston read my hesitancy. He probably thought I didn't have a hundred sovereigns, but that's not what he said. "I'd like to sell them this week because I am going to Surrey for several months—Surrey is my home. Why don't you talk to Tom Chandler and ask if a hundred is a fair price? Let's see what he says, and then we can talk again."

Maybe this was his way of bargaining—appearing to be concerned about the price being fair. The truth was I could scarcely believe he was talking to me, much less taking my inquiry seriously.

"Tom is there now," he added, "and I could walk with you part-way. It might be a good idea to catch him today. Then you can think it over and let me know . . . tomorrow, if that would be convenient."

Maybe I should have said I needed to be somewhere else, that I would see Chandler later, but that isn't how you answer a gentleman. "Thank you, sir. I would be honored."

So, there I was, walking side by side with Sir Francis Weston. He talked about his home in Surrey, the horses he had while growing up, how he came to own these two. Surprisingly, he asked me where I was born, how I had come into the cardinal's service, and where I learned to play so well. He was the first titled person to express any interest in my upbringing.

When we reached the stable path, he said, "I hope we can agree on a price, Mark. I would like for you to have them."

After he left, I visited the horses' stalls before looking for Chandler, my mind swinging between elation and worry about how to proceed. As a child, I had watched gentlemen ride by on fine horses, but none were as fine as these. I could afford them, and I wanted them. But perhaps Paul was right. Maybe they were too grand for me.

Chandler was known for his surliness, but everyone agreed he knew his trade. "What did he ask for?"

"One hundred sovereigns for both of them—he said to ask you if it is fair."

"A hundred? Well, it might be. Who's to say on that?"

Chandler's answer was evasive, and I assumed he thought I was daydreaming and wasting his time. Then he pulled his head back-ward and chuckled slightly. "But I'd wager you can get the pair from him for fifty . . . maybe even forty-five."

"But I don't understand. If a hundred is fair, why would he take so much less?"

"All I am saying is that I think he'll sell them for fifty. I'd say he'll take whatever he can get from anyone who can pay right away."

"What do you mean?"

"He's desperate for money—knee-deep in debt. Moneylenders only wait so long."

"But Sir Francis has lands. He's one of the king's favorites."

"That's true enough . . . but he spends every penny he has—gambling, women, jewels, furs. He owes the stables for at least six months. Word is he's going to Surrey to beg his father to bail him out." He laughed gruffly again. "I am telling you, you can get the horses off him for fifty. If I had fifty sovereigns handy, I'd buy them myself."

I wasn't sure what to make of the situation—that Weston needed money and I had the upper hand in the bargaining. Suppose Chandler was wrong . . . suppose I offered Weston fifty sovereigns, and he was insulted. Maybe I should offer eighty—less than he asked but more than Chandler suggested. I tried out various numbers in my head, thinking that it would be better to speak with Sir Francis than to write to him. That way, I could quickly increase my offer if he seemed offended. Then I knew what I had to do. If Weston and I were of equal rank, I could have bargained for a better price. But he was a titled gentleman, and I was only a player. Offering him less than he asked would be discourteous. He might tell stories about my impertinence.

I returned to my rooms and wrote to Weston offering the hundred sovereigns. Oddly enough, I was overjoyed once I finished the note. For me, it was easier to pay the extra money than risk Weston's contempt. He replied immediately, asking me to meet him at the stables at eight o'clock the next morning. He explained that he would bring papers assigning ownership of the horses to me.

I rose at dawn and counted out the sovereigns, checking my count three times. I put the coins in a small bag and set out for the stables early. I didn't want to annoy Weston by being late.

But he was already there when I arrived, leaning his forehead against the black horse's head and stroking its neck. I saw the bond between them. He looked up when he heard me approach, his smile as unclouded as ever. "I call him Prince, but he doesn't answer to it, so you can call him whatever you like. He's yours now."

"I like Prince, sir. It suits him."

"The mare is Annette—you can change her name too. Maybe something more dignified. What do you think?

"I had thought of calling her Flanders, after the country of my birth, if that seems suitable to you."

"It's a perfect name—Flanders it is. She's a beautiful girl."

I gave him the bag of coins. "I checked the count, sir. I believe it is correct."

I had extra sovereigns in my pocket in case my count was off. He took the bag but didn't open it.

"It certainly weighs enough." He grinned at me, his eyes clear, his face pleasant. As genial as he appeared, I wondered whether he was congratulating himself on getting the better of me. But I was so thrilled to have the horses, I didn't really care.

Weston seemed to want to linger, patting the horses and whispering to each in turn.

"If you ever want to ride them, sir, it would my honor to oblige you. Perhaps you would like to take them out one afternoon when you return from Surrey."

"Thank you. I might do that, but they are yours now. I know you will use them well."

He slid his hand over the perfectly rounded haunch of the mare, her reddish-brown coat shiny and smooth. "Horses have nice backsides, don't they? Almost as attractive as a woman's."

"Maybe so, sir."

This was his waggish side coming out—Weston, the charming rascal whom so few could resist. "I like a nice, round backside on a woman. Do you think Lady Anne has a nice round backside under all those skirts of hers?"

"I wouldn't know, sir. I have to keep my eyes on my lute when I play."

He knew this wasn't true; he played the lute himself. But his laugh was friendly, as if we had shared a joke. "Yes, a very good policy on your part."

He removed a sealed document from his doublet, his family emblem impressed in red wax on the back.

"I believe the papers are in order." Before leaving, he paused at each horse's stall to stroke its neck one last time.

I didn't have a chance to open the document and read it until shortly before I went to bed: "Sir Francis Weston of Sutton Place, Mayford in Surrey, transfers ownership of two horses housed at Greenwich to Mark Smeaton, a musician of the king." The papers described the horses in some detail and guaranteed their good health. Weston's extravagantly grand signature covered the bottom of the sheet.

I guessed that Sir Francis Weston was resting easier because he had money to reduce his debts. And I floated in unaccustomed happiness and disbelief. I had gained what I had wanted since I was a boy of five or six.

❧

From then on, whenever I had free time and pleasant weather, I took one of the horses for a ride. We trotted away from the palace, lazily discovering new paths and fields, the sun shining on my face. Even when I was busy, I rose early to visit them, to ensure they were washed and brushed and always warm and well-fed.

I bought the horses for the joy of riding and caring for them, but I couldn't deny that owning them changed some people's perceptions of me. At court, there were whispers about how much money I had, and a few speculated that I must have done more than play the lute to get it. Outside court, people often assumed I was a gentleman when I rode one of my fine horses, maybe a person of rank. Despite his initial opposition to the purchase, Paul often went out with me. The stable boys saddled the horses and brought them up to the gate, so Paul wouldn't have to use the long, stony path down to their stalls. He rode well, and I liked seeing him astride one of my fine creatures. When he was riding, his malformed foot didn't matter. He was as free and quick as any man.

When Weston returned from Surrey, he greeted me cordially. "Prince and Flanders—how are they? I hope you are enjoying them."

As it turned out, Weston became something of an ally in the months to come. He appeared to think well of me.

⚜

King Henry's court, I had learned, was an ever-shifting battle for power, and knowing someone's weaknesses could be as valuable as gold. If you understood a person's vulnerabilities, you could manipulate them—it might be as innocent as appealing to someone's vanity or as sinister as threatening someone they loved. Gathering and using this kind of intelligence was a master craft, and Lady Anne excelled at it. She used soft, flattering phrases and playful glances to lure both men and women to her side.

But even Lady Anne was bested by Thomas Cromwell, though his methods were far less agreeable. Some whispered that he kept dossiers on everyone who might be useful to him—families, finances, faith, ambitions, vices. He treated members of the court as chess pieces, each with a defined but limited role. His uncanny ability to move these pieces to His Majesty's benefit made him indispensable. Like everyone else, I noted his rise but only from afar. In Cromwell's cunning games for influence, musicians were only pawns.

Since we had both served Wolsey, he recognized me when I first came to court but never spoke to me. Once I began playing for His Majesty and Lady Anne, Cromwell occasionally offered a minimal acknowledgment of my existence, a brief nod of his head.

Late one night, I was leaving the king's outer chambers after entertaining His Majesty and a small group of courtiers and ladies. Cromwell had not been in the room. Yet as I entered the hallway, he appeared at my shoulder and invited me to join him for a drink. He indicated that we would go to another location. My fingers tightened on the neck of my lute as I followed him, my mind abruptly alert.

He led me to a small library not far away, the walls covered with maps and books. A fire crackled in the hearth. Cromwell sat down and gestured for me to take a nearby chair. Before doing so, I rested my lute on a cabinet well away from the fire—too much heat can damage the wood. It was a cordial scene by the look of it: plush crimson chairs in a comfortable room, torches supplying a flickering golden light. A servant brought in a tray with wine and cups and then departed. Cromwell poured our drinks himself.

"You've done well at court, Mark . . . impressing Rochford and Lady Anne."

"They have been most gracious, sir. I am grateful."

"His Majesty, too, values your musical gifts."

"As he values your statecraft, Sir Thomas." I silently asked myself what he wanted from me.

"I hope you are pleased with your new prosperity. Someone told me you bought a fine pair of horses from Weston."

Was this it? Paul had warned me that some would see my purchase as a sign that I didn't know my place. But I was surprised that my owning horses had attracted Cromwell's attention. Why would he even care?

"Fortune has favored me, sir. As a child, I dreamed of having my own horse, and Sir Francis was seeking a buyer . . . I beg pardon if anyone is offended."

Cromwell's eyes lit up, and he nearly laughed. "Well, anyone who complains is probably short of money after wasting it on gambling and silks. If you can afford to keep horses, by all means do so. Those of us who have worked our way to affluence must support each other."

I searched my mind for an appropriate response and took a drink of wine to give myself time. But Cromwell went on. "I was wondering whether you have stayed in touch with any of those who served Wolsey. Cavendish perhaps or Peter Capell?"

"I barely knew Cavendish, sir. To him, I was a boy who worked in the church. But yes, I've had letters from Master Peter. He will always be 'Master Peter' to me."

"Of course, master and apprentice," Cromwell replied. "He appears to have taught you well."

"I learned all my skills from him, and I believe he is proud of my progress."

"And he lives in Cornwall now?"

"Yes, in Cornwall. We exchange letters from time to time." Cromwell's questions could be seen as friendly conversation or the start of an interrogation. I thought it better to be frank.

"And what does he write . . . in these letters to you?"

So, here was the twist—a question that was both ominous and rude. It also showed Cromwell's power and authority compared to my lowly station. I had no choice but to respond. I shrugged, hoping to convey the complete harmlessness of my correspondence with the choirmaster. "Good wishes . . . news about his grandchildren, the state of his garden. I send my compositions to him and ask for his advice."

"Nothing of politics and religion?"

"Nothing at all. Master Peter is a man of music. Not everyone is interested in political matters."

"He protected a boy who insulted the king. His Majesty still complains about it."

"But, sir, this was church law. It wasn't Master Peter's decision."

Cromwell offered a dour, begrudging smile, but a smile, nevertheless. "Don't worry, Mark. I am just curious. No one suspects Capell of disloyalty. He has removed himself from worldly affairs and appears content to live quietly. This is all I know of him."

"Master Peter is not treacherous, sir. I would stake my life on this."

The smile again. "I see you stand by those who have helped you—an admirable quality. I am sure the Boleyns value that as much as your musical gifts."

He raised his cup to me, and I raised mine. There was little else I could do. In the moment, my main concern was about Master Peter—whether someone had accused or targeted him.

"I am sure you wish to write to your old teacher now," Cromwell went on, "to assure yourself that all is well. It is. I was merely interested in your relations with those who served Wolsey and whether you have enough sense to tell the truth when asked. There are so many who resist the need to change with the times."

"I have told the truth, sir." I bowed my head as I had been taught to do, but my resentment of him deepened. *Changing as you have done, Sir Thomas? Putting ambition over loyalty?* But then I had to ask myself if I was any different. Like Cromwell, I had looked for advantage after Cardinal Wolsey had fallen.

"I care nothing about musicians and music," Cromwell went on, "as long as players keep to their domain."

"Then Master Peter would agree with you. He always told me to stay away from politics and concentrate on my music."

"Then he gave you good advice—and not just about singing and playing the lute."

Cromwell emptied his cup, and I drank from mine, thinking only of when I would be allowed to leave.

"You must be tired, Mark. I understand you work very hard, almost as hard as I do." He rose and walked to the door.

"Thank you for the wine, sir." I placed my cup on the tray and picked up my lute before walking to stand before him. *At least I'm not working when I take a cup of wine with someone,* I thought as I bowed deeply to him.

He tilted his head, his expression amused. "I doubt you enjoyed our conversation tonight, but don't worry about it too much. I was simply trying to get to know you better. Ask your friend Paul Markham. He'll explain it to you."

I bowed once again and left him, shaken by the encounter. But it was his last statement, his mention of Paul, that turned my stomach inside out. I wanted to talk to Paul right away but thought it wiser to wait in case someone was following me.

I didn't go to my friend's room until the next morning before breakfast—Paul was fully dressed and reading his Bible. I quickly summarized what had happened, focusing first on my worries about Master Peter.

"I'm sure you didn't tell Cromwell anything he didn't know already. I've never heard any suspicions about Capell, and I've heard suspicions about nearly everyone else."

"But why would Cromwell question me like that? I don't understand."

"You have influential friends now—Rochford, Weston. You're in the king's favor, and you no longer answer to Bray. You've just spent an enormous sum buying the horses, so Cromwell sees someone who wants to rise. He's letting you know he's watching you."

"But why would he hint that Master Peter is suspected, and then take it all back, as if it were a joke. He told me to ask you why—he mentioned you by name."

Paul blinked and glanced at the open Bible on his desk. "Well, that's unnerving, I must admit." My friend kept his hair cut close, almost like a monk, and he rubbed at it before continuing. "Cromwell likes putting doubts in people's minds and setting them against each other—it's one of his most effective weapons. If everyone else is unsure, then he's the only one who knows the truth." Paul's eyes darkened, and his face lacked its usual openness. "Are you suspicious of me now?"

"I would trust you with my life, Paul, and my soul if it comes to that. Why do you think he named you?"

"To show how much he knows . . . to make you mistrustful of me . . . to imply that I am connected to him when I am not. It was a warning; Cromwell is telling you that he has his eye on you and that you should never cross him."

"I have no intention of crossing anyone."

Paul seemed confident about his interpretation of the meeting, and I vowed to be more careful than ever about my conversations. This was an easy vow since I rarely talked to anyone above my station. I arrived, played, and left.

The following week, I was relieved to receive a letter from Master Peter—nothing unusual at all. He wrote of the birth of a new grandson and said he was teaching his oldest granddaughter to play the virginals. He enclosed a musical manuscript, a Mantuan frottola for three voices, and suggested that I adapt it for a single singer and lute. No comments about the king or Anne Boleyn or Queen Katherine or Pope Clement, no remarks or questions about the court or the church or the world beyond his son-in-law's farmlands. None of it mattered to him. I hoped to be like him in a few decades.

14

No One in Particular

1532

Madge Shelton, The Court of King Henry

In the coldest days of winter, the court celebrated the Feast of Saint Valentine—poems, sweets, and dancing before Lent with its dreary weeks of fasting and prayer. The king gave my cousin a drawing rolled up into a scroll and tied with a purple ribbon. We all looked on and cheered as she pulled at the bow and opened the document with a flourish.

When she held it up for us to see, I was disappointed. It was an architectural sketch, one of dozens prepared for the renovation of Hampton Court. The king talked so much about his plans for the cardinal's old palace that it had become tedious. "We'll make Wolsey look like a pauper," he would say. "We'll make the doges envious."

But my cousin's reaction was different from mine. She smoothed the scroll out on a table and traced the drawing's curves with her index finger. She held it up again, making sure we saw the detail—a love knot merging an "A" for Anne with an "H" for Henry.

The notes explained that workers would carve the design into wood paneling in Hampton Court's halls and galleries.

"People will link our names forever," she said as she pressed the drawing to her heart.

⚜

The court passed much of the year at Greenwich while the renovations were underway. After supper, we moved into the king's chambers to hear about the builders' progress. These architectural conversations diverted the king and my cousin during their frustrating wait for the annulment—or, if need be, a more earthshaking solution. The king gloried in describing his plans, asking us what we thought and accepting our praise for his ingenuity and good taste. My cousin talked of his exceptional vision: Hampton Court would include a new hunting park, tennis courts, and enormous kitchens with ornate brick chimneys designed by Italian craftsmen. During these discussions, she and George suggested embellishments while musicians provided accompaniment and attendants offered wine and ale.

"The falcon will appear in stone over the main gate," George said one night as he showed another sketch to the king. Everyone recognized the white falcon, the Boleyn family emblem. [6] "The flowers in its beak represent fertility and the birth of princes," George explained.

The king pushed two fingers into the side of my cousin's breast, and she leaned over to kiss his cheek. His palms traveled from her breasts to her waist to her stomach, as if he were rubbing a magic lantern. That night they left us early, as they had begun to do more often.

My cousin once explained to my mother and me that she could satisfy His Majesty's desires without completing the full sexual act. "It is better if His Majesty has something more to anticipate," she told us, adding that she had learned certain techniques in France and considered them useful. Exactly what they were I could scarcely imagine.

One night, some of us stayed behind playing cards after the king and my cousin disappeared. I was at liberty until she emerged from the king's bedroom several hours later to return to her own chambers—decorum must be preserved. The men drank and joked except for Sir Henry, who was still mourning his wife. My cousin George turned to the musicians. "Mark, why don't you sing? Whatever comes to mind."

An older player leaned back in his chair, his annoyance undisguised. Silas Bray was master of musicians, and, by custom, George should have addressed him first. Others might not care about these niceties, but George did, and he quickly corrected his error. "Master Bray, why don't you begin? We are fortunate to have you here."

"Let's have some romantic songs about unrequited love," Brereton added. "That's what the young ladies like." Sir William was always teasing and winking at women—gentlewomen and servants alike. He was another one with an absent, half-forgotten wife.

Silas Bray played several court favorites and accepted George's compliments before pulling his chair aside. Mark bowed to Bray as he prepared to perform, but the older musician didn't acknowledge him. I had seen rivalries like this among the ladies-in-waiting and the king's attendants—someone falling out of favor, someone rising. Rank was everything at court.

Mark's first song was poignant and told a melancholy tale. A lover delights in the company of a young woman dressed in green, but she rejects him despite his devotion and costly gifts. After the final chord, everyone was quiet. Even the servants had stopped to listen.

Sir Francis placed his hand of cards on the table. "This is wonderful . . . the way the melody lodges in your mind."

Mary began clapping and making a show of herself. "Is the

lady one of us?" She had interrupted Sir Francis, but he too began applauding. Everyone else joined in readily—all except Silas Bray.

"Is it Spanish?" Brereton asked. "It sounds Spanish to me."

"It is perfect no matter where it's from," George said before Mark could answer. "Let's hear it again."

Mark played and sang, his gray eyes shining, his dark hair falling over his forehead, the locks neither curly nor straight. Bray sat back and stared across the room. Despite his noticeable jealousy, he must have recognized the song's uncommon beauty.

George asked Mark the name of the piece.

"It is my own composition, my lord. I haven't given it a name." He angled his body toward Brereton. "But you are perceptive, sir. The song does use a musical sequence common in Spanish music. I hope it does not displease you."

"If Rochford and Weston like it, so do I, and I can see the young ladies enjoyed it."

Mark lowered his head, the model musician. I wondered whether he was pleased or uneasy—he must have sensed Bray's dislike of him.

"Have you lost your heart to a woman in green, boy?" Brereton continued. "I wish you all the luck."

Mark laughed—probably the only answer anyone expected or wanted.

The card playing resumed, and the musicians moved on to other pieces. Sir Henry begged everyone's pardon and left early, stopping on his way out to bow to me. His particular attention made me wonder if gossip about my mother's aims had somehow reached him. In private, she daily pressed her case: "Sir Henry is an excellent match," she would say, smiling and touching my cheek. "Such a marriage would honor you—and bring you contentment in time. It is what your father wishes." She had already raised the prospect with my cousin, who kept saying, "*Peut-être. C'est quelque chose à considerer.*" Letting a few rumors circulate would serve my mother's ambitions, a phenomenon I am sure she understood.

About an hour after Sir Henry left, Brereton pointed to Mark and spoke to him as if their earlier exchange had never ended.

"About your song, young man . . . what's your name, again?"

Mark stood up, his lute in hand. "I am Mark Smeaton, sir."

Brereton's face was pinkish from his many cups of wine. His voice carried throughout the room. "Ah, yes, Master Smeaton . . . well, the Lady Anne favors green, or so I've noticed. Has the Queen of Hearts seduced you like she seduces all the men? Has she trifled with you?"

Someone gasped, while others looked at their cards or squirmed in their seats. George leapt in. "Brereton, your jokes will cause trouble one day. My sister thinks only of His Majesty. She conducts herself as a queen."

"Of course . . . it's just those French ways she has, that's all I was talking about. Every man here knows what I mean."

No one said anything. Mark stood silently, waiting to be addressed or told to sit again. Brereton mumbled an apology for his distasteful clowning and lifted his cup, as if he were giving a toast. He often drank to the point of recklessness, but he was sober enough to realize that he needed to turn the room's attention away from his dangerous words. Again, he spoke to Mark.

"So, my young friend, which of these fair maidens has broken your heart? Who is your song about?"

"It is a poor musician's invention, sir, about no one in particular."

This particular line of questioning was over. Everyone was relieved.

Later that night, when I was falling asleep, I thought about how rumors can start in a moment of drunkenness or bravado—how ill-chosen words can destroy. Brereton's jesting about my cousin had no basis in truth—she was far too occupied persuading the king to marry her. But I wondered if Brereton had revealed his own hidden desires. Men often looked at my cousin lustfully.

And then I thought about Mark's claim that his song was a mere fantasy. Can a man truly write such music solely from imagination? Or was there someone he loved?

Yet whether he answered truthfully or not, his words described only one of love's cruelties—the pain of passion with no return. My own situation was the opposite. I might soon be forced to marry a man who meant nothing to me. I feared I would live my life pretending to love someone I only felt sorry for.

15

PERILOUS ENCOUNTERS

1532

Mark Smeaton, Greenwich and Whitehall

Court gossip had turned to Mistress Shelton and Sir Henry Norris, though no betrothal had been announced. The rumors saddened me, as if I were losing her—as nonsensical as that was.

I had never seen them in any flirtatious conversations. They rarely talked at length. She danced with Weston, Brereton, Lord Rochford, and many others, including His Majesty. Pretending only mild interest, I asked Paul about the rumors.

"It would be a logical match," he explained. "The Boleyns would consolidate power and have another family member close to the king. Besides, Norris is wealthy, and the Boleyns spend well beyond their means."

Still, I thought it a strange coupling. Norris was a dour, solitary widower who spoke very carefully or not at all. Mistress Shelton was luminous. She wrote poems and amusing stories which she read aloud. When her listeners laughed, she laughed too. I wished I could sit near her and talk with her—it would be a small theft of bliss.

cþ

When I wasn't playing or practicing, I rode Prince or Flanders and explored the countryside. Within months, I knew every path, hill, and stream around Greenwich. I saw the country people farming patches of turnips and carrots, wearing the same frayed britches and shirts no matter the time of year. They lived in flimsy sheds scattered near the road, and I knew what these were like inside. Every so often, I imagined my mother standing in the doorway of one of them and my father cutting wood at the back. I envisioned them older and pretended I was returning home after many years—a son with enough money to free them from their ceaseless labor.

One afternoon, I was riding a well-worn trail back to the palace when I saw someone in the distance—a woman leading a horse. This stretch of the road was one of my favorite spots, dreamlike in every season. Large beech trees lined each side, their branches meeting and touching overhead. That summer day, the sun twinkled through the tunnel of limbs and leaves, creating shafts of light in the shade. As I approached, I saw that the woman was young—her light brown hair flowed down her back. The scene reminded me of a legend or ballad—the lonely traveler meets a mysterious maiden, a princess or an enchantress. I knew quite a few songs that begin this way.

Mistress Shelton's horse was limping while she walked slowly beside it, her full attention on the animal. When she looked up, she was startled, as if I were a stranger. Then she blinked before she smiled. "Master Smeaton. . . ."

"Ma'am." I jumped down from Prince and bowed. "May I help you in any way?"

I suspected we were equally surprised. She didn't expect to meet a court musician riding a fine horse in the woods. I didn't expect to find one of Anne Boleyn's ladies by herself on the road, much less the glowing Mistress Shelton.

"One of his shoes is loose," she explained. "I'm afraid that riding him will hurt him."

I knelt beside the horse to check its hoof, my mind sifting through the commandments I had absorbed from an early age. I shouldn't speak freely to a person of higher rank, especially a young lady. "Good morning," "good day," "ma'am," and "thank you" were the limits of conversation.

But surely this was an exception. She was on the road alone, and robbers were not unknown. I had to help her, and to do that, I had to talk to her—to say more than "good afternoon."

The horse's shoe was half off its hoof, making its gait uneven. Riding the poor beast could, indeed, injure him. Mistress Shelton evidently knew enough about horses to see that. The obvious solution was for us to ride Prince together, with her sitting behind my back and her horse walking beside us. But the rules were as clear as water—that would be completely inappropriate. Even suggesting it would be disrespectful.

"Please take my horse, ma'am, and ride ahead," I offered. "I can walk your horse back to the palace." I wanted to do it—I was proud to do it—but there would be consequences for me. Walking the horse back to Greenwich would mean I would arrive after sundown, long after I was due to play for His Majesty. I would have to explain.

She gave me her horse's reins and stood near Prince. "You'll get back late," she said. "They'll be asking where you are. Do you want me to give someone a message?"

"Perhaps you could ask one of the stable boys to ride out to meet me with my other horse—I'll stay on the path." This would save at least an hour. "Ask for Jack—he'll know what to do. We'll take good care of your horse."

"Yes, I know you will. Thank you, Master Smeaton. I'll talk to Jack myself."

She took Prince's reins but looked uncertain. "I'm sorry to cause you trouble."

"Do not concern yourself, ma'am. I am honored to help."

Then I remembered the gruff Welshman who occupied one of the small sheds just beyond the rise. "There's another possibility, ma'am . . . with your permission. I know of a farrier nearby who could repair the shoe. You can ride my horse back to the palace, and I'll get yours shod and ride him back afterward."

She said nothing for a moment, making me wonder what was on her mind. Then she spoke in a gentle, lilting tone, "Let's go together." She laughed a soft laugh that sounded like music. "To the farrier, I mean. It will be an adventure."

I heard her words and understood them. Our meeting seemed real enough. Gripping her horse's reins, I tightened my fingers around the leather, looking for tangible proof that I was awake. Yet her invitation was astonishing, surprising even for a dream.

"He's Starlight," she said. "I named him as a child."

"This is Prince. I hope you'll ride him to the farrier. I can lead Starlight beside you."

"Thank you, Mark." I bowed and nodded while she added, "I am very tired—I've already walked a long way."

I considered whether I should help her mount, but she climbed astride Prince without hesitation, swinging her legs on each side of the horse. At once, she began to explain. "I learned to ride this way in the country, where I grew up. It's a secret."

"A secret?"

"Yes, riding like this isn't proper for one of Lady Anne's attendants."

"No, I suppose not. No one will learn of it from me."

She put her forefinger to her lips jokingly, and it occurred to me that she had to follow rules, too, despite her high social position.

The walk to the farrier passed in an instant. She talked of Norfolk and her childhood at Shelton Hall. When she asked, I told her about Prince and Flanders, saying that Sir Francis Weston had sold them to me.

"The sorrel," she said. "She is gorgeous. I've always admired both these horses—they're the most beautiful at the stables."

Like Weston, she asked about my family and how I had come to Hampton Court. Unlike Weston, she seemed concerned about some aspects of my story. "But you had to leave your family when you were so young. That must have been very hard."

"It was, but my parents wanted me to go to school, and. . . ." I stopped. The depressing details of poverty weren't suitable for ladies of the court.

"And what. . . .?" She waited, as if she truly wished to know.

"There wasn't enough food for everyone."

She hesitated, saying only, "Ah," before looking at me, our eyes locking for a moment. "Do you visit your family now?"

"My father died, and my mother and brother returned to Flanders."

Another pause.

"But you have many admirers and friends at court now. I hope it is compensation."

"Yes . . . I love playing music. In this area of life, I have been very fortunate."

"Even when you have to tolerate obnoxious men like Brereton?"

She rolled her eyes, leaving no doubt what she thought of him. Then she met my gaze and spoke earnestly. "Your songs are very beautiful, Master Smeaton. His Majesty, my cousins, everyone at court delights in them."

I bowed and thanked her. Others had given me similar compliments, but this one pierced my heart and soul.

The farrier did his work quickly, and when he was finished, he turned to me and held out his hand. Evidently, he assumed that

Mistress Shelton and I were married or betrothed or brother and sister, that we were connected in some way. She watched, bemused, while I paid him. Oddly enough, I was elated that she didn't offer to repay me afterward. She acted as if I were a gentleman.

Outside the farrier's shack, she mounted her horse while I got on mine. She brought Starlight around to stand close to Prince.

"If we hadn't met today, I would have had a miserable afternoon," she said. She touched the top of my hand, softly and affectionately, like the tap of a fairy queen. "You appeared when I was exhausted and beginning to be frightened. Now I will remember your kindness and quick thinking."

"It was my honor, ma'am." I tried to sound detached and unaffected, but I wanted to cheer aloud to the angels above. Naturally, I imagined kissing her, though I buried that thought immediately. We went back to the trail with our horses trotting side by side. We passed through the tunnel of beeches, and the sunlight gilded her hair. When we came out into the full light again, we both halted. I knew what I had to say.

"Mistress Shelton, perhaps you should ride ahead. The way to the palace is direct along the path."

"You are right, Master Smeaton. We cannot be seen arriving together."

"I will not mention our meeting."

"Nor will I . . . but thank you again."

The skin where she had touched my hand tingled, as if my flesh were determined to retain the memory. She gently tugged at Starlight's reins, and I watched as she rode away from me. When she was about thirty feet down the path, she paused and looked back to wave goodbye. Everything about her was radiant.

Later that night, I watched her dancing with Sir Henry and several other gentlemen. The next day, a boy delivered a bushel of pears and another of apples to my horses' stalls—these were his instructions, he said. In the weeks to come, Mistress Shelton and I never spoke of our meeting. We limited our words to the polite, contrived exchanges permitted between a lady and one of the king's musicians.

For her, I supposed, our encounter was like one of those chance meetings people have when traveling, interesting but without consequence. For me, my dreams had briefly meshed with reality. Every minute I spent with her glistened in my mind.

Several months later, Mistress Shelton and I would talk again in secret, but under less magical circumstances.

⚜

Mary Shelton was still girlish in figure and awkward. She lacked her older sister's wondrous grace. But she often approached me when I was playing, bubbling with compliments and asking silly questions about the music. I responded politely, as suited my place.

Lady Worcester, the queen's highest-ranking lady-in-waiting, frowned when she saw the girl near me. Lady Shelton admonished her daughter: "Mary, it's time for us to leave." Paul noticed her repeated attempts to talk to me and advised me to avoid her.

About six o'clock one evening—the hour when the ladies change their clothing for the evening meal—someone knocked on my door. Before I could answer, Mary Shelton walked into my room, carrying a lute with its strings trailing on the floor.

"Mark, could you mend this?"

I was resting on my bed with my feet up and my shirt undone. I quickly stood up, fastening my clothing as I bowed. I remained across the room, standing some feet away. She had left the door ajar, and I couldn't decide whether it would be better to close it or open it wide.

"Of course, ma'am, I would be pleased to." I approached her to take the lute from her outstretched hand. "I'll repair it tonight and have it delivered tomorrow morning."

"I want to watch. I can sit here while you work on it." She settled herself in a chair by the window, tossing her skirts around her. Her feet barely reached the floor.

"I do beg pardon, ma'am, but the work may take some time."

"I can wait. I have nothing else to do."

"But won't Lady Anne miss you if you're not nearby?"

"She wouldn't know if I was there or not."

"But Lady Worcester would notice, as would your mother and sister."

"So what if they do? I would rather be with you."

Allowing this ridiculous girl to stay in my room was dangerous. This was no accidental encounter in the countryside—she had deliberately come to see me. If she were seen or told someone she had been in my chamber, few would accept an innocent explanation. As young as she was, I believe she knew this. I think she relished the prospect of a scandal.

"Ma'am, please forgive my frankness, but I believe you should leave now. It is not suitable for you to be here."

She looked around the room and toyed with the beading on her veil. "You have books. Are they yours?"

"Ma'am, I am sure your mother and sister would not want you here."

She stood up and walked to my worktable where she picked up the small wooden horse my father had carved for me. "Is this a toy?" she said, wrinkling her nose. "Why do you keep it?"

"Again, ma'am, I ask you to leave . . . or I will look for your mother and sister myself."

She swirled around, raising her chin. She was angry, but so was I. The girl was either stupid or malicious, possibly both. "Very well, Mark, but I thought you would be more courteous to a visitor."

My anxiety soared as she pranced out. Suppose she invented a story painting me as the lustful villain, a grown man taking advantage of her? Since I was due in the Great Hall at seven o'clock, I had little time to worry. I examined her lute—the dangling strings, all precisely the same length, probably cut with scissors. A sloppy, childish stunt—and my wooden horse was gone.

My mind scurried through options. After my performance, I would talk with Paul—my first step without a doubt. Perhaps I could go to Weston or Lord Sandys if the girl made trouble. I ruled out Lord Rochford, who would naturally take a family member's side. And of course, there was Mistress Shelton. We had walked side by side one afternoon, talking almost as if we were friends. I had behaved honorably, and she seemed kind, even more than kind. Moreover, she had witnessed her sister's lack of restraint on several occasions.

But to me, approaching her was unthinkable, no matter what risks I faced. In my dreams of her, we were equals. I could never go to her as a pathetic supplicant, begging for her protection. And why would I expect her to believe me over her own sister? We had only been together for part of a sunny afternoon.

As events unfolded, the choice wasn't mine. I dressed, picked up my lute, and walked through the garden toward the Great Hall. Mistress Shelton was waiting outside the door. She motioned for me to follow her into an outdoor gallery, deserted at this time of day. In the setting sun, we stood some feet apart, her body silhouetted. I could barely see her face.

Even as I prepared to defend myself, I asked myself why she would choose to speak to me alone. If her sister had accused me, wouldn't the father or Lord Rochford be the one to confront me?

"Mary has told me a story," she said quietly, "but I'm not sure what to believe."

Every muscle in my body tightened while my mind flitted in a dozen directions. My fingers wrapped around my lute, almost as a form of prayer.

"Mary said you asked her to visit your room. She claims you kissed her and took liberties. Have you done this?"

"Ma'am, I have not."

I should have ended my answer there—these were the rules at court. But her sister's lies enraged me, and, for once, I refused to play the humble underling. Mistress Shelton would hear the truth.

"Your sister brought a lute to my room and asked me to repair it. I never invited her there. I suggested she leave, but she delayed until I threatened to come to you and your mother. Nothing passed between us . . . and I believe she damaged the lute intentionally as an excuse to visit me."

Mistress Shelton pulled her cloak closer around her neck and looked through the stone arches to the other side of the courtyard. Darkness seemed to fall more rapidly. I waited, expecting her to dismiss my outburst as a guilty lie. Why should she accept my account? But I had underestimated her. She was far more generous and fair-minded than I had imagined.

"I am sorry this has happened, Mark. I owe you an apology." Her voice was soft but clear. "I saw my sister with the lute this afternoon. I didn't realize what she was doing."

"If you believe me, Mistress Shelton, no apology is needed. You are not to blame."

"No, but Mary is. I will speak to my mother and ensure she understands. My sister is not ready to be at court."

"She is very young, and she let herself be carried away by storybook fantasies."

"She is foolish, and I expect my mother will send her back to Norfolk tomorrow. She will not bother you again."

Even in the shadow of the gallery, I saw that she had raised her eyes to mine. "I should have known Mary's tale wasn't true even without asking. I hope you can forgive her and forget what she has done."

"Of course. I would never speak ill of her."

"Thank you." She bowed her head. "There are men at court who would have taken advantage of her stupidity. Once again, I am grateful to you."

She reached inside her cloak and pulled out my small carved horse. "This is yours, I believe."

I stepped closer to take it and thanked her. I was genuinely grateful for its return.

"Did you carve it? The work is so clever and delicate."

"My father carved it for me before I left my home." For some reason, I felt a boldness I should have suppressed. "He was exceptionally skilled with wood."

"He must have loved you very much to make such a charming gift for you."

"Yes, I believe he did."

I bowed and left her. There was nothing more to say.

PART THREE

---

*The Lady
Becomes a Queen*

16

SECRETS

1532 to 1533

Madge Shelton, The Court of King Henry

*E*veryone keeps secrets, I suppose. Once upon a time, my greatest secret was that I sometimes snuck out of the palace to ride my horse astride. Then I began to keep more forbidden secrets—that I was drawn to Mark Smeaton and imagined myself lying in his arms and kissing him. Even though my mother praised Sir Henry Norris daily, the king's close friend did not appeal to me in that way.

Mark Smeaton was completely unsuitable . . . nothing could come of it. Yet my feelings for him matched all I had ever heard about romantic love. Alone in the forest, far from society's judgments, I had leaned over and touched his hand. I had done this—a breach that would have shocked my mother.

Mark and I kept secrets between us—we had a kind of bond. I knew he would never speak of what had passed between us in the countryside or of Mary's escapade. And I admired his skill and diligence. Unlike the other men I knew, he wasn't born with lands and titles. He had gained what he had on his own.

Most of the time, I forced myself to act sensibly. I avoided him at the dances and sat farther away when he played. I recognized that I was too fond of him, and this could harm both of us. No one should ever know how I felt, not even Mark himself.

But I wasn't the only one hiding my desires and clandestine meetings. The king and my cousin also kept secrets, and theirs would upend the realm.

My cousin supported the new religious ideas from Germany and recommended them to the king. She ordered books and read passages to him as they sat side by side. She chose dresses that revealed the curves of her breasts and mixed teasing whispers into her religious soliloquies.

"The pope is corrupt," she would say. *"L'église de Rome est pervertie."* She would tilt her body so His Majesty could peek into her bodice and sometimes inhaled to give him a better view. "The time has come," she'd go on, fingering her neckline as if she meant to undo the fastenings. "You can create a new English church truthful to God's purposes. You can alter the course of history."

She wasn't the only one advocating a spiritual revolution, though she was the only one I knew of who used sex to advance her ideas. Cromwell and Cranmer urged the king to sever the English church from the Church of Rome. "But it could divide the kingdom," he replied. He worried about making permanent enemies of the pope and the Spanish king. His vacillation frustrated my cousin, and she whispered to George about His Majesty's *manque de colonne vertébrale.*

Then, one morning, a rusted needle in a cup changed all the rules of the game. Nature had intervened.

☙

Shortly after New Year's, my cousin suspected she was pregnant and sent for doctors to be sure. She announced this news to my mother and me without embarrassment or explanation. I wondered whether her French techniques had failed or whether she had chosen to abandon them.

Two gray-bearded men arrived, and little Pourquoi barked at them. She laughed at the dog and spoke softly, *"Tais-toi, mon petit."* She leaned back against a mountain of pillows wearing a nightdress trimmed with Venetian lace. The doctors took turns pressing her belly and placing their ears against it.

"My lady," said one, bowing his head. "There are questions we must ask."

"Bien sûr . . . of course." Her mood was effervescent.

"Are your breasts sore or larger than usual?"

She laughed. "They are as they always are."

The other doctor, after an extended apology, inquired about her monthly bleeding—its regularity and when she had seen it last. They stepped back and conferred urgently in a corner. One approached and pulled my mother aside. "We require a cup of urine."
[7]

I was shocked, but my mother wasn't. She accompanied my cousin to another room and, some minutes later, they returned with a half-filled Venetian goblet. The doctors inspected the urine's color, sniffed at it, and talked among themselves. They instructed my mother to place a sewing needle in the glass, adding, "If it rusts overnight, you can expect a babe."

After they left, my cousin said, "Do as they say, but take the goblet away. I don't want to see it until the time has passed."

My mother smiled as she positioned the glass on a tray and covered it with a cloth.

"And don't look at it yourselves," my cousin warned us, "not before I do."

"Of course not, my lady," my mother answered.

The next morning, we presented the tray to her. I would have lifted the cloth immediately, but she insisted on dressing as usual, a process that took nearly an hour.

"I will examine it myself," she said when she finally approached the tray and stood with her back to us. She lifted the cloth and remained silent for some time. Then she turned and displayed the needle covered with abundant orange rust.

My mother's face beamed with excitement. "The orange color, my lady—this indicates a boy. It has been proven many times."

My cousin visited the king alone—no grooms, no ladies, no musicians, no one to hear anything they said. I waited outside the door, trying to imagine the conversation.

⚜

Some weeks later, we crossed the central courtyard at Whitehall in a frigid predawn dark. To protect the precious babe from the wintry wind, my cousin wore furs from head to toe. She said little as my mother and I affectionately clasped her arms. We stopped at the chapel to pray and light candles before entering the gatehouse and climbing to the topmost floor. Like Hampton Court, Whitehall had once belonged to Wolsey. The dead churchman had palaces up and down the Thames. This one was known for its gatehouse built of light-and-dark stones arranged in a chessboard pattern. The cardinal had ordered the heavy stones brought to London by barge from his properties outside London. [8]

On January 25, in the year of Our Lord 1533, my cousin married the king of England in a hastily arranged ceremony in an ancient edifice rebuilt by her vanquished enemy. Over the years, she must have dreamed of a magnificent wedding at the Chapel Royal or Saint Peter's Abbey—not a paltry event like this one. Since no church had read the banns, the wedding was, strictly speaking, against common law. Even so, the king needed witnesses—my mother and myself, my cousin George, Sir Henry Norris, and Sir William Brereton.

I had expected Archdeacon Cranmer to preside, but George said he hadn't been told—better to reveal the king's second and probably illegal marriage once it was a fait accompli. Thomas Cromwell wasn't there, either. Perhaps a perfunctory twenty-minute ceremony didn't interest him as much as writing edicts designed to create a new church. Perhaps he was too busy planning to close the monasteries and cleanse England's new religion of its holy relics and superstitions. He may have been quizzing his spies.

A few months later, to no one's surprise, Archdeacon Cranmer became archbishop of Canterbury and annulled the king's marriage to Katherine of Aragon. England had a new church leader, and His Majesty was no longer a bigamist. The king was safe from the fires of hell.

17

FANFARES AND POETRY

April and May 1533

Mark Smeaton, London

ord Rochford's servant brought the message before breakfast: "Come to the Privy Council chambers at two o'clock. No need to bring the lute."

Being summoned to the Privy Council was ominous for a player—it was probably ominous for anyone who wasn't a council member. These men advised His Majesty on foreign treaties, taxes, and plots against the realm. I couldn't imagine why they wanted to talk to me. It crossed my mind that Mary Shelton might have accused me. Maybe she was with child by another man. But she had left court more than a year before, surely proving my innocence. I counted the months on my fingers to be certain.

As I walked down the long hall to the council chamber, I gazed at the tapestries to calm my mind: the birth of the Virgin Mary, the Annunciation, the Nativity, a weeping virgin at the foot of the cross. The last scene showed her ascent into heaven, welcomed by golden-haired angels playing harps. Each tapestry was a marvel of color and detail: delicate plants dotting landscapes, rabbits and foxes peeking around the trunks of trees. These tapestries were Flemish, likely from Geraardsbergen. Just one of them cost more than I could earn in a decade.

Two guards opened the ornately carved doors to the council room, and I recognized Lord Rochford's voice—smooth, diplomatic, no hint of catastrophe. He looked up as I entered and motioned for me to sit across from him, next to Sir Francis Weston. Sir Henry Norris was there, poring over a stack of papers. Whispers about his marrying Mistress Shelton had multiplied, and whenever I saw him, I had to conceal my jealousy and sorrow that she would wed someone else.

Also present were Lord Sandys, Sir William Brereton, and Archbishop Cranmer. Charles Brandon, the Duke of Suffolk, was at the head of the table, and Thomas Cromwell stood near a window wearing a fur-trimmed cloak, as if he had just come in from the cold. It was April 1533, and the most powerful men in England had gathered to discuss an issue of great consequence. Rochford reminded the group who I was. Suffolk looked annoyed.

"The king has specified four days of celebration," Rochford continued, "with the coronation on June 1. Since the marriage ceremony was performed in secret, His Majesty has called for pageantry and extravagance that his subjects will remember all their lives."

Rochford spoke matter-of-factly, but he must have been secretly thrilled. After years of doubt and exasperation, his sister would soon be crowned. He himself would benefit, along with all the Boleyns. Maps of London covered the table, along with sketches of planned events. [9] Lord Sandys pointed to four documents titled "May 29," "May 30," "May 31," and "June 1." Each summarized the day's schedule and included notes about Lady Anne's robes and the number of heralds, carriages, and horses needed—all of it fit for a queen.

Weston spoke, his eyes triumphant. "Mark, we need your help selecting music for the events preceding the coronation."

Normally this work would have gone to Silas Bray as the king's master of musicians, but Weston must have persuaded the council to give it to me. This was his thanks for the hundred sovereigns I had supplied during his days of financial desperation. He moved the papers closer to me so I could read them. He began to summarize the key events:

"On Thursday, a flotilla of barges will escort the queen from Greenwich to London. On Friday, she will ride though the city in an open carriage so her subjects can see her and cheer. On Saturday, there will be festivities for the court and entertainments for the people. We need three days' worth of music for these events leading up to the coronation on Whit Sunday at Saint Peter's Abbey."

He arranged some sketches in a semicircle—twelve drawings depicting a variety of Greek nymphs, maypoles, Morris dancers, shepherds, shepherdesses, flower arbors, and an angel descending from heaven to crown a falcon.

"As the queen rides through the city on Friday," Rochford explained, "she will visit twelve pageants staged by the merchant alliances. These are their ideas. Most indicate the music they plan to use, but in a few cases, they haven't suggested any accompaniment. You know what would be suitable and what my sister would like."

I immediately saw that I would need to find or write music for at least five pageants, but this was the easier part of the work. Much of the proposed accompaniment was amateurish, and some of it was absurd. I pointed to one document. "These are beautiful folk songs, sir, some of my own favorites. But they are meant to be sung in small, tranquil settings. Outside, among a boisterous crowd, few will be able to hear the singers. I would recommend consorts with flutes, drums, and cornets—instruments that can play loudly."

No one spoke, although Rochford gestured for me to continue. I turned two of the documents around to face the group. "This one calls for trumpets and drums while children dance around a may-pole, which could produce an odd effect. And this one proposes Morris dances alongside a Greek allegory. Perhaps we could suggest alternatives."

"I told you he would know what we need," Weston said to the others.

"Yes, that sounds right." This was Rochford. "Could you give us some other choices?"

"If I may, my lords, I would like to consider the plans more carefully and review my own musical manuscripts. If it would be agreeable to you, I could return later today or tomorrow with choices for you to consider." I spoke mainly to Rochford and Weston because they had spoken to me. But I noticed that Sandys and some others were listening attentively. Surprising myself, I offered my own suggestion. "Another possibility would be to place musicians on the barges. They could entertain the crowds on the riverbank and play drumrolls and fanfares as Her Majesty nears the city."

Weston and Suffolk responded simultaneously, with Weston saying, "This could be marvelous," while Suffolk didn't bother to hide his irritation. "And what would that cost?" he asked before continuing. "Weston here wants to order a hundred barges, including one with a mechanical fire-breathing dragon. Do you know any music for a mythical, fire-breathing beast?"

I could think of a dozen pieces that would fit a dragon's bursts of fire—some would do so gloriously. But I doubted the duke actually wanted my opinion, so I said nothing. He exhaled noisily and went on. "It's a ridiculous waste of money. This is a coronation, not a traveling theatrical."

The men debated, apparently resuming an earlier dispute. After some minutes, Rochford said to order the one hundred barges and approved the dragon and extra musicians. I naturally remained quiet, but my own view was that the dragon was a brilliant idea. Londoners love a spectacle. Rochford told me to arrange for players on the barges and asked if I had any questions.

"Will the choirmaster at Saint Peter's choose the music for the coronation?" I wanted to be sure I understood my task. The choirmaster was accomplished, and I was confident he would choose well.

"Only English music, and let's have some new songs," Brereton said. "None of this papist warbling your old cardinal used to inflict on us." He looked at me directly, waiting for my reply to his challenge. I immediately thought of John Redford and John Taverner, the best contemporary English composers I knew.

"There are some superb possibilities, sir, music by English composers from our own time. But it might be well to include some traditional music to show continuity, to convey the strength of our history as our new queen ascends the throne."

"No one wants to hear that pompous old stuff anymore—time to get rid of it."

I was ready to defer to Brereton, but Archbishop Cranmer intervened. "Master Smeaton is right. A blend of the old and the new would be better, the traditional alongside the reformist. It will reassure the English people." He spoke to me with surprising respectfulness. "Perhaps you and the choirmaster could confer on the selections."

Cromwell moved closer to the table, looking at Cranmer. "Yes, by all means, have them confer." His tone left little doubt about his complete lack of interest in the topic. He turned to me, evidently eager to move on. "Do you need anything else to do your work, Mark?"

"We will have to hire more musicians, sir."

Cromwell emitted a grudging version of a laugh. "Tell us what you'll need. Paying the musicians will be the least of it. Can you have your recommendations tomorrow?"

"Yes, I will start work immediately, sir." I rose from the table and bowed to all of them. "Thank you, my lords."

I faced a long, taxing night to deliver what I had promised, but my new assignment was a notable advance for me. I would be well paid to do work that was important to the king and the realm. Thousands would hear the music I had chosen, arranged, and composed.

Even so, my growing prominence and prosperity meant little when it came to Mistress Shelton—pursuing her was still a ludicrous idea. Unlike Sir Henry Norris, I had no title or grand estates in the countryside. I wasn't a friend of the king. I was a lowborn commoner who was perhaps exceptionally skilled in music. In the eyes of the world, my worth had barely changed even with my new duties and responsibilities.

I never imagined I would find myself alone with Lady Shelton, both of us waiting to see Rochford who had been unexpectedly summoned to speak with the king. The manservant who greeted us was polite, offering his master's regrets along with comfortable chairs and cups of wine. Both Lady Shelton and I sat down, but neither of us took any drink. I was there to report on my work planning the music for the coronation events. Lady Shelton must have come for a similar purpose. By this time, Whit Sunday was only three weeks away.

All the ladies-in-waiting had roles in the festivities, both tending to the new queen and participating in multiple pageants and processions. Lady Worcester and Lady Shelton had been charged with organizing the ladies' activities and overseeing the preparation and care of Her Majesty's wardrobe. Though Anne Boleyn had not yet been crowned, everyone at court already spoke of her as "the queen." Referring to her as "Lady Anne" might be read as a sign of some lingering attachment to Katherine of Aragon and a lack of enthusiasm for the king's decrees. Within His Majesty's palaces, the new terminology was obligatory.

Rochford's servant left us, assuring us that His Lordship would return momentarily to speak first with Lady Shelton and then with me. Sitting so near her, I couldn't help but notice the similarities between mother and daughter. Lady Shelton was also slender and graceful, a woman who radiated courtesy and confidence. I remembered how she touched her daughter with such motherly affection the day I first saw them together in the chapel at Hampton Court.

"Master Smeaton," she said once the servant had left us.

"Lady Shelton." I had bowed to her when I first entered the room and did so again, this time inclining my torso and head.

"I believe I owe you a debt of gratitude. My younger daughter mistreated you."

I was surprised Lady Shelton would mention the incident, especially given the passage of time. Yet I appreciated her honesty. "My lady, I thank you for accepting my word."

"Madge is the one who spoke up for you, but our entire family is obliged to you for your honorable behavior and discretion. This speaks well of you."

"It was my privilege to be of service." Another bow of torso and head.

I thought this would be the end of our conversation, but Lady Shelton continued. "Still, there is another matter we should discuss while we have this moment of privacy." She softened her tone and looked at me directly. "I believe you are fond of Madge."

She spoke calmly and evenly. She might have been describing the weather from the sound of her voice. But my mind stopped, as if time had paused and my thoughts were suspended—I may have held my breath. In public at least, I rarely spoke with Mistress Shelton, and I never said anything beyond a servant's predictable replies. I assumed my romantic imaginings were undetectable, and I was confused by Lady Shelton's soft manner. She didn't seem outraged or furious, as I would expect her to be. My mind scrambled for a respectful reply.

"Everyone one admires Mistress Shelton, ma'am." I began to

control my breathing as I might do when I was singing—a method to feign confidence and serenity.

"I do not criticize you, Master Smeaton, for admiring her, as you put it. I can even sympathize with you. All of us have hopeless dreams. In a different world, your admiration might be acceptable and perhaps even returned. But we do not live in that world. I am sure you understand this."

"I know my place, ma'am."

"I hope that you do. There is some enchantment between you. I have seen it. I have watched Madge's face when you perform for the court. I heard her speak from her heart when she defended you from Mary's foolishness. You are both so young, but you are old enough to know that nothing can come of this. I expect you to conduct yourself appropriately, as someone of your lower rank should do."

"I believe I have always done so, ma'am."

"That is my impression, but I ask more of you. Madge must marry a man worthy of her station, someone with wealth, connections, and prestige. This is her birthright and duty. She must fulfill those expectations."

"I understand, my lady. I wish only the most glorious future for her."

"Then, you must act in a way that ensures it. You will curtail any exchanges with her, and I will keep watch to see that you do."

Memories of Mistress Shelton surfaced in my brain beyond my control—the afternoon in the countryside, the light sparkling on her hair, my skin tingling when she touched my hand. I envied the way her mother casually referred to her as "Madge." Then a brief wave of resentment flowed through me—even my private thoughts and remembrances were illicit. This was the lot of those from society's lower ranks, as unfair as that may be. Yet I had no choice but to obey Lady Shelton. Any other response was unthinkable.

"Of course, my lady. I will do as you ask."

"Excellent, because I would not like to have you expelled from the king's service. It would take only a word from me. And you can be assured that I will demand your removal from court if I believe that your presence here confuses Madge or complicates our plans for an appropriate marriage. I do not like making threats, but I will protect my daughter's future. I believe it is better to be frank."

Her words were unpleasant, but I couldn't contest them. What she said was true. For me, pursuing Mistress Shelton was make-believe, the stuff of legends and songs. "I take your warning, ma'am," I said. "I would never do anything to harm your daughter."

Lady Shelton was silent for a moment, but then she leaned forward and spoke to me more gently. "Then you and I understand each other, Master Smeaton." She lifted her chin and looked at me with an expression nearing a smile. "I do not wish you ill—quite the opposite. I wish you every success. You have many virtues, and life is long. You will find your own happiness and marry someone else. Madge will disappear from your thoughts just as the morning mist vanishes by midday."

Since "Madge" had dominated my dreams for several years, I found it unlikely that she would quickly "vanish" from my fantasies. Luckily at this moment, Lord Rochford entered, his servant a few feet behind him. I stood and bowed while he offered his apologies for his lateness. He ushered Lady Shelton into his interior meeting room, saying, "Mark, do you want to wait while I speak with Lady Shelton? Or you can return later if you'd prefer." Rochford was unusual in his courtesy even to those of lower station.

"I can wait, sir."

"Thank you. I have some new books if you care to look at them." He gestured to a nearby table and then turned to his servant. "Bring Master Smeaton a cup of wine."

After my talk with Lady Shelton, I was happy to accept a drink. To my own surprise, my anger and resentment disappeared as I waited in Rochford's elegant public anteroom—suddenly I was jubilant. The mother had detected some fondness for me in her daughter's face, this mother who knew her child so well. When Lady Shelton emerged after visiting Rochford, she paused, and I quickly stood and bowed. Her eyes gleamed, just as her daughter's eyes gleam. "I have always enjoyed your music, Master Smeaton. It was a pleasure to get to know you better."

⚜

In the following weeks, work occupied nearly all my hours. Nights and days blended into one as I planned the music for each coronation event—twelve pageants, the parade of barges, and evening entertainments for the court. I composed new music for some of the occasions and met with the abbey choirmaster about the coronation. Paul helped me prepare detailed lists of how many musicians would be needed for each location at various times. He volunteered to play on one of the barges so the crowds wouldn't see his crippled foot.

I turned to John Blanke, the brilliant African trumpeter, to lead the musical honor guard announcing the entries of the king and queen at different locations. Blanke had come to England with Katherine of Aragon when she arrived from Spain so many years ago. [10] Yet he remained one of His Majesty's favorites despite his connection to the toppled queen. I relied on Blanke to choose the fanfares for the four days of celebrations. He knew this music far better than I did.

Sometimes, I accompanied Rochford and Weston to meetings with the red-faced commercial men sponsoring the pageants. Initially I worried they might resent my changes to their plans, but none voiced any complaint. In their eyes, I was one of the king's men, someone to be accommodated. And beneath it all, there was a glow inside me that I had never felt before. Mistress Shelton had some true regard for me. Her mother's worry proved it.

ⵁ

As expected, the king gave me a substantial reward after the coronation. More surprisingly, Lord Rochford presented me with a book of
poems from antiquity. "A gift from my sister and me," he said as he
presented it. The curved strokes in the dedication, "To Mark,"
showed that he had written it.

In the months that followed, the poems in the book would inspire
the lyrics for several songs, but I would return to one of them many
times, keeping its words for myself alone. The long-dead poet
wrote: "When I read my first love story, I began looking for you, not
knowing how blind that was. Lovers don't finally meet somewhere.
They are one before they are born." [11]

I didn't expect reality to shift in my favor. Mistress Shelton
would likely marry Sir Henry Norris as her family desired—or she
would marry some other man with wealth and power. And yet, beneath the surface of life, I had come to believe in a different truth—
that by some incomprehensible, cosmic magic, Mistress Shelton
and I were joined.

18

WHIT SUNDAY

May 29 to June 1, 1533
Madge Shelton, London

*T*he preparations had seemed endless, but my cousin's coronation was finally near. To celebrate the event, the king issued a proclamation permitting drinking on Whit Sunday, and Londoners of all stations rejoiced. On the Wednesday before the festivities began, I helped my cousin try on her garments for each event. This required several hours of tying and untying fastenings on sleeves, bodices, collars, and capes. I held her hand to help her balance as she stepped in and out of various underskirts and overskirts. I presented earrings, necklaces, and bracelets to her so she could try out alternatives and decide which to wear on which occasion. Once she removed an article of clothing or selected a piece of jewelry, I made sure it was placed in the correct location so there would be no confusion in the packing up.

Her French dressmakers had followed her instructions: "*une douzaine de robes qui étonneront les gens ordinaires . . .* I don't care what it costs." Silks, velvets, brocades, exquisite beading and gemstones, silver and gold embroidery—on Sunday, she would wear purple and ermine, clothing reserved for royalty.

Most pregnant women who were getting married would wear a stiff farthingale to press in their waists and make their skirts stand out. But my cousin was the opposite. "Make sure everyone can see my belly," she had instructed the dressmakers, "so everyone knows I carry the prince. I want the Spanish hag to envy me."

The plans called for her to travel from Greenwich to London by barge and lodge in the Tower of London before her coronation. Although many had suffered and died in the Tower, it was a royal residence as well as a prison—some said the massive building housed both heaven and hell. The king had stayed there before his coronation, and my cousin would do the same. The coronation itself would take place in Saint Peter's Abbey, on land where the saint had once appeared to a young Thames fisherman. England's kings and queens had been crowned and buried in the abbey for more than five hundred years.

Lady Worcester and my mother supervised the packing for the coronation celebrations. We placed my cousin's dresses, cloaks, shoes, and undergarments in cases labeled and sorted by destination—Greenwich, the Tower, the abbey. Since the new queen would be preoccupied, Lady Worcester and my mother would carry her jewel box from place to place.

⚜

Early on the first day, I went to the Tower to make sure all was ready for my cousin's stay. In the afternoon, I joined the throngs of Londoners assembling along the Thames to see the barges. Tradesmen, housewives, servants, sailors, beggars—everyone had something to say.

"A hundred boats, that's what I hear."

"One has a dragon that breathes real fire."

"I hear drummers. Look, the king's banners."

A few people standing near me predicted that a bolt of lightning would kill my cousin before she assumed the throne, although there wasn't a cloud in the sky. Instead, the day was hot and sunny, and the king's subjects sweated and looked for shade. Diplomats and dignitaries suffered in their fur-trimmed cloaks and weighty chains of office. The lord mayor of London repeatedly wiped his forehead with a large white handkerchief.

One by one, the barges appeared—a flotilla unlike anything I had ever seen on the Thames. The first glimpse of the dragon set off a hum of expectation. Fathers lifted their children onto their shoulders while the children shrieked and pretended to be afraid. Everyone marveled at the beast's size and ferocity and offered guesses about its height. From the Lord Mayor to the most ragged vagabond, the crowd cheered each fiery blast.

Soon, people pointed to a glittering image in the distance—the white sapphires and silver threading of my cousin's robes. When her barge neared the Tower, trumpeters played fanfares. The most important men in England removed their hats and knelt at her feet as she disembarked. The king appeared, seemingly from nowhere, and a hundred cannon boomed across the city, an earsplitting salute for Queen Anne.

⚜

The next day was the queen's parade, and my cousin crisscrossed London in a carriage draped with gold bunting—she sat on what seemed like a throne. She told me her golden gown was so heavy with pearls that it made her shoulders ache. My mother and Lady Worcester sat on a low bench behind her, wearing drab black clothing so no one would notice them.

I had volunteered to ride with a group of the queen's ladies—twenty of us seated sidesaddle on pure white palfreys, the horses' crimson bridles and barding matching our crimson dresses. Earlier that morning, we had assembled near the Tower, the departure point for the parade. As we waited to begin, I had caught sight of Mark Smeaton giving instructions to different groups of players. If he had been a Percy or a Seymour or a Neville—even a younger son with middling prospects—we could have played at romance.

"Perhaps we will dance the pavane tonight," I would say to him.

"It would be my honor," and he would bow. "And all the dances if you are willing . . . the saltarello and la volta?"

I pictured his hands wrapped around my waist, the thrilling music rushing through my veins. After a while, we would steal away to a room where no one could see us—a kiss, our foreheads touching, our fingers and palms pressed together, whispers, more kisses, and finally our bodies close enough for me to feel his breath. At the time, I hadn't thought much beyond kisses and a man's hands touching my waist or hair. I had only a vague notion of "wedded bliss."

This delightful fantasy faded when Sir Henry greeted me, standing near my horse and placing his hand on its neck. "It is a great day, Mistress Shelton, is it not?" he said. "And soon, we'll celebrate the prince's birth."

"Indeed, my lord. The prince will be used to noisy processions even before he's born. Today's parade is good training."

Sir Henry's face didn't change—no smile, no relaxation in his cheeks. As always, he was reliably dull, and when he returned to his duties, I saw him standing next to Mark. One of the two seemed tired and soft, with a lifeless, washed-out face. The other was straight and well-proportioned, with something romantic and perhaps even dangerous in his bearing. Only the forbidden one stirred my dreams.

At eleven o'clock, church bells rang out across the city, and the procession began threading through London's streets. A fanfare sounded as we approached each pageant, and my cousin stood up in her carriage to wave. The crowds roared, and whole casts of dancers and players paused to kneel to her. Little children brought her flowers, and stout men presented scrolls with poems. Every so often, amid the cheers and church bells and fanfares, I heard someone yell, "French concubine" or "Satan's whore." I thought back to the boy who had thrown the rat and wondered how many others shared his taste for rebellion and his visceral hatred of my cousin. I doubted a coronation would change their minds.

⚜

On Sunday in Saint Peter's Abbey, the June sun sparkled through stained glass windows. The sound of the organ filled the church. The abbey priests wore golden copes, and the bishops entered in mitered hats. England's dukes and earls filed down the center aisle, every county and shire represented. When all were assembled, my cousin stepped inside the nave, followed by six ladies in silver dresses. I was one of them, and we all kept pace with the stately music.

She knelt when she reached the altar, and all six of us bent down to arrange her purple cloak so the velvet spread out gracefully. The archbishop of Canterbury spoke the age-old words and balanced the Crown of Saint Edward on her head. The king looked on with Thomas Cromwell. The Kyrie, Gloria, Credo, Sanctus, and Agnus Dei rose and fell throughout the abbey. After years of waiting, my cousin allowed her subjects to gaze upon her. Seen beneath the crown, her face emitted a light that compelled everyone to ponder her rise. In her womb, she carried the blessed prince. I expected that the king would order an equally impressive celebration to mark his birth.

ᘓᕽᘈ

Before she began her lying in, my cousin decided that my parents should formally pursue my betrothal to Sir Henry, but only after the prince was born. Until then, she didn't want to hear about it.

"All thoughts must be on the baby's birth," she said, "and the prince's christening. Madge can get married next year . . . if Sir Henry really wants her."

My mother accepted the delay philosophically and ignored my cousin's slight.

"I have seen Sir Henry glance at you," she told me once we were alone. "I can tell he has marriage on his mind."

"I am content to wait . . . as I'm sure you know."

She positioned her thumb and forefinger to lift my chin and stepped back to look at me. "You're my beautiful child. You think I chose Sir Henry solely because he is rich and powerful, but I have other reasons too. He is a man who can love a wife. I know he will be kind to you."

"If he doesn't bore me to death."

"When you have your own daughters, you will understand. Protecting them is all that matters."

"And what about their happiness?"

"As Sir Henry's wife, you will be a respected woman. Your children's love will compensate for any disappointment. Romance is a trifle."

Despite my protests, I knew she was right. Meeting Mark Smeaton in the countryside had been a trifle, to use my mother's word. Yet I remembered everything he said and did that day, and I could still summon the mysterious pleasure of being close to him. Sometimes, I reconstructed the entire adventure from beginning to end before I fell asleep at night. It was a pleasurable but illicit mental exercise.

Reality has paused for me for a moment one magical afternoon. But I accepted that my life would continue along the path set out for me. There were rules, and I had to follow them. I could never shame or disappoint my family. Knowing this to be true, I began to push my fantasies of Mark Smeaton out of my mind the second they emerged. I distracted myself by reviewing my tasks for the queen that day. I forced myself to read or sew.

My cousin George and Sir Francis spent considerable time with Mark, the three of them talking about music and trading books. I watched them from afar as they laughed and drank while planning concerts and masques. But such a friendship was unthinkable for a woman, and Mark himself seemed increasingly far away, though I couldn't put my finger on what had changed.

Once upon a time, I had ridden with him on a sunny afternoon. I had reached out and touched his hand. We shared some secrets, but we lived in separate worlds. Any love between us was a fairy tale.

19

THE CARDINAL'S HAT

1533

Mark Smeaton, London

Rochford and Weston stood in my doorway, both splendidly dressed and at ease.

"Come with us," Rochford said. "We're going to The Cardinal's Hat." His face was flushed from drinking malmsey wine. "He'll be quite a gift for the ladies, eh, Weston? This fetching young player of ours?"

I had spent hours with them during the fevered preparations for the coronation and was often surprised by their friendliness.

"The coronation was a triumph, and my sister is pleased. It's time to celebrate. Madame Margaretha will bring out her best ladies for you, whatever you like—young, old, slim, plump."

Weston was laughing. "I ask for the French ones myself."

Most musicians who weren't married visited Southwark's brothels regularly. In our circumstances, paying for sex was generally the most prudent choice. The king's palaces teemed with eye-catching kitchen maids and seamstresses who readily offered themselves to any man of even modestly higher rank. But most were illiterate, and an unlucky pregnancy could tie you to one of them for a lifetime. The queen's ladies were the daughters of dukes, earls, and landed gentlemen, like Mistress Shelton. They were not women a musician could pursue.

⚜

The Cardinal's Hat was a nobleman's brothel, more refined than any I had visited before. Luxurious furnishings and younger, prettier women—I was astonished to find myself there as Rochford's guest. George Boleyn was married, although it was universally known that he enjoyed feminine companionship wherever and whenever he pleased. Weston's wife and children lived in the country, though I had never heard him speak of them—not even a passing reference. Instead, he flirted with the ladies at court, and I assumed some number of these flirtations went beyond playful conversation.

My evening at The Cardinal's Hat turned out to be the first of many—all that Rochford and Weston had promised and more. Madame Margaretha showed us her ladies, each posing seductively on various chairs and cushions. Some wore silken gowns pulled down to show their breasts or up to show their legs. A few were completely nude except for a transparent cloth draped over their privy parts.

Madame Margaretha led us to rooms upstairs, presenting her house with pride. Mine was spacious and well-appointed, featuring a large bed hung with painted cloths depicting Mount Olympus—the mostly nude goddesses were as rosy and shapely as women come. A silver ewer with wine, silver cups, a bowl of plums, and a platter of small cakes sat on an oaken table.

Madame Margaretha was at least forty with a mass of dark red-dish hair—no modest French hoods in her profession. Her scarlet dress ensured that no man could fail to notice her ample breasts, possibly the largest I had ever seen. She entered the room and greeted me in a Flemish accent.

I bowed. "Madame Margaretha."

She curtsied. "Lord Rochford must be very pleased with you. You're to have whatever lady you want, several if you like. Or a boy if you prefer?"

"A lady will be fine . . . one at a time, I think." I had never been in a brothel where they were so mindful about gratifying your desires. "Not too old, I guess, nor too plump . . . maybe someone who likes music."

She looked at me curiously, and I tried to think of what Weston would say. I pictured him amiable and carefree.

"Are you Flemish, Madame Margaretha?" I remembered my first conversation with Weston and how flattered I was when he asked me where I was from.

"I caught the boat from Antwerp the day I turned twelve."

"I am too. My parents came to England right after I was born, so I don't remember my country. I sang Flemish folk songs as a child."

Her face opened, and her eyes glittered. She nodded with a surprisingly lovely smile. "Then you shall have the best of my house. I have a young lady, someone new to London. She is a beauty, and she dances."

⚜

Dark glistening eyes, chestnut hair, slender, and as soft as the morning dew—Maria Isabella was Spanish by birth, from Andalusia. She spoke little English, but she was intent on pleasing me, more than any woman I had ever encountered. Despite her calling, she had an air of innocence and refinement, and I spent many evenings with her after that. I made her laugh practicing the bits of Spanish I had learned from singing. Sometimes, I brought my lute and played for her after our lovemaking—Spanish songs that were out of favor at court. Maria Isabella loved them. I often saw shades of memory in her eyes when I played her country's music. I, too, had left my home to make my way in the world, and my path was considerably easier than hers.

I didn't love her, not with the incandescent joy I felt at the sight of Mistress Shelton. But since this was the only romance I would be allowed, I decided to pursue it. I comforted myself that women in expensive brothels were more lightly used than those in the common houses. Still, other men stroked her and took their pleasure with her—this was the reality of her life. Some men were rough with women in her position, especially if they had paid dearly for their services, but I never saw any signs of this on her body or in her manner.

Over time, I began to pay extra to Madame Margaretha so Maria Isabella could stay the night with me. I liked waking up to hear her breathing and seeing her stretch her body as she woke. Occasionally, I took her out riding, and we spent entire afternoons beneath the sun and sky. On these days, I forgot my life at court and imagined what it must be like to be free of having to please everyone. Yet I must admit that I sometimes pictured myself riding with Mistress Shelton, even though another woman was at my side.

With Maria Isabella, I compromised in love, as many people do. I didn't long for her or write music thinking of her. She wasn't the woman of my dreams. But she was alluring and willing and seemed enamored of me.

I never asked her about the others she served—presumably they were titled men like George Boleyn and Francis Weston. After some months, she told me she had only one other client, someone well born and well-connected. "*Es poderoso*," she said, with some admiration. This much Spanish I understood—he was an important, powerful man. So, in the end, even my compromise had an element of risk to it. I persuaded myself it was minimal.

20

A Princess Is Born

September 1533

Madge Shelton, Greenwich Palace

When I tried to wipe her brow, the queen pushed the cloth away and stared across the room. My mother silenced the two midwives who were cleaning the wailing babe and whispering as if it were malformed.

"No . . . you are wrong," my cousin said, her face flushed from her lengthy labor. "Give the child to me."

One of the midwives presented the newborn, pink and already punching the air.

"The child is perfect, no flaws or defects of any kind," my mother observed.

My cousin took her baby in her arms and examined its tiny female form. She inhaled and convulsed briefly, saying only "*Mon Dieu.*" She returned her daughter to the midwives for swaddling and sat silently for several minutes. When she finally spoke, her voice was as smooth and calm as I had ever heard it.

"His Majesty may enter when I am ready. Bring me clean clothing and a mirror. Madge, you will fix my hair."

An hour later, she presented the infant to the king. "Your Majesty, your daughter," she said with a smile. *"Je crois qu'elle ressemble à votre famille plutôt qu'à la mienne."* When the king didn't accept the babe immediately, she continued, "I thought to name her Elizabeth. It means 'promise of God.' The name will honor your mother."

He took the babe and held it, his face immobile.

"Shall it be the Princess Elizabeth, Your Majesty?" my mother asked, bowing deeply.

"Elizabeth . . . yes, the promise of God. That is a good idea." He spoke as if he were distracted or unbelieving. After several minutes, my mother took the child from him, remarking on its beauty and coloring and strong resemblance to the ruddy Tudors. The king directed his words to her.

"And the next time, Lady Shelton, we'll find a boy between her legs . . . I am sure of this." He kissed his wife's forehead and patted her hand before going hunting for the afternoon. He needed fresh air, he said.

oto

We all understood His Majesty's point of view, and his was the one that mattered. Henry VIII had enraged the pope, disgraced a Spanish king's daughter, and risked rebellion in his realm because my cousin had promised him a son. The English people expected the new queen to accomplish what the old queen could not. The infant Princess Elizabeth was a dumbfounding disappointment.

That evening, far from my cousin's chambers, I heard some other ladies speculating about her mistakes. She must have eaten a forbidden food or stood too near a window or failed to pray every night. Since Pourquoi had been with her during her confinement, many blamed the small dog for the unfortunate outcome. One suggested killing him, as if a cruel, pointless revenge could change the baby's sex.

The court made the best of the situation. Gentlemen and ladies assembled to drink to the baby's health. The king ordered a High Mass of celebration, and messengers departed Greenwich carrying announcements for the world's rulers and diplomats. Scribes had worked throughout the day to correct the illuminated proclamations to read "Princess" rather than "Prince." [12]

The king's men promoted the most favorable interpretation: that the birth of a princess confirmed the queen's fertility. Soothsayers forecast another royal pregnancy within the year. This time, the seers said, the alignment of stars and planets was even more favorable. Few said what I suspected they really thought—that my cousin had lied to the king.

The next day I walked in the town and listened as the people spilled their scorn.

"So, the French whore gave him a daughter after all," a merchant sneered. His colleagues added insults of their own.

A well-dressed woman said, "The concubine can't change God's will any more than good Queen Katherine could. Now we have this harlot on the throne."

Nearly everyone had an opinion, and the opinions were much the same: "God punishes evil . . . this is the Devil's plot . . . the whole of England will suffer for the witch's sins."

I walked from street to street listening and heard not a single word of cheer. Even my cousin's friends whispered, "I don't understand what happened. I was certain she would birth a boy."

On September 10, 1533, the flower of English nobility assembled at the church of the Observant Friars for the baby's christening. [13] Candles flickered, and incense spiraled into the air. Still puckered from the months within her mother's womb, the Princess Elizabeth wore a satin gown embroidered with lilies and encrusted with pearls. She didn't cry at all.

The ceremony bore all the signs of a great royal event: the stately church, lords and ladies, silver basins, heralds, trumpeters, torch-bearers. The king didn't attend, nor did my cousin. Still resting after childbirth, she was secluded within the palace walls.

21

REVELS FOR THE QUEEN

Late Summer and Fall 1533

Mark Smeaton, Greenwich Palace

I had more time to myself during the queen's confinement, so I often rode in the countryside. Mistress Shelton spent her days within Her Majesty's chambers, so I rarely saw her, not even from afar. Yet every time I traveled through the tunnel of beeches where we met, I relived our time together. Once again, I felt her fingertips tap the back of my hand, and I heard her carefree laugh. And then, to keep myself from brooding, I visited Maria Isabella. At least she was real and not a daydream.

During this period, I worked on my music, creating several new songs for the lute and my first composition for a small consort. I began to sketch out a masque. A week after the princess was born, His Majesty ordered revels for the queen's birthday and asked me to compose a piece to honor her. He said he wanted to celebrate his love for her. When I told Paul, he saw a more practical purpose: "It's not surprising. He needs to show his loyalty to her despite her failure to bear a boy."

For the queen's birthday, I created a fantasia for three lutes and flute, choosing Duncan as the woodwind player. He was a superb musician and a jolly, easygoing man. With a wife and four sons, I knew he would welcome the extra money the king would give us. I planned to play myself and invited Paul to join the group, although he initially tried to talk me out of it. I also decided to ask Silas Bray to be the third lutenist—this would be a peace offering, I hoped.

"The man detests you," Paul said. "Why would you ask him to perform your music?"

"I thought it might help. We'll be very well rewarded."

"He will think you're gloating. He used to be the favorite, and now it's you."

"I never pushed him out. I just put myself forward."

"That's not how he sees it."

"But he's prosperous, respected. I admire his playing myself."

"Be careful, Mark. He resents you, and he spies for the Boleyns' enemies. He brings the Seymours every tidbit of gossip he hears."

"There's not much to gossip about in my life. What could he possibly say?"

"It doesn't have to be true to damage you. You should stay away from him."

Paul paused and looked at me, his dark brown eyes earnest with a friend's concern. Then, he caught my arm and took a breath before he spoke again.

"This is a wonderful moment for you, Mark, to perform your own music for the king and queen on such an important night. You don't need to include me. It will bother some people; we both know that."

I didn't hesitate, not for a second. "No, I want you there beside me. I don't care what anyone thinks."

I wrote to Bray asking if I could speak with him privately. I received no answer, so, three days later, I wrote again. He sent a message saying he would be in the music room early, before nine o'clock. When I entered, he was standing by the windows with his back to me. He must have heard my footsteps but left it to me to announce my presence.

"Master Bray, good morning. Thank you for seeing me."

I remembered the day I first met him in the music room at Hampton Court. He was antagonistic even then. Still, what could I lose by trying to be cordial. I presented my idea for the queen's revels as modestly as I could, describing the composition and the other players.

"I would be honored, sir, if you would play with us. You would bring luster to our group."

"You want me to perform this little improvisation of yours?"

"There is a solo, sir. You would play it brilliantly." When he didn't respond right away, I had begun to hope he might agree. "I am sure the king will reward us generously."

"You do have a knack for attracting money," he said with a smirk, "especially from George Boleyn."

"The king commissioned this piece in the queen's honor, for her birthday."

"I want no part of this."

It was a contemptuous dismissal, and for once, I refused to be dismissed. "Could I ask why, sir?"

"Why should I help you impress the king?"

"To show your skill. Everyone will admire your performance."

"Sitting next to your crippled friend? Do you think the king and queen will be pleased when you display him like that? You have my answer. I want no part of this."

Paul had been right. Approaching Bray had been a terrible idea. Instead, I sought out Oliver, who was seventeen and impressively talented, though he was new to court. I reserved the most intricate passages for Paul and myself, worried that Oliver might be nervous in his first performance for the king and queen. But he learned so quickly and was so diligent—I saw some of my younger self in him. Master Peter and Cardinal Wolsey had given me opportunities when I was his age. In the end, I assigned him the solo variation I had offered to Bray.

In this piece for the queen, I imagined four different strands of music—the flute and each of the lutes—sometimes coalescing, sometimes mirroring each other, sometimes diverging to follow separate paths. I had labored over the piece and sent an early copy to Master Peter, asking for his advice. I kept the letter he sent back all the rest of my life. It contained little counsel on the music but glowed in my hands with his words of affection and reassurance.

On a gusty November evening, my players performed flawlessly and to great acclaim. The king lifted his hand in a sign of approval, his heavy rings sparkling ruby red and emerald green. The queen smiled brightly, which pleased me—she had been much quieter since her daughter's birth. Mistress Shelton sat beside Sir Henry Norris as she frequently did during this period of time. Their betrothal was not official, but I had accepted that this man would take her.

To close the concert, each of my players approached the queen and knelt before her. One by one, we pronounced our good wishes and presented a small gift. When Paul walked toward her with a white Tudor rose, his hobbled gait was evident, as I knew it would be. I glanced at the king—he seemed more startled than anything else. But the queen was suddenly radiant. She remembered Paul's name, signaling that he was one of her favorites.

"You play so beautifully, Paul. I hope we can enjoy your performances more often in the future."

She turned toward me and nodded her head in thanks.

In the months to come, the queen's sorrows would change her. Disappointment and fear would steal her grace. But at this moment, she was wondrous—brave and independent, an intelligent woman who loved art and music and admired those who create it. This was the Anne Boleyn history should remember. She was no ordinary queen.

PART FOUR

The Saga of
Birth and Death

22

THE BIRTHING GAME

1533 to 1534

Madge Shelton, The Court of King Henry

he midwives advised a month of rest, but my cousin dismissed their counsel. She resumed her wifely duties two days after the princess was born. She visited His Majesty's chambers nightly and sometimes returned after midnight, trembling and in tears.

"It is not as easy as it was," she whispered to my mother and me as we helped her get ready for bed.

My mother suggested skipping a few days. "It will increase the pleasure, Your Majesty, and the king's desire. We all know this to be true."

"No, I must continue. I have no other choice."

One morning when my mother bathed her, I saw bruises on her arms and thighs. Later, I asked my mother, "Has the king harmed her?"

"He is angry . . . and sometimes rough. He believes she has deceived him."

"But it's not her fault the child is female."

"The king thinks it is."

My mother must have seen my face because she quickly added, "This will not happen to you, Madge. This is one reason I pray that you will marry Sir Henry, who is a temperate man—and he already has a son."

"Is having a son so important?"

"Men need sons to inherit their lands—or rule the realm in the case of a king."

"But some countries have queens—Egypt had Queen Cleopatra."

"I doubt she inspires much confidence, Madge. Cleopatra was defeated and lost her kingdom, and then she killed herself."

◌̣

In the first quarter of the new year, my cousin despaired when her monthly bleeding came. The week before her normal time, she inspected her linens hourly, praying to find them pristine and then sobbing when she saw blood. But in the spring, her doctors confirmed another pregnancy, and the soothsayers promised a boy. With her own future considerably more promising, she turned her attention to mine.

"This match between Madge and Norris," she said one morning, "*Cela pourrait nous être bénéfique.*" She laughed and spoke to my mother in a mock whisper. "It's time to nurse it along."

My mother took on the task with determination and subtlety.

"I know he admires you, Madge," she told me more than once. "He must be lonely. Soon, he will speak to your father . . . I am certain of it."

One afternoon, through my mother's wiles, we sat with Sir Henry in the garden, watching his children who were visiting him at court. Willy was a sturdy seven-year-old, his cheeks flushed from play. His younger sister was a bouncing child who informed me that her name was Lettice and that she could count to ten in French. The children had devised a made-up game with a small black dog and a yellow ball. At one point, the dog whizzed past Sir Henry's feet, the ball firmly in its mouth. The boy caught up and nuzzled his pet before patiently retrieving the ball. He gave it to his father who laughed and advanced the game by throwing it across the lawn.

"He's a lovely boy," I said as the play resumed. He had the curly blond hair of an angel in a tapestry, and I could easily imagine myself kissing these two children as they went to sleep at night and watching over them during the day. I had begun to daydream about what it would be like to have babes of my own, likely the result of caring for the squiggly Princess Elizabeth. From time to time, Sir Henry talked of his first wife as if he still mourned her—as if he would love her all his life. Oddly enough, this drew me to him. His loyalty to his children's mother reassured me he was a caring man, as my mother had said. Sir Henry served the king but wasn't like him.

A week later, my mother came to me, her face alive with pleasure and pride. "Sir Henry has told your father that he desires you for a wife."

I nodded and smiled, though in truth I wanted to cry. *This is it*, I thought, *the true end of my fantasies of Mark Smeaton and my dreams of a romantic life.*

My mother took my hand and kissed it. "Madge, this is for the best."

⚜

My cousin's second pregnancy seemed troubled from the beginning. She was anxious and slept poorly and complained that her stomach burned. Some mornings she awoke to small smatterings of blood on the bedclothes, and I watched her cringe and weep. But the doctors and midwives decided it wasn't enough blood to worry about. "Nothing unusual," they said.

In late summer, she began her lying in, and her female servants sealed the windows to prevent "bad air" from harming the babe. They cleared dogs, cats, and birds from an entire wing of the palace, and little Pourquoi whimpered when they took him from my cousin's arms. I tended him for her and described his silly antics when I spoke with her. I even wrote a story about Pourquoi traveling around England in his own coach and magically helping the village people complete their chores.

As the weeks crept by, we all tried to keep her comfortable, but we couldn't open the windows to reduce the heat. She wanted music, but the musicians weren't allowed to enter the birthing rooms. A few ladies played and sang passably. But it was her separation from the king that preoccupied her, and she repeatedly asked where he was and who he was with. She wrote letters and copied poems for him. His Majesty responded with gifts of jewels and a letter describing the silver cradle he had ordered for "my son, England's prince." [14]

During this time, His Majesty visited the noble houses of England—riding, hunting, jousting, feasting, enjoying his normal routine. He spent a week at Wolf Hall, the Seymour family estate, and commented on the family's graciousness.

⚜

"Madge, you must bring me something precious," my cousin said one morning when we were alone. "It will be our secret."

"Of course, Your Majesty."

I thought she wanted to see Pourquoi, and what harm could it do? Blaming a pup for a child's sex was ridiculous, and I was sure his jumping and bouncing would entertain her.

"At Westminster," she whispered, "the monks keep it . . . the Virgin Mary's sacred girdle."

This was an unexpected and bewildering request.

For centuries, the queens of England had wrapped this braided leather belt around their bellies during labor, believing the Virgin herself had worn it. Some said it guaranteed the Virgin's blessings for both mother and child, but many queens and babes had died, nonetheless.

"Ma'am, I am not sure what you want," I said, though I understood her perfectly well.

"The Virgin's girdle at Westminster . . . I dreamed of it. It will ensure I bear a boy."

"But it is a relic, ma'am. Archbishop Cranmer has preached against relics and those who believe in them."

Until this moment, my cousin had complained about the monasteries and their papist relics as much as any reformer I had ever heard. She must be very afraid, I thought, to reach for this kind of comfort. I felt only pity for her.

"I have to try it—it might help. *Qui peut dire?*" She pressed her palms into her belly. "This child must be a male."

"But kissing a relic, ma'am . . . praying to the Virgin. Some say it is a heresy."

"Would you deny me? *Je suis désolée* . . . You will do as I say."

"As you wish, Your Majesty."

I went to Westminster that afternoon, carrying a small sack of silver coins in case some payment was required. But the monks claimed they no longer kept the Virgin's belt and didn't know where it was. This had become common—monks hiding their relics so the objects wouldn't be seized and destroyed. Each week, new decrees laid out new definitions of heresy, and the king's subjects struggled to understand them. Some began praying to the Virgin in secret and hiding prayer books and saints' medallions among their linens. Since reformers often disagreed about what was holy and what should be banned, accusations of sacrilege were commonplace. Some preachers claimed that reciting a prayer or psalm in Latin was blasphemy and deserved a sentence of death.

Not knowing what to tell my cousin, I described my visit to Westminster to my mother, who held the queen in her arms and shushed her.

"Your Majesty, your mind is clouded. You must not speak of this again."

⚜

My cousin's hopes ended one cloudy morning, her sheets, gown, and body covered in blood. As tradition dictated, the midwives dripped pure water on the shapeless mass of tissue: "I christen thee in the name of the Father, the Son, and the Holy Ghost." We all prayed for the infant's soul, although no one could say whether the child was a girl or a boy.

This time, the king didn't visit—he spent the day and evening inside his privy chamber. News spread quickly at court, but no public announcement was issued. Since no child was born, there was nothing to say.

23

CAVALCADE OF DEATH

1534 to 1535

Mark Smeaton, London

I entered His Majesty's inner chambers shortly after he learned the queen had lost the babe. The king's men thought music might help ease his grief and called for me to play for him. He sat alone, drinking, his burly form collapsed against his chair's high back. I never spoke to him unless he addressed me first, but that day I took the risk.

"Your Majesty, I am deeply sorry about the child. The whole court grieves for you."

He responded, saying, "Play the old English music, Mark—in memory of my son who never breathed life. I had hoped to name him Edward."

For a while, the king brooded alone and stared into the fire. Then his closest companions gathered: Norris, voicing sorrow for Her Majesty; Suffolk, urging hope. Rochford brought a sealed message from the queen which the king said he would open later. After Rochford left, he read it and tossed it in the fire.

Cromwell arrived to say they should prepare for public discontent when the news seeped out, as it surely would. Many saw Anne Boleyn as a heretic and usurper, he warned. Unrest and rebellion were possible.

I knew His Majesty's face well by this time. He was not a man who disguised his thoughts. I stopped playing and watched his cheeks redden before he said, "Then we must ensure the people's obedience."

Cromwell knelt. "Your Majesty." The others knelt as well.

The king's pronouncement was clear to all who heard it: "Anyone who doubts the new church or the queen's legitimacy is a traitor. I want no questions—none—from anyone. See to it."

Then the killing began.

Over the years, I had met a surprising number of those who found themselves condemned. Elizabeth Barton, the Holy Maid of Kent, had visited Cardinal Wolsey after she first reported seeing visions—I was only thirteen or fourteen at the time. She attended a Mass where I sang a solo hymn, and I remembered the roundness of her face and the rosy blush of her cheeks. But after England left the Church of Rome, she rejected the new religion and called the king an apostate, prophesying that he would lose his kingdom and writhe in hell. Her arrest surprised no one, but her execution did. Her head was placed on a pike after she was hanged at Tyburn—no one remembered this being done to a woman before. I made sure I never saw it, even if I had to walk far out of my way.

Bishop John Fisher was beheaded for opposing the new religion. The old churchman had visited Hampton Court many times. Once, the cardinal had introduced me to him, saying, "This boy's father was a penniless carpenter, but the child has a gift for music, despite his humble birth."

The bishop must have sensed my embarrassment. "Our Lord Jesus Christ was a carpenter," he said to me. "God blesses those who labor."

After he was beheaded, the executioners left his body lying on the scaffold, assuming that people would come to laugh and point at him. Instead, his supporters gathered to pray for his soul. Then the king's men put the bishop's head on a pole on London Bridge, but again, the old man's remains attracted sorrowful followers who mourned and prayed for him. After several days, soldiers took the head down and threw it in the Thames. [15]

Bishop Fisher's execution troubled me—I kept imagining the axe and the spewing blood. The king called him stubborn, and Cromwell said they needed to make an example of him. I kept my own sorrow hidden, even from Paul.

Two weeks later, Sir Thomas More was beheaded for refusing to disavow the pope and recognize Anne Boleyn as queen. The famous scholar had been lord chancellor only a few years before, and his trial was a sensation—the most powerful men in England judging one of their own. Yet, the jury took only fifteen minutes to find him guilty and pronounce a sentence of death. When I heard about the verdict, I remembered the king's words to Cromwell: "I want no questions—none—from anyone. See to it." [16]

The less prominent suffered more gruesome deaths. The Carthusian monks had taken vows of poverty and charity and spent their days in study and prayer. But when ordered to recognize the king as the supreme head of the church, these men of God resisted. Like Fisher and More, they chose to die for their faith. After days of torture, they were dragged through the streets of London to Tyburn, to be hanged, drawn, and quartered. Executioners disemboweled them before they reached the refuge of death and cut their bodies into parts. Yet people in the crowd said the monks died singing God's praises and crying out words of forgiveness to their executioners. In prior years, the king had sported and laughed with one of them; Sebastian Newdigate was once a courtier. [17]

All these people were traitors—that was the story we were told. Important nobles attended their executions and described them to the king and queen, who nodded their approval. Human remnants hung on scaffolds and bridges throughout the city, sometimes a half dozen at a time. Out on a daily walk, you could easily see the rotting head of someone you had joked with over supper.

George Boleyn, Lord Rochford—the gracious courtier who loved music and poetry—witnessed the execution of Carthusian monks; Sir Henry Norris did too. They both watched a man boiled to death for his crimes, a punishment so pitiless that some observers became ill and had to be led away. How could these kind, courteous men stomach such unspeakable cruelty?

During these dark months, torture, death, and dismemberment became the subjects of court chatter. Some enjoyed the savagery, attending every execution and taking their children to watch. Some saw it as God's just punishment for traitors and those holding false beliefs. Some accepted it reluctantly—the price to pay for order in the realm. Others were sickened by it.

♔

In late October, Paul and I went riding, giving Prince and Flanders rein to run freely in the autumn air. Afterward, we trotted along, enjoying the open skies and golden trees. Forty or fifty swallows swirled above us. They swept upward as if they were about to fly away and then plunged down again. Paul smiled as his eyes followed their loops of flight. His face was flat and sharply triangular, and his thin, brown hair stuck flush against his head. But I loved the curved lines around his mouth and the way his eyes crinkled when he laughed. The man's kindness and grace improved his dull appearance.

When we were alone on the road with only birds and horses for company, Paul leaned forward in his saddle and spoke quietly. "Do you think they deserved to die that way . . . Fisher and More and the monks, I mean?"

"Well, no . . . not really."

Paul and I had never talked about the killing, though I noticed we both avoided the tavern talk where people joked about the dying men's screams. I told Paul about Bishop Fisher and how much his words had meant to me when I was a boy.

"Sebastian Newdigate was my father's patron," Paul said in return. "He adored masques and Christmas revels. For my tenth birthday, he gave me a prayer book blessed by the pope."

"Do you know why he became a monk?"

"I think he wanted a different life . . . something more honest. I still have the prayer book; I read it the day he died."

"Paul, you need to be careful."

"It's well hidden, don't worry. I only wondered what you thought . . . about all the executions."

"I try not to think about them."

"The king assumes that fear of death will stamp out the old beliefs," Paul went on. "But people don't abandon their faith so quickly, especially a strong faith."

Paul was cautious—I was rash by comparison—but his words worried me. He often read his Bible and went to chapel in the mornings. In the evenings, he prayed with an old family rosary. Religion was important to him, far more than to me.

"Well, no one cares what players think," I said, mainly to convince myself.

"It's meaningless to you, isn't it? You can't imagine someone dying for his faith."

"I don't understand it the way you do, but I admire them—Newdigate and the others—the way they died. I'm sure they are at peace."

To be honest, I wasn't sure. How could anyone know whether they were at peace or not? At the time, I hadn't thought much about how a man approaches death or makes his peace with God. I said this to comfort Paul.

⚜

Apparently, the king and Cromwell believed that people would accept a new church and a new queen the way a man puts on a new cloak. But there was always someone, somewhere who wouldn't submit. They were fearless, these men and women who clung to the old religion.

As for myself, I lived comfortably among the king's glittering subjects—courtiers, ladies, learned travelers, successful merchants, philosophers, diplomats, poets—all of us floating above a cesspool of terror and death.

24

ACQUIESCENCE

Summer and Fall 1535
Madge Shelton, Whitehall

I had known Margaret Roper since we were children, long before anyone imagined my cousin would become queen. Sir Thomas More's eldest daughter had married young and become a scholarly woman who translated Erasmus. Her letter to me described her mother's despair over her father's coming execution. She said little about her own feelings.

She wrote that she had tried to persuade her father to sign a document accepting the king as the head of the church and my cousin as England's queen. She had signed it herself, but her father stood by his convictions. To him, the Church of Rome was the universal church and the pope its rightful head.

By this time, everyone in England had become accustomed to seeing those who rejected the new religion imprisoned, exiled, or executed, depending on how outspoken they were. The general view among those I knew was that obeying the king was far wiser than arguing over ecclesiastical fine points. But as the deaths multiplied, the court split into segments. Some championed the dreadful executions, either because they truly believed the old religion was heresy or were resolutely loyal to the king. Some drank, gambled, flirted, and joked as they always had—they simply looked away. But some, and I was among them, fell into a deep unease. I read my own mother's doubt in her eyes.

"We must say nothing about Sir Thomas, Madge. Our opinions do not matter."

⚜

Sir Henry had attended More's trial, and I decided to ask him about it. If we were to marry, I should come to know his mind. It was early July, and we met in a garden near sunset, as we often did during these warmer months. We talked of his children, who had returned to the countryside.

"My sister cares for them," he told me, "but I long for the day when you will be their mother. My daughter says you are as beautiful as a princess in a fairy tale."

This was as close to romance as he got.

He gazed over the greenery at the thick bands of pink clouds and sky formed by the setting sun. He seemed preoccupied, and we spoke in clichés, as if we were actors in a play.

"Your children are delightful. I hope they will welcome me."

"I believe they will do so eagerly."

We could have continued like this, commenting on the children, the weather, the summer blossoms, the cool of the bubbling fountains. But I believed a man and wife should be able to speak frankly and exchange views on worldly matters. My mother and father did.

"May I ask you about the trial?" I ventured.

"This is a dreadful subject, ma'am. What do you want to know?"

"Do you understand why Sir Thomas defies the king?"

"He says he obeys a higher power—or at least this is what he claims."

"You don't believe him?"

"I think he wants to create a spectacle . . . to die for God . . . to secure his place in history." Sir Henry tightened his fist for a second, and I noted his heavy signet ring, a symbol of his service to the king.

"But no one wants to die," I said. "Not as a traitor . . . not in the midst of life."

"For some, suffering on Earth guarantees entry into heaven. This is a dangerous belief. His wife and daughter begged him to bend. The Tower warden told me his wife was pitiful when she left his cell."

"Couldn't he be exiled? His only crimes are his beliefs."

"It's not possible. If men like More and Fisher flout the law with no consequences, others will follow. There could be civil war."

Sitting beside me in the glorious twilight, he seemed exhausted.

"When will it be?" I asked.

"In two days' time."

"And will you witness it?"

"Yes, I watch traitors die and assure the king the danger is past."

When he paused, I deliberately caught his eye.

"I had hoped More would relent," he said quietly. "I often wonder how many more will die before . . . I should return to His Majesty now."

He stood and bowed and kissed my hand. "Try not to think of these matters, Madge. Perhaps More will be the last."

I watched him walk into the palace, understanding even less about him than before. My future husband spent his days soothing the king of England. Acquiescence was his muse.

On the sixth of July, Sir Thomas More was beheaded. Among the people I knew, few spoke of him again.

❦

"Play cards with us tonight, Madge. You can entertain us with your stories."

Sir Francis caught up with me as I was leaving the queen's apartments. He pulled at the veil of my hood and put his lips close to my ear.

"So, is it true, my lovely Madge? Is Her Majesty with child again?" Placing his hand at my elbow, he ushered me into the queen's library where he could speak to me alone.

"This would be a cause for celebration . . . a lifting of the darkness. Should we prepare to dance and sing again?"

"You'll get no secrets from me, sir."

"Not even a hint? How disappointing."

Of all the king's men, Sir Francis paid the least attention to politics. He spent his days gambling, sporting, and planning outings and balls. He excelled at light conversation. During these gloomy months, these particular talents were useful. His florid proclamations of courtly love amused my cousin while she prayed for another pregnancy. His banter and willingness to lose at sport diverted the king, whose temper was unpredictable.

"I will play cards another night," I said. "I should be with the queen."

"Then she must be with child. Otherwise, they'd be at it, and you could join us. They're like rabbits, aren't they? Unfortunately, without the same results."

He often made outrageous jokes like this—jests that captured what others thought but were too afraid to say aloud. When I didn't answer, he winked and tugged at my veil again.

"Mark will play for us. Doesn't that tempt you?" His blue eyes gleamed as he touched my chin. "I wish you looked at me the way you gaze at Master Smeaton. All the ladies flutter their eyelashes at him."

I carried a constant fear that someone might notice my lingering fondness for Mark, and my stomach somersaulted. "I have never done anything like that, and you know it. I am betrothed to Sir Henry Norris."

He blinked, smiling. "Ah, but does your heart follow the rules?"

"Who are you to question me?"

My reply was sharper than I intended, probably reflecting my guilty thoughts. He stepped backward and raised his hands as if he were surrendering in a battle. These kinds of conversations diverted him, and his expression was jubilant.

"Don't worry, my beautiful Madge. I am teasing you. I would never tell such a tale. Besides, I like Mark too. He's a polite, gifted boy."

"Are you so much older than he is?"

"Maybe not, but he is a romantic with his head in his music, whereas I am a man of the world."

I had lied and evaded his questions, as I had to do, but my denials caused me pain. My memories of Mark were precious to me, and I felt I was erasing them.

Weston changed his theme, but he hadn't finished with his roguish games. "If you would like to be a better wife to Sir Henry, I can teach you about marriage's delights. It could be our secret."

"You are impossible."

"I hope so."

He patted my cheek and walked to the door but turned back to me before leaving the room. "Now that I think of it, I am mistaken. It was your sister who was so besotted with Mark, wasn't it? You, my dear Madge, keep your sentiments well hidden."

⚮

Weston's guess about the queen was accurate. On her doctors' advice, she began another lying in, this one much earlier than required. Locked away from court, her moods alternated between anxiety and euphoria, and I prepared myself for months of tantrums and extravagant demands. Like all the Boleyns, I prayed she would give birth to a healthy boy this time.

One damp, foggy day, I decided to step outside for a few minutes before beginning my evening duties in my cousin's airless rooms. Given the weather, I didn't expect to see anyone outside, except maybe a guard. But a man and woman stood near a fountain, and I recognized both. His Majesty bent over to kiss Jane Seymour, one of my cousin's ladies, and slipped his hand beneath her overskirt. She nestled closer and laid her head on his chest as he rubbed her buttocks. Based on her reaction, this seemed to be something they often did.

25

THE NEW COMPANION

Summer and Fall 1535

Mark Smeaton, The Court of King Henry

ome months ago, officials had posted the proclamations in every village square and in country churches and public houses: "Henceforth, all will describe His Majesty's former wife as the Dowager Princess of Wales. His older daughter is the Lady Mary."

Those who could read had explained the rules to their un-schooled neighbors: "Queen Anne is England's only queen, and her daughter is the only princess . . . So, don't call Queen Katherine 'Queen Katherine' anymore because now it's against the law."

But people change slowly, and even within His Majesty's palaces, occasional references to "Queen Katherine" or "Princess Mary" slipped out. Word spread of an older cook at Eltham who was thrashed for her forgetfulness. She had served the old queen for twenty years.

Queen Anne wore the old queen's jewels. The demoted Lady Mary was shunted away. Once, the former princess would have married a king or a prince in another royal family. In her new circumstances, spies watched her and read her letters.

Many considered these measures mean-spirited, insisting that "this is Anne Boleyn's doing—not the king's." Even His Majesty seemed to tire of reassuring the woman who had once beguiled him. More than once, he complained to Norris and Cromwell, "No matter what I do, she is never satisfied."

Throughout the year, I had watched the king take his leave in the evening to join the queen in his bed. He lifted himself heavily from his chair, showing little appetite for what was to come. I suspected he would rather drink and joke with his companions than fulfill his marital office.

The whole court twittered and speculated about the size of the queen's belly and the pallor of her skin. Everyone knew time was running out, although few said as much. The queen was near the age when conception is less likely and giving birth becomes more precarious. I began to feel sorry for her.

In the fall, she disappeared into her chambers, another lying in. In the towns, gamblers organized the betting—no baby at all, another girl, or the long-awaited prince. The odds favored another miscarriage.

About this time, the king began walking in the garden with Jane Seymour and sending her letters and poems. I had long since abandoned any choir-boyish notions about married life. Men at court were rarely faithful to their wives—certainly not those who wed for land and wealth. And few expected the king of England to subdue his manly needs while the queen was unavailable. Not even Anne Boleyn should have expected that.

But His Majesty's choice seemed strange to me—a stiff young woman who rarely spoke. She was so pastel in coloring that she sometimes faded from view. Still, I was relieved the king hadn't decided to amuse himself with the glowing Mistress Shelton. Other than that, I didn't care.

✦

With the queen's lying in, Paul and I had more leisure, and we left the palace one night to take supper at an inn. Bursting with travelers and country tradesmen, this was a place where we could relax and speak more freely. We reviewed the afternoon's remarkable events.

Hours earlier, we had been playing in the king's chambers with Silas Bray, a conventional trio, nothing unusual at all. A half dozen of the king's men had gathered to gamble and talk politics. The wine flowed freely, and His Majesty was jovial. "Find Jane Seymour and bring her here," he had ordered. When she arrived some minutes later, he coaxed her onto his lap. The king's men continued their discussions and games.

Our waitress appeared, bringing cups of ale. We ordered our dinner and glanced around the noisy tavern after she left us. No one was near enough to listen to what we said.

"It was unseemly," Paul began, "everyone watching him paw over her."

"Well, the king does what he wants."

"Do you think they're lovers?"

"Maybe—I expect they'll get there. You're not shocked, are you?"

"No, but he used to be more discreet."

"It's almost as if he wants to humiliate the queen—to punish her for disappointing him."

"Do you think he will push her out if there's no male babe, just like he did before?"

"And marry Jane Seymour, you mean? She's as drab as they come."

"Her brothers are powerful, and she's a decade younger than the queen."

Paul's question didn't surprise me—the possibility had occurred to me as well.

"So, both queens end up living in drafty old castles up North," I said, "because neither produced a prince. It would be sad twist of fate, wouldn't it? At least from Anne Boleyn's point of view."

We ate our meal—a succulent oxtail soup—and called for another round of ale.

"Did you see Bray this afternoon," Paul asked, "when the king had Jane Seymour in his lap?"

"No. Was there something to see?"

"Everyone else was pretending nothing was happening—even Suffolk and Norris."

"Well, it was vulgar."

"But Bray watched, and I think it pleased him."

"A vicarious thrill, you mean? With Jane Seymour? Do you think she tempts him?"

"No, but he'll have good news for the Seymour brothers. Bray's probably telling them while we're having supper."

I pictured Bray bringing his morsel to his patrons, and the brothers chuckling and gloating and congratulating themselves. An unpleasant thought, but most wealthy families used their sisters and daughters to improve their prospects. None of it mattered to me.

⚜

Just before she began her lying in, Her Majesty urged the king to choose a royal match for the little princess who had become a happy, prattling tot. The queen's choice for her daughter was the seventeen-year-old Dauphin of France.

"She's still a babe," the king said. "We'll decide after the prince is born."

Once, the king would have spoken these words with a twinkle in his eye and a playful pat of his wife's breasts. This time, he added, "Leave it for now. . . I decide, not you, and I'll decide whenever I'm ready to."

The queen argued with Thomas Cromwell about the match, and with her uncle, the Duke of Norfolk. According to reports from people in the room, she berated Norfolk, using language unfit for any woman. Once she was secluded for the remainder of her pregnancy, Cromwell raised the matter with the king.

"The queen might have a son," Cromwell said. "This would be glorious news, and the child could be matched to the kingdom's advantage. Her Majesty might bear another daughter who would also have some value for the realm, although it would be trivial. But my counsel is that we shouldn't reach any decisions until we know the situation. Then we can weigh all our options."

"You are the master of options, Thomas. What shall we do if she fails again?"

"Your Majesty, your choices are limitless. The queen might die in childbirth or relinquish the crown due to her failures. She might cease to be queen for reasons we don't even know about yet."

"I need a son."

"And England needs a prince. One way or another, it will be."

26

MY COUSIN'S SORROWS

Winter 1535 to 1536

Madge Shelton, Whitehall and Greenwich

The December weather seemed especially dreary that year, and the servants lit the fires in the birthing chambers in the early afternoon. With the doors and windows shut to keep out dangerous vapors, my cousin's rooms were stuffy and hot. Only a half dozen ladies and midwives tended her, along with the women servants. With God's grace, a prince would be born within these walls by spring. Every night, I watched my cousin and mother pray for this.

My cousin got fully dressed every day, even when pregnant. In the morning, she would choose a gown, skirts, sleeves, jewels, and hood, and I would help her put them on. Since she never saw the king or other important visitors, I wondered why she spent so much time on her appearance. She often tried on garments and jewels in different combinations, changing her mind repeatedly. She sometimes gazed in the mirror as if she were convincing herself that she was beautiful, still pleasing enough to tempt a man.

One afternoon, my mother and I arrived to find her playing cards with my little sister, who had recently returned to court. Mary's "second chance" followed a series of motherly lectures: "I expect my daughters to behave modestly and avoid scandal. If you can't conduct yourself properly, you'll be back in Norfolk before you know it." Mary did seem chastened and more grown-up, but I kept my eye on her. She had just turned seventeen.

On this day, my cousin was particularly animated. She placed her hand of cards on the table and stroked her stomach, saying, "*De plus en plus grand, n'est-ce pas?*" She looked at her belly and rearranged the folds of the dark green silk flowing over it. "I've sent all the servants away until supper. *Marie, verse le vin.*"

My sister filled the cups, laughing when she splashed wine onto the embroidered tablecloth. Her giggling and reddened cheeks made me question how long she'd been with the queen and how much wine she had already drunk.

"I felt the quickening this morning," my cousin announced, "the burly kick of a boy."

"Such good news, Your Majesty," my mother replied. "God bless your firstborn son."

My cousin spread her ringed fingers across her belly again, perhaps reassuring herself by gauging its size. "I have a plan to discuss with all of you," she said. "Madge, search the outer rooms."

We all knew Cromwell hid his minions among the servants, the women who scrubbed the floors and changed the beds. They reported to him on the queen's condition and listened at doorways whenever they had the chance. I had recently encountered a maidservant pausing near my cousin's inner room and asked her why she was there.

"Beg pardon, ma'am," she said, bowing to me. "I was sent to shake out the blankets."

This might have been true, but I sent her away anyway. She could have been Cromwell's spy or someone else's.

A careful tour of my cousin's apartment assured me that we were alone. When I opened the door to return to the inner chamber, I heard my mother's voice.

"Mary, I thought you were putting Her Majesty's wardrobe in order for the colder weather as I asked you to."

"I sent for her," my cousin explained. She patted my sister's hand and looked at my mother with some sharpness. "I have heard about *la chienne*."

All the ladies had concealed the rumors about Jane Seymour— the midwives warned us to avoid upsetting the queen. We confined ourselves to pleasant topics, such as the charms of the Princess Elizabeth, George's diplomatic successes, and the elaborate plans for the prince's christening. My cousin turned away from my mother, angling her body toward Mary. "Well, *ma petite*, what do you know about His Majesty and this Jane Seymour?"

"She sat in his lap. Everyone was talking about it."

"Anything else?"

I was surprised my cousin was so calm.

"He gave her a diamond bracelet . . . and maybe some other jewels."

"Well, we knew this might happen."

My cousin's voice took on a silvery, philosophical tone. "The king is only a man. All men have their needs." She ran her fingers over her stomach again, unable to resist the need to feel its bulge. She directed her words to my mother. "But we need to keep this Seymour woman away from him . . . in case anything goes wrong."

"She is no substitute for you, Your Majesty. The king will quickly tire of her."

"She is young, and her brothers will encourage the king's lust for her. I suspect Cromwell will, as well."

My mother frowned. Unlike me, she rarely showed her feelings. "Do you think so? Cromwell has always been on your side."

"Cromwell is on Cromwell's side."

My cousin tilted her head and looked at me. "And what have you heard, Madge? About the Seymours and their plans? What does Sir Henry say?"

"Very little, Your Majesty. I have heard that the king sometimes walks with Jane Seymour. I know nothing of the brothers."

Some of this was close to the truth. Since I spent most days inside the birthing chamber, I hadn't heard much gossip at court. Sir Henry was reserved and didn't talk about the king's private habits—he was the model groom. But I had omitted what I had witnessed personally: the king had slipped his hands inside Jane Seymour's skirts and rubbed her behind as if he did it every day.

"All of you must listen more intently—you will be my eyes and ears." She took Mary's two hands between her own, smiling and looking at her carefully. "You have grown into such a pretty girl—our très jolie Marie. Perhaps you could distract His Majesty and entertain him sometimes in the evenings?"

My mother's body stiffened, but she didn't speak.

"Mary is young and agreeable," my cousin went on. "She is not promised to anyone, so one will object. What do you think, my dumpling? Could you flirt with the king?"

By this time, I had grasped the full idea.

My mother's face was passive. "What would you like Mary to do?"

"Not nearly as much as you fear."

My cousin kept her gaze on my bubbling little sister and instructed her. "You can smile at the king and flatter him . . . Wear dresses that show off your breasts. Lean over so he can peek inside your gown . . . just a little. Sit near him and accidentally brush your leg against his . . . You will do this for me, my Marie?"

"Mary is not experienced," my mother said.

The queen refilled Mary's cup herself. "Most evenings, the king is drowsy and sated by ten o'clock. If he takes her to bed, she can pleasure him, and he'll fall asleep before the act. We can tell her what to do."

"And what of Jane Seymour? Isn't she likely to be nearby?"

"I will require Jane's presence here in the evenings—every evening, all evening long. The scheme will proceed as I have planned."

"I want to do it," Mary cooed. "The queen thinks I'm pretty enough to please the king."

She stared at my mother with a defiance I hadn't seen before. "You think Madge is prettier . . . you always have."

My mother's eyes glistened as she wrapped her arms around her ribs. My cousin moved on to describe the plan's additional benefits. "And afterward, Mary will marry a duke or an earl. I will arrange it myself . . . Madge and Sir Henry will marry this winter before the baby is born. This will ensure that Norris stays with us."

At this point, she appeared to tire, as if her plotting had drained her strength. "And how is my sweet Pourquoi?"

I was minding the little dog again. "He jumps and plays as always, ma'am."

She dismissed us, and we rose as one. Only Mary was happy.

⚜

Several days later, I entered our family apartments to see my mother sitting at a side table with Sir Thomas Cromwell. Their voices were low, producing an even buzz of indistinguishable words. My mother looked up and smiled while our visitor stood and bowed.

"My congratulations, Mistress Shelton," Cromwell said. "I hear you will soon wed. I wish you and Sir Henry every happiness." He placed his brown feathered hat near his heart and inclined his head. "But now I must return to His Majesty. I am glad we talked, Lady Shelton. We will talk again."

As far as I knew, Cromwell had never entered our chambers before. The man was hardly a family friend. His mannerly "I am glad we talked" could mean anything. Once he was gone, my mother began reviewing the wedding plans.

"Does Sir Thomas have business with us?" I asked.

"Nothing to do with you, my dear, and nothing for you to worry about."

⌀⌀

Mary tempted the king regularly, but he rarely summoned her to his bed—only a few times when he was drunk. "The plan is succeeding wonderfully," she gushed to my cousin. She made sure to add, "His Majesty yearns for you."

When my sister and I were alone one night, she said, "He doesn't really do anything. I don't think he can."

"You should be quiet about such matters."

"Well, do you want to know what happens or not?"

Of course, I wanted to know.

"I undress, and he sits on his bed drinking and tells me to walk around the room. Once, he made me come closer and said, 'Bend over.' Then he kissed my bottom and fell asleep with his big stomach bulging through his nightshirt. He looks like a country hog."

"Mary, don't. You can't talk about the king this way."

"I'm not stupid, Madge. You're the only one I've told."

⌀⌀

When I wasn't tending to my cousin or spending time with my family, I tried to escape with Starlight for the afternoon. Even as the weather worsened, I went riding, visiting spots I already knew well and discovering winding trails I had never traveled before. I would wear my warmest cloak and hat and glory in my freedom—I didn't mind the cold. For several hours, I didn't think of the court at all, except that I always thought about Mark.

Late one afternoon, I returned to the palace and encountered Sir Francis standing just inside the doorway. He toasted me with the goblet he held.

"Ah, the alluring Mistress Shelton." His cheeks were flushed, and his eyes were bright. He took my wrist with his free hand but laughed and let go when I pulled away. "You must be cold after being out in this weather," he said. "Let's sit by the fire and share a cup of wine. I have much to tell you."

Before I could respond, I heard a woman's voice ahead of us. "The queen is waiting for you, Madge."

Jane Boleyn, Lady Rochford—George's wife—had emerged from a side door. She spoke with some urgency. "Be quick. You must go now. You'll have to change your plans—you can visit with Sir Francis another day."

At first, her reaction puzzled me. Did she think I intended to meet with Weston?

But Sir Francis was quicker and tried to salvage the situation. "I had hoped to persuade her to sit with me, but I've had no success. We've just met at the door. But, perhaps, Lady Rochford, you would join me in a cup of wine. We haven't spoken in a while."

She answered him briefly by saying, "Sir Francis, I must attend the queen." She then directed her words to me. "Madge, you should be on your way."

As I nodded and turned to leave, Weston began some thread of light conversation, perhaps hoping to charm Jane Boleyn out of her prickly mood, but his efforts evidently failed. I heard her footsteps behind me, and I waited for her, trying to think of what to say.

"You must be careful," she whispered once she caught up. "You're betrothed to the king's best friend." She slid her hands down her skirt until her fingers reached the small prayer book she carried on her belt. "Our enemies are spreading rumors and lies about us—all the Boleyns, including you. You shouldn't be spending time alone with him."

"Of course not. We only met at the doorway, just as Sir Francis said."

She stared at me before she replied. Her tone was more insistent than before. "I believe you, Madge, but others may not. I advise you to be on your guard."

She seemed overly upset by a minor incident, and I knew I had done nothing wrong. I was sure she was exaggerating the danger—I wasn't important enough to inspire court gossip.

My cousin lost the child in January, and this time, the midwives were certain it was a boy. She swore us to secrecy until she could rise from her bed and walk to the king's chambers: "I will tell him myself."

A few hours later, I helped her dress, assuming she would wear mourning in memory of her lost son. Instead, she chose a gown of burgundy, its brocade overskirt and bodice studded with tiny silver beads. She asked for the ruby necklace the king had given her for Seigneur du Bellay's ball, in the days when he itched for her.

"I cannot look ill, Madge. His Majesty must envision me as I was."

People gasped and whispered as we walked through hallways toward the king's privy chambers. Anyone who saw her immediately realized that she had lost the child. The king stood up when she entered, his arms hanging limply at his sides. He stared past her and walked across the room to the door. "Leave us while I speak with my wife alone," he said.

As I was going, I glanced back at her, thinking she must be afraid and still in pain. The king used all his considerable strength to slam the door shut. The sound echoed down the hall.

27

A TEST OF LOYALTY

Winter 1536
Mark Smeaton, Greenwich

On one of my days of leisure, I rode Flanders along the Thames from Greenwich toward Chiswick, the icy river coming into view whenever I climbed a hill. I stopped in a small village with a single tavern and a rough stone church. A few scraggly boys played near the road, and one approached.

"Your horse, sir, what's her name?"

"She's Flanders. Would you watch her while I'm in the tavern?"

I gave him a coin, though I was sure he would have watched her for the pleasure of petting her. I used to be like him.

The stable boys at Greenwich exercised Prince and Flanders daily, but even when I was busy, I took each horse out as often as I could. I liked escaping to little towns like this one where life was slow, and people's rhythms matched the seasons. The villagers talked about their crops and animals and complained about too much rain. No one ever mentioned the Seymours or the Boleyns.

When I returned Flanders to her stall later that day, I saw a reedy, red-haired man drinking with the stable master. Both had their feet up, their muddied boots resting on bales of hay. Nate Gage wore the Seymour livery—I had seen him around, but never spoken to him beyond "good morning" or "good day." The stable master told me Gage had once asked him who I was: "I told him you played for the king. That's all I know, anyway."

A boy brought fresh water for Flanders and checked her hooves for stones. I removed her saddle and wiped off her lustrous red-brown coat. I heard Gage creep up behind me.

"Where'd you get her?" He slapped her haunch—it wasn't a hard slap, but I didn't like it. I kept my eyes on her and calmed her as I answered him over my shoulder.

"I bought her from Sir Francis Weston—and the black stallion. I've had them several years."

"Weston? I hear he's quite the sportsman—and a ladies' man."

"Apparently." I rubbed the cloth over my horse's back and wished Gage would go away.

"And one of the queen's favorites," he went on. "I've been told he visits her every day."

"Does he? I never heard that." Gage followed me as I circled Flanders and continued drying her coat.

"But you must see them together all the time . . . I bet you could tell a tale or two."

I was used to fending off drunken busybodies, most of them more subtle than Gage. "Honestly, I don't remember Weston being there more than anyone else."

"But she has her group, doesn't she? Weston, Norris, Brereton—all of them sweet-talking her."

"I play a lute in the corner. I doubt I could tell you anything you don't already know."

"No? That's surprising." A gold earring glittered through the oily strands of his matted hair. "These two horses must have cost you a pretty penny. Are players so well paid?"

After spreading a soft blanket over Flanders' back, I moved to Prince's stall to stroke his neck. I smelled Gage's sweat as he followed me. "Musicians have many opportunities," I replied, "but we must work day and night to profit from them. In fact, I'm performing this evening and should leave now. Please forgive me, Master Gage."

A few days later, he reappeared, leaning against a garden wall near my quarters. "Mark, my good man, join me at the tavern. You will be my guest."

"I'm sorry . . . it is a generous offer, but I'm leaving shortly for a performance at Lord Rochford's."

Gage placed his hand on my upper arm, his dirty fingernails digging into my sleeve. "Another time, then? You play for the queen. You play for Rochford. You could benefit from talking with me."

"How is that?"

"Some would pay well to know what you hear. Other players profit this way."

"I am sorry, Master Gage. I have more employment than I have time for." I bowed, but he wasn't finished.

"The king wouldn't object. In fact, His Majesty might be grateful. Think on this, Mark. You want to be on the right side now that she's lost another one. I'll be at the stables all week."

I had little time to wash and change, but I went to see Paul anyway. "Gage said to find him if I want to do it," I told him. "Maybe he'll back off if I ignore him."

"The Seymours must have sent him—he wouldn't try to recruit you on his own."

"I'll tell Rochford tonight."

"It might be better to stay out of it."

"But shouldn't Rochford be warned?"

"He knows there are spies, and he knows who pays them."

"But I would feel better if I told him."

"Be careful, Mark, you may be choosing between the king and queen."

⚜

I walked to George Boleyn's house near the palace, firm in my decision to report what Gage had said. Lord and Lady Rochford met me
at the door standing arm in arm, as if they were bound with rope.
After the usual greetings, I asked if I could speak to him after my
performance.

"We could talk now if you like," he said. "My guests have not
arrived."

But Lady Rochford showed no sign of leaving, and my news was
for him alone.

"If we may, sir, I would prefer to talk afterward. I hope it is not
inconvenient."

"Certainly—as you wish."

⚜

As I played that night, Gage's words rose up in the back of my mind.
To my relief, Rochford approached me as soon as I was done, his
cloak tossed over his shoulders and his hat in hand, along with my
own cloak and hat. "Let's walk in the garden . . . the weather is mild
enough," he said.

His house and garden reflected his rank as the queen's brother—
Italian paving stones, French statues and fountains, hedges grown
in elegant patterns. Even in winter, some plants were luxuriant,
chosen to thrive in the colder months. We walked along pathways
scented with jasmine and lined with urns of snowdrops and
heather. He listened to my report and asked me to repeat Gage's
words about the king.

"Thank you for telling me." He looked to the horizon where a
new moon hovered in a sky that was nearly black. "The queen and I
are in your debt."

"What Gage said about the king, sir . . . it may be nothing. He's a braggart who likes telling tales."

Rochford smiled. "Let's hope that's true." He put his hand on my shoulder. "You are one of us now."

When we returned to the house, Lady Rochford was waiting in the hall. Most of their visitors had gone home. Although the evening had been festive, with excellent food and drink, several important guests had not appeared. I remembered the days when everyone at court coveted the chance to dine with Lord and Lady Rochford. But with the Seymours' rise and the queen's difficulties, some thought it better to stay away.

I bowed to her. "Thank you, Lady Rochford. It is an honor to play in your house."

She replied pleasantly but seemed uneasy. As one of the queen's ladies, she understood the court's plotting and maneuvering as well as anyone. She must have guessed the nature of my news. I didn't see Gage in the following weeks, but I noted a change in Rochford's behavior. He visited the king more often in the evenings, bringing small gifts from the family and bits of diplomatic gossip. His Majesty welcomed him heartily but never invited him to stay to play cards or join in the conversation—those days of camaraderie were gone. If I noticed this alteration in the king's attitude, I was sure George Boleyn did as well.

⚜

From our first meetings, Maria Isabella was curious about Her Majesty's dresses—the colors, laces, velvets, beading, the lush Italian brocades. Since the queen's gowns were designed to be noticed and talked about, I thought little of it. I described them as well as I could. Once or twice, she asked me who had visited the queen that day and what the visitors were like. Her questions seemed to reflect the common fascination with life at court. I ignored them and began the sex, and she happily complied.

But after the queen had lost the prince, Maria Isabella began probing the details of Her Majesty's daily activities—who she saw, what she said, and where she went. Quite suddenly, my sultry paramour wanted to know all about Rochford and Weston and other gentlemen of the court as well.

"You're very inquisitive lately," I said one night. She stared at me, tilting her head to the side, so I tried what Spanish I knew. "*Eres una mujer muy curiosa.*"

She smiled like she smiled the first night we met. "I improve my English." She made a noticeable effort to pronounce each word correctly. "No one talk to me."

"It's 'talks' . . . 'No one talks to me.'"

"No one talks to me." She stressed the "s" to be sure I heard it and concluded the conversation by wrapping her arms around my neck. During our lovemaking, I tried to convince myself there was no cause for worry. The next morning, I visited Madame Margaretha.

"Ah, Master Smeaton, my good friend, sit with me. We can have breakfast before the girls wake up." She grinned as she tore a huge chunk from a loaf of bread. Three sizzling sausages filled her plate. "Some ale? The best in the city."

I took the cup, mainly to be polite.

"Perhaps you have tired of our Spanish enchantress," she went on. "Or perhaps you wish to take her away with you?" Reading men's moods is a madam's specialty, and her face changed as she studied mine. "What is wrong?"

"Maria Isabella's other visitor . . . could you tell me who he is?"

"I keep the confidences of all who come to my establishment."

"I am sorry . . . I do need to know. She told me there is only one."

Madame Margaretha placed a sausage on the bread, which turned orange from the juices and grease. She drank from her cup and then spoke without looking up. "There are two now, brothers. Both use her, but they are often away."

There were dozens of possibilities—gentlemen brothers were common enough—but I knew the two she meant. "Are they often at Wolf Hall?"

"Yes, I believe they are." She bit into her sausage and bread.

"Thank you . . . I am grateful. No one will know of our conversation."

"But you will not see Maria Isabella again."

"No, my time with her is done."

⚜

Paul went home to Devon during his father's final weeks. He was unusually quiet when he returned. I considered his preoccupation natural—I was silent for days after they told me my father had died.

One afternoon, we talked in his chamber, and I noted, as I always did, how few possessions he had: a few clothes, his lute, some music, a Bible, and several books of prayer and meditation. I sat in his single chair while he leaned against his rough-hewn desk.

"I have made a choice," he said.

"What kind of choice? Are you in love?"

"In a way. . . ."

"Well, who is she?" He had been attracted to several young women over the years but didn't visit the brothels. He seemed prepared to wait for a wife.

"When I was in Devon, I began taking orders. By the summer, I will be ministering to parishioners in a small church near the sea."

I absorbed the news—I was surprised but shouldn't have been. Paul had often mentioned his faith in God and admiration for those who devoted their lives to Him. Still, I felt that slow thickening in the throat that comes with the news of loss. My first thought was that I would be alone again. My second was for his safety.

"Are you certain?" I asked. "To go from the king's palaces to some parish in Devon . . . there are more cows in Devon than people." I regretted my scoffing the moment I saw the deep, soft brown of his eyes. "I'm sorry, Paul, I didn't mean to question you."

"I've questioned you often enough." His whole face crinkled as he laughed. He moved to stand closer to me. "I know this is unexpected, but apart from our friendship, there's little I value at court."

"But you are playing more. The queen praises you. I could speak to Rochford about more money. . . ."

"No."

His gaze was as honest as any I have ever known. I knew his mind was set.

"You thrive at court," he continued.

"In some ways."

"You perform. You write music. You live an accomplished life. You give people pleasure, and your music will outlive you. Unless I do this, my life won't matter to anyone."

"It matters to me."

"We will be friends even when I'm a priest in a muddy village in a church the size of this room. And you're right about the cows. Devon does have more cows than people."

I swallowed. "We'll be friends all our lives."

I forced myself to be enthusiastic about the future he had chosen. This is the rule for friends. But when he was gone, I sat alone in my room, surrounded by luxuries I had never imagined as a child. To me, his departure was like a death.

PART FIVE

So I Hear

28

SUSPICION AMONG FRIENDS

Winter and Spring 1536

Mark Smeaton, The Court of King Henry

The queen wasn't the same after she lost the prince, although she reigned as she had before. She glided through her days served by adoring courtiers and obedient ladies. She wore sumptuous dresses and costly gems. She attended feasts, jousts, and dances and visited with foreign dignitaries. At official ceremonies, she sat beside His Majesty wearing a diadem.

But her sorrows had changed her. In private, she quarreled with the king and accused him of betraying her. She began to openly question her ladies and her friends, and her suspicions poisoned the court. No one trusted anyone. Everyone was on their guard.

I recalled a country song from my childhood about a beautiful woman in every season of the year. In spring, she dances among flowers; in summer, her kisses are sweet. Near the end, "the days grow old and winter cold. She draws her cloak around her." [18]

This is how I saw the once-gleaming Anne Boleyn—alone, surrounded, and fearing every whisper.

✝

Few people at court were surprised when the king postponed Sir Henry's wedding to Mistress Shelton after the death of the unborn prince.

"This winter," he said, "we will mourn my son. They can marry in May."

The delay seemed appropriate, and of course I welcomed it—a short suspension of reality. I had always understood she would marry someone else. I knew this from the start.

But as the days passed, court gossips began talking of scandal—a supposed liaison between Sir Francis Weston and the lady. No one could say exactly what had happened, but some claimed that Mistress Shelton had "misplayed her cards" and caused her family great distress. The story was that Sir Henry was having second thoughts.

I didn't believe it—perhaps I didn't want to believe it. I had never seen signs of a romance between Weston and Mistress Shelton, and I still watched her far more closely than I should have. Besides, Weston was too smart to meddle in Boleyn family business. He could have a dozen beautiful women for the asking. Why would he risk angering his friend, Lord Rochford, and aggravating the queen?

Yet Her Majesty believed the most damning rumors the minute they reached her ears

"This stupid girl and Francis running around with his cock out," she said to her brother. "They could ruin our plans." She sat rigidly in her heavy oak chair, drumming her fingers on the sides.

"It's not true," her brother reassured her. "Someone is spreading lies."

"You don't think he would jump into bed with her?"

"Not in these circumstances . . . Sir Henry and Madge will marry as planned."

But Anne Boleyn refused to be comforted. "*L'imbécile*—Sir Francis Weston will learn the rules."

"Anne, leave it alone. Weston has done nothing wrong and Madge even less."

The queen snatched at her veil and turned her face away. By this time, not even her brother could give her advice.

⚜

The king, Norris, and most of the court had left for Hampton Court that morning. Much of the rebuilding was complete. Mistress Shelton and her mother had journeyed ahead to prepare Her Majesty's rooms, but the queen had unexpectedly complained of tiredness, saying that she would travel the following day. Weston, too, stayed behind at Whitehall, as did Brereton and a few others.

The men hunted in the morning and played cards after the midday meal. They gathered at a gaming table while servants refilled their goblets many times. Stationed at benches by the windows, Oliver, Bray, and I played Venetian fantasias, mainly for ourselves.

We all stood and bowed when the queen entered, and Weston raised his drink to her.

"Your Majesty, we welcome your presence—the room now glows with your light."

"Francis, we haven't seen you for days."

In recent months, her voice had lost its alluring musicality, and her tone was brittle and thin. She turned and spoke to Lady Worcester and Lady Rochford who trailed behind her. "I ask myself, 'Has he abandoned us?' Perhaps one of you knows the answer."

The women curtsied and looked at the floor. We all remained standing, waiting for permission to sit. Everyone sensed a brewing storm. [19]

"Go ahead . . . resume your game."

She clutched a silk handkerchief and waved it as she spoke. Brereton offered her his cards. "It's quite a good hand, Your Majesty. Perhaps you wish to join?"

"No, I am content to watch. Well, Francis, where have you been?"

Weston shuffled the cards and replied in a carefree voice. "Irksome matters of commerce, ma'am . . . selling some property to an obscenely rich German—obscenely fat as well." He dealt the cards, his tone confident. "They live well, these German merchants, and they still have money to spend."

At first, his response seemed to amuse the queen, but soon she began twisting her handkerchief. Weston noticed and placed his cards face down on the table. He rose and approached her. "In truth, Your Majesty, I was counting the days until I could gaze on you." His blond hair rippled forward as he bowed again. "Given any choice, ma'am, I always prefer to be at your side . . . and at your service."

The queen jerked her head back, inhaling before she spoke. "I hear you've been seeing Madge—bringing her poems and sweets. She is betrothed to Norris, and you will keep your distance. This is my command."

"Your Majesty, I have rarely spoken to her . . . I swear it on my mother's soul."

"Do you think I'm a fool?" She grabbed at the sides of her chair, and her handkerchief fell to the floor. Lady Worcester started to pick it up but decided to stay seated. Oliver, Bray, and I stopped playing, fearing the queen's anger might settle on us.

Nothing in Weston's expression suggested his thoughts. His cadence was measured and relaxed. "Then I swear it on my father's soul . . . or on my new greyhound's soul . . . and that, Your Majesty, is a serious oath. You know, that pup is the most wonderful creature." He fell to one knee and placed a hand on his heart. "Your Majesty, I will stay on my knee until sunset to convince you I speak the truth."

"Are you mocking me?" Her voice quivered, as if she couldn't control it. Brereton sat stiffly while Lady Rochford pretended to sew and Lady Worcester pretended to read. All of us had witnessed the queen's recent fits of temper. The only surprise was that the target was Weston. "You will regret it if you cross me, Francis. Madge is family. She will be unknown to you."

Weston remained on his knee but raised his eyes. "Your Majesty, you alone are the goddess who reigns in my thoughts. On my very soul, I swear I adore you above all others."

His words didn't shock me. I doubt they shocked anyone in the room. Gentlemen of every age and nationality used the language of courtly romance to seek the queen's favor. She collected flamboyant declarations of eternal love the way other women collect hats or gloves.

Lady Worcester kept her eyes on her book. She hadn't turned a page since the dispute began. The queen pulled her shoulders down and lengthened her neck. "Don't be silly, Francis. Just do as I command."

For all his swagger, Weston understood it was time to leave. He bowed deeply, nodded to the rest of us, and backed out of the room—the time-honored sign of deference and obedience.

I glanced at Silas Bray a few feet across from me. He had the look of a triumphant cat with its claws on an unlucky mouse.

⚜

"Joan, what is it?"

Joan the Fool sat on a low bench outside the queen's chambers. She was sobbing and bent over at the waist. I had never liked her clowning—her most frequent act was to mimic the pope or the king of Spain and pretend to fart or pee. She used to hobble and snort like a donkey when Paul entered the room. He said her jests didn't bother him, but what else could he say? She liked to joke that musicians always coupled with other men, as if all musicians were the same. "Oh, so pretty, like a little girl," she squealed at me once. "If you were really a man, you would kiss me in front of everyone and take me to your bed." I avoided her as much as possible.

But here she was in front of me, crying and distressed. I rested my lute against the bench and sat beside her. She heaved noisily before answering. "She slapped me . . . she's crazy . . . she slapped me . . . I didn't do anything wrong."

"Who slapped you?"

"The queen. She was laughing, and then . . . all of a sudden, she hit me. She said she didn't want to hear any more."

Unfortunately, Her Majesty's tantrums had become daily fare, and Joan's cheek bore a faint red mark. The queen had also struck Lady Worcester and screamed at Lady Rochford, all of this in full view of others. During these incidents, most of the servants nervously performed their duties and left the queen's line of vision as quickly as they could. But others lingered and listened, likely reporting to Cromwell or the Seymours or someone else. Bray was notably eager to play background music for the queen's inner circle, work he had previously avoided.

I assumed that stories about the queen's abuse of Joan the Fool would be repeated and then embellished. Her Majesty's enemies would use them to show that she was cruel and unpredictable, that she wasn't fit to be queen. I signaled to a passing servant to bring a cup of wine for Joan and stayed with her while she drank it. She must have feared that her days at court were numbered, but she returned to her clowning the next day.

A few weeks later, I heard one of the kitchen boys entertaining a couple of maidservants with one of the story's more lurid versions: Joan the Fool had burst in on the queen and Rochford—Her Majesty in a nightdress and her brother lying on her bed. The kitchen boy winked and rolled his eyes. He was thirteen or fourteen, trying to scandalize his listeners and show that he was an experienced observer of the wicked ways of the world.

I interrupted him. "Who told you this?" The boy glared at me.

"Lots of people say it, sir."

"This is a lie."

"How do you know?" The question, though insolent, seemed to reflect genuine skepticism.

"I talked with the fool myself. She never described anything like that." The boy was silent, and the young women looked at their aprons, one of them fiddling with the ties. I doubted that my first-hand evidence impressed them. Still, my higher rank would likely be enough to ensure that this one boy wouldn't tell this particular story again. "It's not true, so don't repeat it," I told him. "You'll regret it if you do." They all bowed and scampered away.

In the past, I would have told Rochford about the slander, thinking he could counter it. But this vile story was already beyond anyone's control. I was sure he had already heard it.

29

Unforeseen Complications

Winter and Spring 1536

Madge Shelton, The Court of King Henry

I didn't love Sir Henry as I had expected to love a man, not the way I had dreamed about Mark Smeaton. But I convinced myself the time had come to live in the world as it truly is. I had no need of motherly lectures—I often lectured myself: *These dreams of Mark Smeaton are childish . . . you must live honorably, as you have been taught . . . You can't disgrace your family.*

I would soon become Sir Henry's wife, and I saw my parents' pride in me. My little sister talked about the wedding without end. My cousin George said, "He's the king's closest companion and as rich as Croesus, thank God. He's a better man than most."

And the truth was that serving my ill-tempered cousin had become tedious. I was looking for an escape. As Sir Henry's wife, I would manage my own household, watch over his children, and have babes of my own in time. I avoided envisioning the intimacies of marriage, though my mother had explained them to me. I had heard that women often picture another man while having sex with their husbands. This is what I would do.

Even so. I was relieved when the king delayed the marriage, saying, "Now isn't the time . . . I've just lost my son. The court should mourn his death." A postponement seemed appropriate and would give me more time to adjust to reality. No one asked me for my opinion.

♂♀

The change in Sir Henry was sudden and inexplicable. He delayed signing the marriage contract drawn up between him and my family, claiming he was busy with other affairs. He greeted me coldly whenever we met. After I'd spent so many months persuading myself to marry him, his abrupt reversal upset me. I talked to my mother about it.

"I don't understand," my mother said. "He has always been so fond of you."

"I thought so too . . . until a few weeks ago."

"Have you quarreled?"

"I have sometimes asked questions, but not disrespectfully. He has never taken offense."

She brushed the backs of her fingers against my cheek. "No, neither of you is easily angered. Someone has interfered."

"What do you mean?"

"Someone wants to prevent the marriage . . . to divide Sir Henry from us."

"The Seymours?"

"Perhaps, but they are not alone. You have more influence with Sir Henry than anyone else. You must speak with him."

That same day, I sent him a note. "Soon we are to be man and wife," I wrote. "I have missed your company."

ⴲ

He arrived at my family's chambers before supper, and we all greeted him cordially. He kissed my hand and sat some feet away. Mary offered him malmsey wine. We had been keeping Pourquoi again while my cousin was preoccupied. The little dog jumped up and down and then rolled onto his back and put his paws in the air, right at Sir Henry's feet. My mother's face mixed hope and tenderness as she said to my sister, "Mary, take Pourquoi with you," and then to Sir Henry and me, "We will leave you now."

He began by describing His Majesty's plans for the May Day jousts and a trip to Calais in the spring. He spoke dully, as if he were filling time, and I detected a thread of resentment in his words. I had resolved beforehand to speak frankly, whatever the cost or risk. With some nervousness, I raised the question. "Sir Henry, if you have doubts about our betrothal, please tell me. I would wish for your happiness nonetheless."

He blinked. "If I have doubts, ma'am, I will raise them with the king and your father. This is not a conversation we should have."

"But it is a conversation about the rest of our lives."

"I am not sure it is."

I thought of the many times I had wished to be rid of this man— how I had longed for Mark and yearned to be free to love whomever I pleased. Yet faced with the prospect of disappointing and embarrassing my parents, I prayed to salvage the betrothal. My family was relying on me.

I tried again to get some kind of explanation. "I hope you will be honest with me, sir, as I have tried to be with you."

His tone sharpened. "Have you been honest, Mistress Shelton?"

"As honest as I am able."

"This is not what I have heard."

I was so startled I could barely reply, absurdly fearing that Sir

Henry might have read my mind. I had desired Mark Smeaton but told no one. How could anyone know of my fantasies? I finally mumbled, "Sir, what do you mean?"

He looked discouraged. "You ask for honesty, ma'am? There are rumors you have lain with Weston."

"Sir Francis?"

I remembered Jane Boleyn's warning, the one I had so casually dismissed. But how could Sir Henry believe I would be so wanton? I generally avoided Sir Francis . . . I wasn't even sure I liked him. These rumors were based on nothing but air, and yet I felt ashamed.

"Who told you this, sir? Someone is lying. I hope you will trust my word over malicious gossip."

"You are young, and Weston is charming. What would you have me believe?"

"I would have you believe *me*, sir." Though the accusations were outright lies, I was humiliated by them—and angry that Sir Henry had accepted them so readily. I considered asking him to leave, which would have been my right, but if I created a scene, only dishonor and more gossip would come of it. Righteous outrage wouldn't help my family.

I looked around the room, the setting for my family's daily joys and petty squabbles. I could have sketched the chairs, tables, rugs—all of it—from memory. The familiarity of my surroundings bolstered my confidence. I tried the truth again. "Whatever you have heard, Sir Henry, it is a lie."

"The report came from a worthy gentleman."

"There is nothing between me and Weston. I have never lain with any man . . . I swear this on all that is holy. I will swear it on a Bible if you wish."

"That is a serious oath."

"And I am not afraid to take it, sir." I briefly worried about swearing on the Bible, given my secret and improper thoughts about Mark Smeaton. But I had never acted on my fantasies. Surely taking an oath wouldn't be wrong.

For his part, Sir Henry seemed far away, as if he were recalling other incidents and conversations. Perhaps he was remembering his first wife and the years when his life was certain and full. They must have been deeply in love.

More for my family than myself, I said to him, "Sir Henry, I am not so unwise . . . nor so deceitful."

After a long pause, he said. "No, I don't believe you are. I have been manipulated."

We both sat silently, and I heard Pourquoi barking and scraping at the door.

"Let him in," Sir Henry said. "Even if we create misery for ourselves, we should try to make children and small dogs happy."

After I let him in, Pourquoi raced around the room before sitting near us, his triangular ears straight up. The dog's entrance was an odd but welcome disruption. Sir Henry patted his head, and Pourquoi curled up beside his boot.

"When men get older," he said without looking at me, "they can be foolish in matters of love." He straightened up and gazed at me. "I hope you can forgive me, ma'am."

"I do not think you are foolish, sir. Someone has lied to create mischief."

"The gossip came from Sir Edward Seymour. My foolishness was in listening to him."

He rose and moved to sit closer to me; Pourquoi roused himself and followed. "Sir Francis is young like you, and handsome, so doubt came easily to me. But I should have trusted you and believed you without question. I ask you for another chance."

"Then all is well between us?"

He approached and kissed me on the lips. "It is . . . if you still agree to be my wife."

I agreed—this was what I had sought. Pourquoi jumped up and down as if cheering.

Later that night, as I prepared for bed, my mother kissed my forehead and ran her fingers over my hair. She smiled and thanked God that all had turned out well. A few days later, I returned Pourquoi to my cousin, who hugged him and teased him in French. I secretly thanked the little dog for his aid in saving my betrothal to Sir Henry. His innocent antics had broken the spell.

A week later, Sir Henry gave me a locket with his family emblem in rubies and gold. "My first wife wore this," he said, "but now it is yours." He signed the marriage contract, and the date for our wedding was set for the end of May. Still, this episode confirmed what I had known from the beginning. Any affection between Sir Henry and me was fragile and pieced together. We might form a bond and create a family, but this man still loved his dead wife, and I loved someone else.

⚜

My serving woman woke me before breakfast.

"Please come downstairs, ma'am," she whispered. "Her Majesty will be so upset."

I dressed quickly and went with her. "Are you sure he's dead?"

"I believe so . . . his body is cold."

I could see his fluffy coat from the window, startlingly white against the garden soil.

"Should we move him, ma'am?"

"Get a coverlet. Let's wrap him up and bring him inside."

I went out and knelt beside him, placing my hands against his ribs. My fingers touched his chilled, matted fur; there was no warmth or breath. I had spent enough time with Pourquoi that I cried to find him like this. When the serving woman returned with the cloth, I picked him up, and his head fell over as if his neck were broken. We swaddled him like a baby.

When he heard of the little dog's death, the king said he must

have fallen out the window, and most people accepted this explanation. The queen cried as I had, but she was also suspicious. "He was
sleeping beside my bed last night, and he wouldn't have left my
apartments on his own. How could he just 'fall' out of a window?
Someone killed him."

She told Cromwell to find out who had done it, and he agreed
but never questioned anyone. I had doubts about several servants
because my cousin had become harsh with those who waited on her.
At one time or another, most had felt the lash of her tongue.

A few weeks later, Brereton gave my cousin a greyhound named
Urian, making a great show of presenting an enormous basket and
asking her to guess its contents. He supplied some clues like "fast"
and "gray," and she predicted a falcon. He lifted the lid, and the
greyhound jumped out. The creature was surprisingly sweet for a
sporting dog, but my cousin never cared for him. I walked him in
the garden and let him stay in my rooms to sleep by the fire. After a
while, he began following me everywhere and putting his head on
my foot when I read or sewed. I renamed him Galahad and considered him my own.

I asked George whether we should find a dog that looked more
like Pourquoi, thinking that a similar puppy might ease my cousin's
grief.

"I doubt anything will make her happy now. We must give her
time and keep her safe."

During these days, my service to my cousin became more onerous
than it had ever been before. She was angry when she woke up in the
morning, and her anger thickened throughout the day. She spewed
her rage at His Majesty, and not only privately. In front of a half
dozen people, she screamed at the king of England: "You can't go a

week without sticking your cock into some stupid little bit . . . even that pathetic Seymour woman!"

Almost daily, she demanded new titles and honors for the princess, herself, her father, and my cousin George. If the king loved her, she said, he would do as she asked. Instead, he stormed out of the room. Sometimes, the rage in his eyes frightened me.

When His Majesty wasn't there, she turned her anger on those close to her—George and my mother most of all.

"Why don't you defend me?" she demanded. "Why don't you stand up to the king? Why don't you fight for our family like the Seymours fight for theirs?"

The rest of us assured her that the king's affection for her would soon return, but Katherine of Aragon's ladies must have said the same.

I understood my cousin's unhappiness. Tricks of nature had ruined her plans. Age left her little time—I'm sure she knew this. I pitied her, but her lack of judgment astonished me. Panic, fury, and too many cups of wine loosened her tongue and made her reckless. One day, she called the king "fat," "smelly," and "impotent" while her listeners stood by astonished. On another occasion, she described him as "a stinking, greasy sausage of a man." She goaded Weston and Brereton into joining her as they all drank together, and the men flattered her.

"I admire your fortitude, ma'am," Sir Francis said, "trying to couple amid all that fat."

My cousin laughed, but no one else did. I looked around the room and wondered who among us would repeat the queen's words to her growing list of enemies.

30

ILL-FATED CONVERSATIONS

Early Spring 1536

Mark Smeaton, The Court of King Henry

One quiet afternoon, Oliver and I were playing for Her Majesty while she read poetry with only Lady Rochford and Lady Worcester attending her. Sir Henry Norris arrived with a message from the king—nothing unusual at all. As one of His Majesty's grooms, Norris often carried the king's most important messages personally. [20]

His marriage to Mistress Shelton had been rescheduled—contracts signed, dowry paid, the banns to be read in May. Among Her Majesty's ladies, conversations revolved around the bride's dress, flowers for the church, and everyone's wishes for a sunny day. The queen frequently described the match's advantages: "The Boleyns will be tied to the Crown by unbreakable bonds, as I am one with the king."

For me, the saddest and most relevant news was that Mistress Shelton would leave the court to live on Sir Henry's estate and care for his children. Soon, she would be a memory, like so many others who have been dearest to me.

That afternoon, Sir Henry bowed before speaking to the queen and extended his hand with a letter, the king's red wax seal showing on the back. She took it without reading it, apparently planning to ignore it for the moment.

Norris bowed again and spoke evenly, "It isn't urgent, Your Majesty. Tomorrow's diplomatic ceremony has been postponed."

"Why is that?"

"Some delay in the ambassador's arrival . . . bad weather and flooded roads."

"Is that the true reason?"

"I believe so, ma'am. His Majesty asked me to ensure that you knew about the change."

The queen's face was immobile, but we had all learned to read her rigid posture which suggested both resentment and anxiety. On this day, she seemed to make an intentional attempt to cheer herself and summon the grace and humor that had once charmed everyone.

"Have you visited the lovely Madge today?" she asked in a purring tone, much as she used to speak. "My young cousin pines for your company."

"I would gladly visit, ma'am, but I cannot today. I am engaged in the king's affairs."

"And what affairs are those?"

"Arranging for the May Day games, the trip to Calais, this summer's progress. There is always much to do."

"No one has spoken to me about the summer progress. Will it include Wolf Hall?"

This kind of drama had become commonplace: an ordinary conversation unexpectedly becoming ominous—the sky darkening with thunderclouds. One moment, the queen was the witty, elegant woman who had won His Majesty's heart. The next, she was angry and broken, a betrayed wife lashing out. Nearly every day, she questioned the king about Jane Seymour and pressed her ladies for information. Abandoning her dignity, she interrogated pages, court visitors, and even tradesmen. Had the king sent Jane Seymour letters or gifts? Who paid for her new feathered hat?

Norris responded as he always did, with phrases chosen to soothe. "There are no final decisions, ma'am. His Majesty will likely consult you directly."

But rather than calming the queen, his diplomacy provoked her. She signaled to us to stop playing. "No, Henry, you're hiding something. You're secretive—you always have been. What is it that you do all day *avec ce visage mélancolique?*"

"Only the king's bidding, ma'am . . . as is my privilege and duty."

She tried to speak playfully, but there was a manipulative edge to her words. "Ah . . . but I hope you are my friend as well."

"Of course, ma'am. I am at your service."

"How can I be sure of that?"

"Your Majesty, I am your ardent and devoted servant."

"Ardent and devoted?" She laughed a coquettish laugh. "I hope that is true, Sir Henry. Indeed, I hope you are more than that." She touched her fingers to her veil, running her thumb and forefinger along the edge before pulling it teasingly across her lips. Her breath lightly stirred the silken fabric as she spoke "Perhaps Madge bores you . . . perhaps you yearn for a more sophisticated woman of the world?"

Norris smiled, his hands dangling uneasily at his sides. "Mistress Shelton is lovely and gracious, Your Majesty. I am honored she will be my bride."

"Is this your declaration of love for her?" The queen dropped her veil from her mouth and cocked her head. "*Pas de mots d'amour?* Perhaps you have wished the king wore dead men's shoes so you could marry me instead. Is that what you want?"

The room was soundless, and Norris stood oddly still. He looked down, his eyes blinking rapidly, his face conveying his shock. Speaking of the king's death was a crime, and people had died for it.

He acknowledged her, saying only, "Your Majesty, I have no wish to lose my head."

The queen stood up, her book of poems clattering to the floor. She lowered her voice and lifted her chin. No one else moved. "That was an absurd and meaningless jest on my part. Sir Henry, please forget my words."

She looked at her ladies. "All of you, please, forget what I said."

They nodded, pantomiming obedience. The queen continued, but her voice had lost its strength. "Sir Henry, we will both pray for the king's long life and good health. I do so every night."

Norris bowed deeply and left. Lady Worcester rushed to pick up the queen's book, speaking instinctively as she curtsied. "Your Majesty, do you wish to continue your reading?"

"Put the book away . . . I need to think. Everyone, leave me now."

Oliver and I stood, along with the ladies, all of us moving as one single being. As we made our way out, I heard the queen say to Lady Worcester, "Send for my brother. I wish to speak with my brother."

"Of course, Your Majesty. I will do so immediately."

I wondered what her brother's advice could possibly be. The queen had talked of the king's death, and she had done it with half a dozen people listening.

⚜

His Majesty grew heavier and clumsier and developed a weeping ulcer on his leg. He cursed his doctors and ate and drank to excess to dull the chronic pain. He avoided the queen when he wasn't quarreling with her. More than once he said to Cromwell, "I risked my soul and my kingdom for this woman. What did I get in return?" Most evenings, he wanted to be alone. The queen, Rochford, Norris,

Weston, Brereton, musicians, attendants, even Jane Seymour—all of us were sent away. Only Cromwell and Suffolk stayed.

Given the spiteful mood at court, I escaped whenever I could to ride in the still wintry countryside. I followed noiseless trails where bare brown branches closed over my head. When I had a few days to myself, I visited the chapels in Cambridge and Oxford to hear the choirs. The music was unforgettable, and the boys reminded me of my youth at Hampton Court. In town, I called on the stunning, red-haired Nuala who replaced Maria Isabella—Madame Margaretha had chosen well. During my liaisons with Nuala, she barely spoke and never asked me anything. I had no complaints. I wrote to Paul and planned to visit him in the summer. I sealed my letters with wax but omitted most of what worried me. Letters could go astray.

31

THE MUSIC LESSON

Early Spring 1536

Madge Shelton, Greenwich

espite his disappointment about her sex, the king doted on the Princess Elizabeth. She had pets and jesters to entertain her and toys from around the world. The Doge of Venice sent a child-sized, three-stringed lute, which she held in her lap as she tried to copy the players' movements.

One afternoon, while other musicians accompanied the court, Mark sat beside her, whispering to her and showing her how to pluck the toy's strings. She laughed and smiled, as he did himself. After some minutes, the two were ready.

"Your Majesty, the princess would like to play for you," he said as he bowed to the king. "Her Highness has learned a new song."

His Majesty beamed and clapped his hands before motioning for everyone to be quiet.

Mark played some intricate pattern and then nodded to the child to pluck a note. Whatever she played, he added harmonies and embellishments to create a melody for all to enjoy. At the end, the toddler princess curtsied to the king, and Mark stood behind her.

"Ah," the king said, "we have two brilliant musicians." Everyone applauded. He turned to Mark. "You will be her teacher when she is older."

"That would be my honor, Your Majesty."

Some days later, I had watched Mark perform with a consort of musicians during an elaborate masque that had been arranged for foreign dignitaries. Near the end, he played a solo of astonishing beauty and complexity. The room was completely still, everyone listening and then applauding, even though the masque was not yet finished. I recalled meeting him at Hampton Court, the choirmaster's pleasing apprentice, his future up in the air. Since then, he had prospered and gained influential friends such as my cousin George. I continued to daydream about the day I had encountered him on the road. I remained grateful for his kindness in protecting my foolish sister and secretly cheered every success that came his way.

After the masque was over, he approached me, his black velvet clothing elegant and subdued. He bowed and smiled, and although I was soon to be married, I felt the same fluttering of the heart I always had in his presence.

"Mistress Shelton, I wish you every happiness. I understand you will leave court in May."

"Yes, to care for my husband's children. I will miss your music."

"And I will miss your stories, ma'am."

That was all. He bowed again. I had the chance to say more but didn't. I had convinced myself that I should be content with Sir Henry—that "romance is a trifle," as my mother said.

Yet my hidden feelings told a truth my brain had caged. I adored Mark Smeaton and admired him. His rise in life had been against all odds and far different from the easy paths of the court's gentlemen. Men like my cousin George floated along, taking full advantage of their names and family wealth. They lived as if whatever they sought should be gladly handed over to them. Mark had earned his place through his rare musical gift and hard work.

And the reality was that I longed for him with sensations I don't care to describe. I had no doubt that I would picture him while having sex with my wellborn husband. To be honest, I had already imagined it.

⚜

Late one afternoon, I received word from the stable master—sad but expected news. They had found Starlight's body in his stall that morning. He was nearing the age when horses die, so I had prepared myself.

"Would you like to go down to the stables?" my mother asked. "I will ask Lady Rochford to tend the queen. I know you loved the horse."

The stable master was apologetic. "I tried to save him, ma'am . . . I used all my skill."

"I know that, and I am grateful. I would like to see him if I could."

He lay on the ground on his side, covered with a blanket of gray wool . . . my beautiful Starlight, his body cold and hard like a stone. I moved the material to the side and kissed the white star on his head. That's when I heard a noise behind me and looked around to see Mark Smeaton standing at the gate.

"I am truly sorry, Mistress Shelton. The stable boy told me. I know you rode Starlight as a child."

"Yes, we were old friends." I stroked the horse's ear. "In many ways, the best of friends."

"Yes . . . he was loyal and trusting. The bond between you was clear."

"I was prepared. He was at the end of his days."

"But you will miss him . . . I can see that."

I stood up and backed away from Starlight. It was time to leave him behind. Mark knelt and placed his hand on the blanket over the horse's shoulder. He remained there quietly for several seconds and then rose and turned to me. "This is a hard day for you. I could walk you back to the palace, or perhaps part of the way?"

"Thank you, but I'm not ready to join the others yet. I'll stay here for a while."

"As you wish, ma'am." He bowed, his manner poised. He adopted the cloaked gaze of those who serve. He shifted his stance, preparing to leave, when my grief and loneliness spoke for me.

"But I would welcome your company, Master Smeaton."

He stood still, his tone easy and composed. "Then I will stay with you."

We walked far away from the stable and palace grounds to sit side by side on a low wall of heavy stones. The chilly night ensured that few were outside to see us. The darkness protected us—the only light was the pale glow of the moon.

Mark pointed to a pattern of stars scattered in the East, where the sky was black. "It is Pegasus. Do you see him, the divine stallion? The winged horse of the Greeks?"

I looked in the direction of his pointing hand and listened as he explained how the stars formed a horse's shape. I could barely make it out, but the sound of his voice comforted me.

"Perhaps Starlight has already joined him," Mark said, "and Pegasus and Starlight will soar across the heavens forever, their souls linked as they gallop side by side."

"It's a lovely thought . . . thank you."

After a pause, he took my hand, saying only, "May I?" He knew my answer would be *yes*.

Based on what I heard among the ladies, sexual desire is the province of men. Yet what I felt in this moment must have been desire. There is no other way to describe it.

"But doesn't the Bible say that beasts have no souls?" I asked. "Did Cardinal Wolsey teach you differently?"

"I don't remember. I paid more attention to my music teachers than the priests and their catechism. But all good creatures must find peace after their lives on Earth, especially your Starlight."

"Yes, I will think on this." His hand was warm around mine, and on impulse, I raised his fingers to my lips. "We first met years ago," I said, "and I have spent all this time wishing to know you better."

I felt completely at ease with him. By some magic, our hearts and minds had united, as if we spoke every day. Sir Henry and I shared few interests, and in the last months, our conversations had been careful and artificial—my thoughts centered on preserving the match. But that night, in a time of sadness, Mark and I were irreversibly joined. For years, he had been a fantasy—young, handsome, exciting. But here he was beside me, kind and reassuring. Only the present mattered.

The kiss itself was brief. His fingers lingered at the back of my neck where he had slipped his hand beneath my veil. I felt shivers down my spine.

"I will be sorry to see you go," he said, "to see you wed another . . . although I know that this must be."

"It is the way of our world. Sometimes I fight the idea of it, but I see no other choice."

"Nor do I. We cannot wish the rules away."

We sat there, saying nothing, both of us certain that our thoughts were the same. He took my hand again and smiled. "Since we have kissed, I will call you 'Madge,' at least when no one else is near."

"And when you address me as 'Mistress Shelton,' I will hear 'Madge' instead and know that we are friends."

Until that night, I had planned to avoid the court after marriage. I was eager to escape its rivalries and politics. But the advantages of regular visits suddenly occurred to me. Other wives came to court from time to time, and I was certain Sir Henry would agree. He would never wish to keep me from seeing my family.

"My mother and sister are remaining at court to serve the queen. Even after I've left, I will return to visit them, and I will see you then. I will be a matron, a country wife." I grimaced, and he laughed. "And in time the mother of children," I added. "This, I look forward to with gladness."

"You will be the cleverest and most beautiful mother the world has ever known."

I weighed my words before I said them. To my own surprise, I said them anyway. "Sometimes married women enjoy freedoms that maids do not. Their families do not watch them as closely. What they do is better hidden."

At first, he didn't move or say anything. He looked at me and spoke evenly. "Yes, I have heard that this is so." His gray eyes seemed to soften. "Are you leaving me with hope?"

"That is my intention, sir . . . if you wish it. I believe we should express our love."

He touched the lace at the cuff of my sleeve as he answered, "Ma'am, I believe you must be right." His finger strayed onto my wrist, and we kissed again. I rested my head on his shoulder, and we remained there quietly for some time, both of us happily amazed.

He walked me halfway to the palace that night, and we parted, standing yards apart. Our words were formal, as courtly life required. The stable path was public, and even the lightest of kisses or an affectionate gesture could cause a scandal that would endanger us both.

I walked on alone through the courtyard and the gardens of Greenwich Palace, my mind turning from the loss of my dear Starlight to the astonishing promise I had made. Not so long ago, I had sworn to Sir Henry that I was "an honest woman." But that night, sitting in the moonlight beside Mark Smeaton, I had agreed to violate my marriage vows.

In the days that followed, I found myself thinking through the practical questions: How soon could I return to court after my wedding? Where could Mark and I meet? My cousin George had rooms at Whitehall that he never used. This was a possibility. Since George had his own secrets to keep, I was confident he would agree to provide any arrangement that might be required. And George was fond of Mark too—I believed he would protect us if need be.

For myself, I found a lilting freedom I had never felt before. I had finally chosen my own destiny and was secretly proud of my boldness.

32

AN INFERIOR PERSON

April 1536

Mark Smeaton, Whitehall

I didn't return to the palace after she left that night. I wandered under the stars, sometimes in utter aimlessness. At one point, I raced down a hill just as I had as a child—running in a wild outburst of celebration, my feet pounding the soil. When I reached the bottom, I was glad no one had seen me. My madcap dash meant I had to climb up again. But I didn't mind—I felt victorious. There's no other way to put it.

I had broken my promise to Lady Shelton by going to the stables that night. It was something of a risk. But I had seen Mistress Shelton's tender care for the horse and knew she would grieve for him. I don't remember what I expected to happen, only that I wanted to see her and speak some words of sympathy. And yet, in this moment of sadness, one of love's miracles brought us together. Later, I asked myself what I had done to deserve this wondrous stroke of luck.

After this surprising improvement in my romantic prospects, I lived in a haze of happiness for weeks. Mistress Shelton and I followed the rules of court and addressed each other formally. Even when we were in the same room, we stayed far apart. But I had kissed her and called her Madge—the stealth increased the thrill. In my mind, Mistress Shelton became "Madge," no longer only a vision. Despite all the sad songs I had written, perhaps I was to be lucky in love after all.

Don't get carried away, I told myself. Stolen kisses, whispered words, promises made under a silvery moon—these can create the illusion of love. The liaison might never happen. If it did, it would be months away, maybe a year. Whatever might pass between us would be occasional, even if it were glorious and passionate. This is a precarious basis for contentment.

And yet I trusted her—I sensed that our bond was fundamental. Even the court chatter about her upcoming wedding and the lands the king was giving the newlyweds couldn't dim my clandestine joy. I began a flurry of composing, music flowing out of me, the melodies lighter and sweeter than before. Rochford noticed the change.

"This piece is wonderful," he said. "If I didn't know, I'd say you were in love." He seemed to be aware that I was seeing Nuala. "Are you? Is it the Irish one?"

"Yes," I answered. "She has enchanted me." An easy, plausible lie.

For weeks, I enjoyed one of life's graces—the blush of a budding romance, secret though it was. Those I worked for were less fortunate. The king and queen battled daily, vitriol poisoning whatever affection remained between them. Men like Rochford and Weston had married for wealth and position. They tolerated and managed their wives.

I had come alone to entertain Her Majesty and her ladies on a quiet, cloudy day. Madge was there, and I watched her tend the queen and the spirited little princess. Occasionally she spoke quietly with the other ladies about their families, the health of elderly relatives, the weather, their dressmakers—all the usual topics of friendly conversation. Every so often, she glanced my way as if to confirm our assignation, whenever it might be.

That afternoon, the queen complained she was cold. Then she complained she was bored. Then she complained her ladies weren't doing enough to amuse her. Lady Rochford suggested cards, but the queen said the game would be tedious with such a dull group of women.

The once sensuous Anne Boleyn was thinner and perhaps not completely well. The princess scampered around the room, stopping beside each of the ladies one by one. The women pretended to be surprised by her arrival, and the child giggled in return. She soon fell asleep on her wine-colored pallet which was as plush as a royal throne. Madge pulled a coverlet over her and adjusted it to cover the princess's chubby arms.

The queen repeated her usual complaints: They were all keeping secrets from her. They knew more about Jane Seymour than they said. They were reporting back to Cromwell, twisting her words and making up stories. She couldn't trust any of them. Lady Worcester pressed her lips together and gazed up at the ceiling. It wasn't hard to read her thoughts: Soon, the queen would unleash another of her tirades, but this time, she appeared not to want an audience.

"Get out, all of you, with your gossiping and conniving . . . I would rather be alone."

Madge picked up the sleeping princess to take her to the nursery. The other women put their needlework away and smoothed their skirts. I rose to leave as they filed out.

"No, Mark. You stay here. Come, sit next to me." [21]

I bowed and pulled up a chair, considering which musical

pieces might distract and cheer her. "What should I play, ma'am? One of the lullabies? Or I have a new song—Your Majesty would be the first to hear it."

"Yes, the new one. Sing it for me."

The song was a recent work touching on the unexpected ways of love. I had adapted the words from a Flemish nursery rhyme I had learned from my mother: a young woman entices her sweetheart by planting a garden and giving him a new bloom every week.

"This country romance," the queen said, interrupting me after the first refrain. "I don't want to hear about other people's happiness. Sing the one about the man who longs for a woman—his lover who has cast him off despite his costly gifts to her."

I immediately knew which song she meant. Brereton once joked that I had written it because I longed for the queen. But I had composed the music thinking of Madge when she seemed unattainable and then invented verses to disguise the circumstances. From time to time, the king sang the piece when he was at his leisure, and over time, some assumed he had written it for Anne Boleyn during the months when he fell in love with her and gave her priceless jewels.

That afternoon, the queen watched me as I performed, her face suggesting fears and sorrows beyond my understanding. I felt sorry for her but turned my eyes on the lute's richly burnished wood. As her servant, I avoided her gaze. When I finished, I saw that she was crying, and I wanted to say some comforting words. But it wasn't my place to act in such a familiar manner. I waited for her to speak.

"I am lost, Mark. I know it. I have squandered the king's love."

"Forgive me, Your Majesty, but I do not believe this is so. Only yesterday, I saw the king look at you, and his eyes were full of love."

This was false—I had made it up—but I judged that a lie would be kinder than reality. She reached out and touched my hair. Her fingers slid down to my cheek. "You're a sweet one, aren't you? Give me your hand . . . I will tell your fortune."

I was startled, and my breathing quickened—touching her was

against the normal rules. But I wrapped my left arm around my lute and extended my right hand as she ordered.

She ran her fingers over my palm, and I recalled the first few times I saw her. Once, she had been radiant—a woman who fascinated one and all. But over time, she had become damaged, seemingly desperate to be adored again. Like most of those around her, I regretted her troubles, especially the loss of the babes.

"Most of your life will be fortunate," she said as she cupped my hand in hers, "nearly all of it. When you die, you will die as a gentleman, on an equal footing with titled men." She looked up at me, triumphant, as if she were giving me a gift.

I laughed, not sure what else to do. I expected she would dismiss me soon. Instead, she held onto my hand, retracing the lines in my palm with her fingertip. I was uncomfortable and wondered how long she would continue. She seemed trapped in thoughts of her own.

The room was still, so Lady Worcester's return was noticeable—I heard the click of her steps and the swoosh of her skirts behind me. She approached the queen holding a cloak draped over her forearm. She ignored me, her face unreadable. "Pardon me, Your Majesty, you said you were cold. I brought this for your warmth."

The queen pushed my hand away, and I spontaneously withdrew my arm, a reaction suggesting guilt—I'm sure that's how it looked. Her Majesty often read men's fortunes: Weston, Brereton, her brother, the king. Both Lady Worcester and I had seen her do it many times. This kind of banter and playfulness was acceptable between the queen and one of the court's noble gentlemen, but it wasn't customary with a common player. I felt I had been caught in a sinful act.

The queen spoke coldly. "I never asked for a cloak. Get out! And you too, Mark. Leave me alone."

Lady Worcester bowed quickly and retreated. I stood up and bowed, preparing to go. The queen raised her voice to make sure

Lady Worcester could hear her clearly: "You act as if you think you are a gentleman, Mark, looking at me with this longing gaze. But you are an inferior person—a common, base-born servant. Your behavior offends and sickens me."

Her slap was strong enough to force my head to turn, but the sting was less painful than her words. Derision came to her so readily . . . that I was inferior . . . that my behavior offended her . . . that touching me sickened her. I stepped away. I had no doubt Lady Worcester was listening at the door.

The skin on my cheek tingled and burned even as the seconds passed. I bowed to the queen and tried to speak as the rules dictate. "Forgive me, Your Majesty. I do not seek conversation. A look from you will suffice."

Yet even as I heard myself pronouncing these words of submission, my resentment and fury mounted. The queen had created this scene, and I had only obeyed her instructions. What choice did I have? I had served her loyally for years, and she had shamed me and put me in jeopardy. Moreover, she had done it solely to protect herself from embarrassment, ignoring the risk to me.

I should have waited for her to dismiss me. I should have apologized again. I should have addressed her as "Your Royal Majesty" and knelt at her feet. But I didn't. I wasn't an inferior person—Madge didn't see me that way.

"Fare thee well, ma'am." I said, allowing my anger to show. I bowed, and then I turned my back to her and immediately left the room.

As I entered the hall, I saw a swatch of blue satin—Lady Worcester's dress as she rounded the corner ahead of me. She must have heard every word of the queen's false accusation, along with the smack of the slap.

The queen had slapped Lady Worcester and Joan the Fool. She routinely screamed at servants who had done nothing wrong. She berated her uncle, the Duke of Norfolk, and Cromwell and even His Majesty. In my case, it was obvious that she was startled by Lady Worcester's entrance and responded impulsively.

But she had implied that I had tried to seduce her—the king's wife—which was a grave accusation against any man. I could only assume it was a hanging offense. And I had made matters worse by turning my back on her in a moment of anger and pride. That alone could jeopardize my position. I had heard stories of servants who were flogged and thrown into prison for turning their backs on the king, although I wasn't sure they were true.

In my room, I placed my lute in its case, my hands trembling as I fastened the leather straps. I sat on the bed and stared at nothing, my muscles as tired as if I had been laboring since dawn. I must have sat there doing nothing for half an hour, my thoughts darting in different directions. As time passed, I began to persuade myself that I was taking the incident too seriously. The queen's tempests passed quickly—she raged, and then she didn't. If Paul were still at court, I could have gone to him for counsel, but he was miles away in Devon.

Despite my attempts to calm myself, my encounter with Anne Boleyn planted itself in my brain. I repeated the dialogue in my mind and heard Lady Worcester's footsteps as she entered the room. Hours later, I could still feel the sting of the queen's hand hitting my cheek. That night, I dreamed about the episode, my dreams taking shockingly different paths. In some, the queen held my hand and touched my cheek. I pushed her veil aside and kissed her neck and then her mouth. Then the queen was Madge, and then she was the queen again. We made love, her hands guiding mine as I loosened her clothing and took full pleasure in her body's silky curves. When I woke up in the darkness, my heart was pounding—not with desire, but with horror. Why had my mind conjured up this forbidden dream? The queen wasn't the woman I desired.

In other versions of the dream, the queen took my hand to read my fortune, and guards burst in to drag me away. In one, she said: "No, let him go. It is nothing." In another, she said: "I am sorry, Mark. I must save myself."

During the night, there were hours when I thought my panic would suffocate me. I considered leaving England—taking my money and my lute and my horses and heading for Portsmouth. English and Flemish musicians worked all over the continent, and I could start a new life somewhere else, perhaps entertaining a different king and queen.

But to throw my life away after Madge and I had talked in the moonlight . . . to leave England just when this luminous romance was within my reach? And my beautiful horses—what of them? I could ride them to the coast, but the practical course would be to sell them and use the money to start anew. Just picturing someone leading my horses away crushed me. Why should I lose everything because of a few hasty words spoken by the queen in a conversation that barely lasted a minute?

When the sun filtered into my rooms in the morning, I got out of bed and walked to the window. I stood there and decided I couldn't leave. In the garden, the hedges formed elegant patterns. Half-open flowers sparkled with dew. If I fled, Madge and I would never meet again.

I tried to think of what Paul would advise. Was my situation really so dangerous? What had passed between the queen and me wasn't a crime—it wasn't anything close to a crime. Surely any misunderstanding could be explained.

Around ten o'clock, the queen sent a message asking me to play for the princess while she and some of her ladies readied themselves for a trip to Greenwich. I saw this as a gesture of kindness and normality, if not quite an apology. Afterward, when she dismissed me, she smiled, saying, "Thank you, Mark. Your music is beautiful as always."

She looked so fragile as she said goodbye, her dark eyes shining, perhaps with the possibility of tears. I bowed and wished her a pleasant journey. I never saw her again.

PART SIX

Partings

33

A TRIP TO STEPNEY

April 30, 1536

Mark Smeaton, Whitehall and Stepney

Most of the court was attending the May Day celebrations in Greenwich, so I had a fortnight at Whitehall to myself. The palace was quiet, its unseen work proceeding without pause. Gardeners trimmed the hedges, and housemaids swept the floors. I watched a group of women carrying baskets of linens to be laundered and dried in the open air. These would be stored with bunches of lavender until the king and queen returned.

The weather was tranquil—neither cloudy nor bright—and I planned on riding later in the week. I had become prosperous enough to bring Prince and Flanders with me whenever the court moved from place to place. This meant I could ride and enjoy them, no matter where the king wanted to be.

But on this last day of April, I worked on my music. The incident with the queen had receded in my mind. My newly acquired optimism had returned. I revised a short piece I had composed to accompany one of His Majesty's poems, preparing a version that was simple enough for the king to play and another more intricate one. I would perform the more demanding piece in a concert once the king and queen came back. After stacking the musical pages in order, I checked them one last time.

I also worked on a choral piece—my first, despite having been a chorister as a child. My favorite composer, John Taverner, had died recently, leaving behind glorious sacred works that stirred and motivated me. I had an idea in mind, and my pages showed the scratches of my progress and hesitation. I had reworked several sections multiple times, and they were not yet satisfactory. But others were better, and a few were exactly as I had hoped. The work was beginning to take shape.

⌀

"Sir?" The red-haired boy who served me cracked the door open and poked his head inside. "There's gentlemen to see you."

He stepped aside for two men who removed their hats and bowed to me from the waist. One was Thomas Cromwell's clerk, Rafe Sadler, serious and sandy haired, not much older than me. He shared my love of horses and rode a handsome white palfrey—we sometimes spoke at the stables. Standing beside him was Gilbert Cromwell, one of Thomas Cromwell's distant relations who had joined his kinsman's retinue. Like his more famous and powerful relative, he was dark and square, his beefy strength oozing from his solid frame. I didn't know him well.

"Beg pardon, Mark. Are you busy?" Rafe spoke, his demeanor relaxed.

"I am just finishing. Please be seated, sirs. How may I help?"

I tried to be cordial while questions popped up in my brain: Why were Cromwell's men here? Did they know the queen had accused and slapped me? I remembered the blue triangle of Lady Worcester's dress as she turned the corner. Was she in Cromwell's pay?

Neither of Cromwell's men sat down. They stood side by side, Sadler slowly turning his hat round and round, his fingers moving methodically along its edge. "My master asks if you are free to play tonight in Stepney, since the king and queen are away. He is entertaining foreign visitors. Perhaps you could stay the night and return tomorrow. I am sure he will reward you generously."

This could be the truth, and I tried to convince myself it was. But Cromwell had never asked me to play before.

"Yes, I am honored," I said. Given the man's importance, I could hardly refuse. "I would like to change . . . if there is time . . . I'll ask the boy to bring my horse around."

Sadler answered. "It's Flanders, isn't it? You can go ahead and get ready. We'll tell the boy."

I nodded, somehow flattered that he remembered my horse's name. "Yes, thank you. I won't take long."

They left to speak to the boy, and I quickly gathered my work from my desk and placed it in the oaken box where I kept my compositions. I wrapped my lute in a soft cloth and set it inside its wooden traveling case, so I could sling it over my shoulder during the ride. I quickly washed up and changed my linens and shirt. I selected a doublet more suitable to performing and put on my best boots. I tried to relax, telling myself that Cromwell's request wasn't unusual. Like other court musicians, I often played for high officials when the king and queen were away. I expected Sadler was right—I would receive a sizable gift for my performance.

The three of us set out for Stepney late in the day, the sun unexpectedly radiant after the dull afternoon. Sadler and Cromwell both thanked me several times for agreeing to come on such short notice. Sadler talked of traveling to Calais with the king and the Privy Council after the May Day jousts. Gilbert Cromwell told me

he envied people who played musical instruments well. Pleas-
antries. Polite conversation. Not a ripple of menace.

 cĺɔ

We arrived in Stepney about seven o'clock under a late-day sky of
pink and gold. During the ride, Sadler's words circled in my mind:
"My master asks if you are free to play . . . Perhaps you could stay the
night . . . I am sure he will reward you generously." It all sounded
harmless enough.

Cromwell's house was imposing, its halls and public rooms
ablaze with candles and scented with exotic spices. I walked past
paintings, tapestries, maps, and collections of leather-bound
books—the belongings of a rich, well-traveled man. I didn't see
any musical instruments, but Cromwell wasn't known for his love
of song. The man himself ushered me into the room where I would
play—plush chairs, a table set for eight, pewter plates, silver goblets,
bowls filled with Spanish oranges and dates. At the back, servants
stood ready with pitchers of wine and ale, and Cromwell offered
me a cup. But I never liked to drink before playing, so I said I
would gladly take something later. He hoped, he said, he had not
inconvenienced me by asking me to come to Stepney. He hoped,
he said, I would stay to dine and pass the night. I agreed and
thanked him.

Cromwell didn't dress to show off—his clothing was costly and
dark. He was plain-featured, clean-shaven, brown-haired, and
barrel-chested. Even those who disliked him recognized his superior intelligence. Many said he was the most brilliant man ever to
serve an English king.

The guests began arriving—foreign bankers and merchants,
mostly German and French. One was a Flemish mercer. I had the
impression this group had gathered before to talk of politics, banking,

and trade. Before and during the supper, I played music from France and Germany in honor of Cromwell's guests. After they ate, I performed songs from many countries, including several Flemish works. The mercer saluted me, holding his drink in his hand. A serving girl paused in her work, momentarily captured by the music. It is not uncommon for the lowborn to have as fine an ear as the rich and powerful. From time to time, Cromwell paused in his exchanges with the others and gazed at me, although he didn't appear to be listening to the music. His face showed no emotion at all.

After the entertainment, the group applauded, and Cromwell raised his hands high as he clapped, a tribute of a kind. Then, an attendant escorted me to a smaller room to eat my own evening meal. Ample food and wine, fine bowls and plates—my supper equaled that of Cromwell's guests.

As I finished and the servants cleared the table, Cromwell entered holding a goblet. At first, he appeared to be joining me for drink and social conversation. But Rafe Sadler stood in front of the now-closed door, and Gilbert Cromwell, in all his thickset heft, took a bench nearby. A nameless owl-eyed man sat down beside him. Thomas Cromwell chose a chair opposite me and placed his goblet on the table. "The Boleyns are falling out of favor, Mark, as someone as observant as you must surely know."

My mind snapped to attention. This was no leisurely after-supper talk.

Cromwell pressed his carefully tended hands onto the table, spreading his fingers out and glancing down at them. He wore a heavy signet ring on his right middle finger—I knew it to be a gift from the king.

"The queen has failed to give His Majesty a son," he continued, "to give England an heir, as she was expected to do. I am sure you have witnessed their quarrels. I myself have advised the queen to check her discourteous behavior—to avoid baiting and berating her husband, especially when others are present."

I searched my brain to think of a safe reply. "Yes, Her Majesty seems most unhappy . . . to lose another babe when all are watching and waiting for a son . . . These must be terrible days for her."

It was a cautious response, I thought. Nearly everyone serving the queen had said something similar. It wasn't a criticism or be-trayal—merely a statement of well-known fact.

"But, as you know, there is more to the matter than that," Cromwell went on. "I hear the queen has taken lovers and talked of the king's death. She has suggested the man she would marry if the king was no longer alive. Perhaps you know more of this? I would like to have the facts."

I sat without moving, trying to appear unworried. I could easily guess the story's origin—the day the queen talked to Norris about the king wearing "dead men's shoes," one of her many careless conver-sations.

"There are many malicious rumors about the queen, sir. Some say she has six fingers on her right hand. Some say she's a witch."

"Yes, that's true—we live in a world of slander and falsehood. But this is something more, I think. If you are loyal to the king, Mark, you will tell me all you know."

I knew quite a bit, and much of it reflected badly on Her Majesty—her dangerous words to Norris, her strange quarrel with Weston. I had seen her talk with Brereton in quiet corners, her hands resting lightly on his forearm, both of them whispering so no one else would hear. The queen sometimes sent her ladies away and spent time alone with these men. I myself had been near enough to her to un-derstand how she might have enticed them. I had seen her tears and felt her fingers tracing along my face and hands. Had one of these men consoled her with more than words? But I had no proof the queen had betrayed the king with anyone—not with Norris, surely.

Cromwell waited, giving me time to savor my unease.

"I am a musician, sir," I said. "Not the one to answer questions like these."

"To the contrary, Mark, I believe you're precisely the one to answer. I've been told you're one of the queen's lovers yourself."

A spasm of dread gripped me so powerfully I could barely breathe. Seconds passed while I tried to shape an answer, while I tried to force my tongue and lips to move. "But this is ludicrous, sir. Who told you this?"

Of course, he didn't reply.

"I am the queen's musician, nothing more than that."

"But you're a very handsome musician. And you appear to have a great deal of money. Your horses are finer than mine."

Cromwell glanced at the other men, his face illuminated by candlelight. He sipped his wine and added, "One of the queen's ladies has reported that she saw you with Her Majesty and that the queen was caressing your face. Do you deny this?"

So, Lady Worcester was spying for Cromwell—this was the only possibility. I tried to think of an explanation that wouldn't blame the queen. My bowels churned in fear.

His manner shifted, and he projected a veneer of concern for me, presenting himself as a man who valued justice and impartiality.

"In addition to being the king's counselor, I am a lawyer, and I believe you should know the charges against you. One of the queen's servants will testify that you visited Her Majesty's bedchamber alone and stayed there until the next morning—and that you have done this many times."

"This is a lie . . . I have never stayed the night in the queen's private quarters." I could hear my own voice echoing outside my body, as if someone else was speaking. "Do you think I am so reckless, sir? Do you think I am so stupid?"

He looked at me calmly, his demeanor almost kind. "Mark, the queen herself has implicated you. She told me personally that you have looked at her with longing and spoken lustful, immoral words. She is the king's wife—it is an offense with a sentence of death."

This is a trick, I thought. He is trying to frighten me and make me doubt the queen. She hadn't talked to Cromwell about me. She wasn't cruel. She wouldn't tell an out-and-out lie that would put my life at risk. And yet, I had seen her quickly devise a story to shield herself. She had done it freely and without qualms.

"I have never done this, sir . . . never. That is not what happened at all."

Cromwell's eyes flickered, and he waited before speaking again. "Then what did happen? You would be wise to tell the truth, Mark."

I doubted the truth would protect me, and it would undoubtedly harm the queen. Cromwell placed his index and middle fingers on the base of the silver goblet in front of him and rotated it slightly to the left. The tightening of a noose? The turn of the rack? Again, he allowed the silence to gather before he began again.

"Did Her Majesty initiate the relationship with you perhaps? Was she unchaste with you? If you accosted the queen, that is treason . . . a slow and terrible death—I wouldn't wish it on the kingdom's worst enemy."

Everyone in the room was fixed in place.

"It was nothing, sir. Someone is spinning tales based on nothing at all. The queen touched my palm to read my fortune. Sometimes the queen is playful . . . you must have seen her tell men's fortunes by looking at the patterns of the lines on their palms. It was nothing more than that."

It wasn't the complete truth, but I hoped it would be enough. It wasn't even close.

Cromwell then expanded his insinuations and accusations, even as my denials became more desperate.

"I have never entered the queen's bed. This is not true . . . this is a vicious lie." I repeated myself dozens of times and searched my brain for arguments to prove my innocence. Sometimes, I thought back to my dream of making love to the queen. It was a dream—I knew that—but the images flared in my mind and increased my terror.

I had no idea what time it was. Nightmares that seem to last hours last only minutes, they say. At some point, Rafe Sadler was gone, and Gilbert Cromwell and the other man were leaning forward—the two of them sitting side by side, two pairs of eyes watching and waiting. Then Cromwell approached the subject from a different angle.

"The queen is going to lose her crown. The king has already decided this. She will be sent to France where she will live out her life in splendor and ease. But the men who have lain with her will die dreadful deaths, even if she tempted them. I could make an exception for you, Mark, if you are sensible."

"But I have done nothing, sir. I am completely innocent of what you say."

"Are you willing to die a gruesome death for the queen, after she has implicated you?"

Cromwell pushed his chair back, looking at me, his eyes appearing to glisten with sympathy. He stood, preparing to leave. "You are entangled in this treasonous business somehow—regardless of whether I believe your claims of innocence or not. You don't seem rash enough to have done this on your own. I always like to think the best of people."

He remained quiet for some minutes while I continued, probably pathetically, to babble that I had done nothing wrong.

"Let me think on this," he said at last, "and see what can be done. Stay the night, and we will talk again tomorrow."

Gilbert Cromwell and his silent partner stood on either side of me. The owl-eyed man gripped my elbow, and I noticed the coiled rope hanging from his belt. The two of them led me out of the room and down the stairs. We proceeded through a long hallway to a chamber at the back of the house—a sparsely furnished room with a bed, a table, and four chairs. A fire blazed in the hearth and a pitcher and cups sat on the table—it was a reasonably comfortable room, I thought as we entered. After my talk with Cromwell, I yearned for rest and sleep. I walked unsteadily toward the bed, fatigue and confusion overwhelming me. Gilbert Cromwell placed one of the chairs near the hearth and sat stirring the fire with a poker. "Don't pay attention to us, Mark," he said. "Go ahead and lie down." The other man sat at the table. I assumed they would guard me until the morning.

So was I tortured? Not as cruelly as some—not as cruelly as the Carthusian monks. As soon as I dozed off, they woke me, laughing at my panicked reaction. Then they pulled me off the bed and made me stand with my arms tied behind my back. The owl-eyed man enjoyed pulling the rope tighter until I moaned from pain. Then he loosened the bindings and entertained himself by pulling them tight again.

My shoulders and arms ached, and my fingers tingled because my wrists were so tightly bound. Occasionally my body reeled from side to side from weariness. At one point, the owl-eyed man began punching me in the stomach, causing me to double over and fall to my knees. My abdomen convulsed from the pain that traveled through every muscle in my body. In time, I sank to the floor and lay on my side while Gilbert Cromwell kicked my spine repeatedly. I curled my hands into fists and held them against my stomach. If I couldn't protect my hands and fingers, I might never play again.

"Our job is to make sure you give my master what he wants," the owl-eyed man jeered. Laughing, they dragged me back to the bed, and I crawled on top of it. When I dozed off—or passed out, perhaps—they threw cold water on me. Cromwell grabbed my hair behind my neck and pulled my head backward. The other man approached, holding the searing poker from the fire, and brought it near my cheek.

"What a shame to scar such a handsome face," Cromwell whispered close to my ear. "You'll look like a monster if you don't play my master's game."

I pictured my skin blistering and roasting, then smoldering and turning to ash. I was mumbling—I don't even know what I said. I felt tears escaping from the outer corners of my eyes and dripping down my face.

Then Gilbert Cromwell let go of me, allowing me to fall back on the bed. "Think about it, pretty boy: What it will feel like when your skin starts to burn. Think about what will happen when the very sight of you disgusts people. You won't be playing concerts anymore." He spoke to his partner—"I think Mark is beginning to understand us" —before he turned to me again. "In this house, we set the rules, and you obey them. I think you're bright enough to see that."

Later that night and into the morning, they repeated their performance, joking about whether it would be more effective to gouge out an eye or press the hot poker against my cheek. My side of the conversation was less imaginative: "It's not true . . . Why are you doing this? Please, for the sake of God, I beg of you. . . ."

That's all I could manage to say.

Around noon, Thomas Cromwell entered the room carrying a document ready for my signature. He sat down at the table and placed the paper on it. A servant brought in a pen and well of ink. I stood before him while his two men held my arms.

Cromwell's voice was as smooth as cream. "If you sign this confession, I will give you gold and get you out of the country. If you don't, my associates will continue encouraging you to cooperate."

The two men pushed me into a chair. Gilbert dipped the pen in ink and put it in my hand. Cromwell pushed the paper across the table, positioning it in front of me.

"You will sign this confession, Mark. You can do it now, and I'll make plans for your escape. Or you can do it later after more persuasion. And then I will turn you over to the law to be eviscerated. That's your choice—a new start in another country or torture and an excruciating death."

For a moment, the words on the paper blurred and ran together. I didn't need to read it. I could imagine what it said.

Cromwell nodded toward his brawny underlings. "You don't want these men to continue with their work, do you? I don't want that."

I looked at the pen resting in my fingers. I heard one of the men behind me shift his weight. I spread my left hand over the top of "my confession" to block out the words. With my right, I wrote my name.

When I had finished, I asked one question. "But why me? You know this is a lie."

"Someone mentioned your name. You are often near the queen. You have no family of importance. Since you are lowborn, I can do whatever is needed to ensure your cooperation. As you know, custom prevents the torture of gentlemen of rank. Getting your confession was the simplest first step."

Cromwell left the room—time to turn his attention to his next victim, whoever that might be. They brought me something to eat, but I didn't touch it. Already, regret devoured me. I had snatched at a slim chance to survive, but once I had done it, I didn't care whether I lived or died.

Later in the afternoon, Gilbert Cromwell and several other men led me down the hall, one of them carrying my lute.

"You'll stay in the Tower until the situation is resolved," Gilbert Cromwell told me. "We'll go to London by boat."

As we left the house to walk down to the river, I saw Rafe Sadler standing nearby, a vacant expression on his face. I wondered how much he knew of what had happened to me. On impulse, I spoke to him. "Could you ask someone to take care of Flanders? My horse . . . will someone look after her? And Prince, my horse at the stable?"

"I will take her back to Whitehall myself," he said. "Don't worry about either of them. I will see to their care and safety, no matter what the future brings."

In the boat, Gilbert Cromwell sat next to me. My eyes connected with his, but he looked toward the shore before he returned my gaze. "We would never have burned you," he said. "I wouldn't do that. But we had to have your confession. My master needs it." I suppose he was trying to convince himself he wasn't a torturer. I hated him even more.

He added, perhaps to settle his own mind, "He will get you out of the country if he is able to. He told me so himself."

In less than twenty-four hours, all I had cherished had been taken from me. The life I knew was gone.

34

THE MAY DAY GAMES

May 1536

Madge Shelton, Greenwich

I had attended the May Day games many times when I was a girl, back when my father jousted and frequently won. One year was unforgettable. When I was five, my father triumphed, and I watched him remove his helmet and wave to the cheering crowd. Then he brought his horse round to the place where my mother and I were seated. He lifted me up to the saddle, and I rode onto the field with him. Everyone applauded, including the king and queen—Queen Katherine at the time. With its games, balls, and royal processions, May Day was a time of celebration. People brought their entire families to Greenwich to join in the merrymaking.

My mother and I had arrived a day early to organize my cousin's clothing and inspect her suite of rooms. We unpacked a dress and cloak of silvery Venetian brocade for her to wear during the games and a gown of yellow and gold for the evening's dancing. My mother spoke with the housekeeper to ensure that the queen's requirements would be met. Once we were certain all was arranged, I had an evening free to read and think of the promise I had made to Mark— how we would meet once I was married and how I would prove my love for him.

The next morning, my cousin appeared—she was skittish and preoccupied as she often was since losing the unborn prince. She said little, but asked almost on arrival, "Is Jane Seymour here?" Lady Worcester told my mother that the queen had quarreled bitterly with His Majesty shortly before he left for Greenwich. This was hardly unusual—they quarreled bitterly every day. [22]

cjo

Scores of groundsmen, gardeners, and carpenters had labored for weeks preparing the Greenwich fields for horse races, archery, and jousts. The workers constructed viewing stands and trimmed them with bunting in the king's colors. A hundred pennants flew from flagpoles bordering the fields—the dragons, lions, and fleur-de-lis of His Majesty's coat of arms. At the center of the viewing stands, the builders erected the royal box which was much higher than the spectators' benches. Anyone in Greenwich for the May Day festivities would want to see the king and queen.

During the opening ceremony, His Majesty had paraded be- fore the crowd in flowing white-and-golden robes, his subjects roaring at every wave of his hand. On the fields, the fathers and sons of England's great families competed, all wearing the royal colors and those of their chosen ladies. During the games, the spectators cheered and groaned for the players while enjoying the sunlight and a cool feathery breeze. The king and queen posed and smiled, shimmering and untouchable. My mother and I sat behind my cousin, ready to help if she needed anything. Sir Henry arrived from Whitehall later than expected, his horse exhausted. The king loaned him one of the royal stallions so he could ride in the jousts.

Just as the afternoon matches began, the king received a sealed message, glanced at it, and left the royal box. The Duke of Norfolk took His Majesty's place beside my cousin. William FitzWilliam, Earl of Southampton, moved from his seat farther away to sit on her other side. Southampton was known as the king's "enforcer," and I viewed him as one of the least pleasant men at court. Rumors circulated that he practiced the arts of blackmail and extortion on the king's behalf and often on his own.

The competition was lackadaisical, the riders not especially skilled. The day grew warmer, and my cousin removed her dove-gray cloak and handed it to me. A page delivered another message to Norfolk who read it without reaction. He leaned forward, nodded to FitzWilliam, and then circled his fingers around my cousin's upper arm. With no warning, the three stood up to leave. I rose too, assuming my mother and I would accompany the queen to another location, perhaps to meet the king. But my mother stopped me, whispering, "We'll wait here, Madge."

My cousin didn't resist or ask questions, not that I could see. As they escorted her from the royal box, she seemed like a delicate ornament trapped between two towering men. I saw no concern on her face.

On the field, the remaining jousters rode back and forth until one of them prevailed. Afterward, workers set up targets, and some two dozen archers assembled. Arrows whizzed, the crowd cheered, and small boys ran up to clear the boards for the next set of contenders. I held my cousin's cloak during the long succession of games, thinking I would return it soon. My mother left to speak with someone unnamed. At four o'clock, the day concluded with a blare of trumpets, but neither the king nor the queen appeared to congratulate the day's winners. Sir Henry wasn't there, either.

Back in our quarters, I began to arrange my own clothing for the evening ball when my mother reappeared.

"There has been a change in plans, Madge. The queen is returning to London, and we must leave tonight."

"But why . . . isn't she attending the ball?"

"The dances have been canceled and tomorrow's games as well. Your cousin will be taken to the Tower, and starting tomorrow, I will tend her there."

"What?"

I stood near a wardrobe, the door half open, thinking that I must have misunderstood. My mother sat down on my bed and motioned for me to come and sit next to her. She spoke quietly, her voice as measured as if she were listing our daily tasks. "I will tell you what I can."

She lightly touched my cheek and hair. "Tonight, we go to London, and then you and Mary will travel to Shelton Hall and remain in Norfolk for a while. This is with the king's permission, and it will be better for everyone."

"But why?"

Her eyes were gentle when she looked at me but clouded when she looked across the room. Then, her tone became motherly. "You are quiet, my darling, but you are strong, and you will need all your strength in the coming days. There will be no marriage to Sir Henry. Your cousin will lose the crown."

I began asking questions such as "What do you mean?" and "How can that be?" It took me several minutes to absorb such inconceivable news. Queen Anne would soon be Anne Boleyn again and likely be sent to France or the Low Countries. "Does she know that?" I asked.

"I expect they will have read the charges to her by now. You must prepare yourself. There is proof of her adultery with at least two men. Sir Henry is one of them."

"That is not possible." This charge was ridiculous to me. "Sir Henry is the last man at court to do such a thing. This is a mistake."

"They say he has admitted his guilt, Madge."

She took my hand and pressed it to her cheek. I briefly wondered how she knew all that she was telling me. It's strange, isn't it? What flies through your mind in moments of disbelief?

"Sir Henry has never lain with her," I said. "I would stake my life on this."

"It may seem so, but there is proof that she spoke to him as if they were lovers plotting the king's death. Several people overheard the conversation."

"And who is paying these people? I don't believe one word of this."

"Another man has confessed. Others will soon be named."

"But who?"

She spoke in a whisper, and I saw the pain she felt for me.

"Mark Smeaton confessed to Cromwell."

I stared at my fingers resting on the folds of my skirt. Images whirled in my brain. I pictured Mark that night, kneeling beside me, his hand gentle on my Starlight's neck. I remembered our kisses and the promise I had given him. My mind was so confused that my thoughts unraveled before they could take any meaningful shape. All I said was, "That can't be."

My mother cupped her hands around my face. "This is the way of things, my dear. There is nothing to be done."

"People are lying. This is wrong. What do you mean there is nothing to be done?"

Though I resisted at first, I let her place her arms around me. I was too shocked to weep. Then she leaned back to look at my face. "Mark signed the confession," she said. "Others have reported intimate conversations between them." She continued as if she were describing the plot of a fable or masque, some story about characters unknown to me. "I doubt that Sir Henry or Mark started the affairs—I suspect she lured them. Since the king has scorned her, she has been desperate to prove that she is still desirable. She demands flattery and yearns to be wanted as His Majesty once wanted her. I believe this is what has happened."

"Where is he? I want to see him."

"He will be taken to the Tower before trial. You cannot visit—it would not be good for either of you. If His Majesty pardons anyone in this sordid business, it will be Sir Henry."

I said nothing. She squeezed my hand and went on. "Sir Henry has known the king since they were young. His Majesty may be merciful."

"That's not what I meant."

She waited, her expression tense. After some seconds of silence, she asked me, "What did you mean?"

"I meant Mark Smeaton . . . I want to see Mark Smeaton."

She let go of my hand and stood up slowly, her movements rigid and contained. She stepped some feet away and then turned to stare at me. "Madge, I have noted your fondness for him. I had hoped it had faded with time. Why do you want to see him?"

I considered the most acceptable answer. To say that I loved him and had promised myself to him in secret would have been absurd. "He is alone. The others have family and connections. I want to help him. I know he is innocent."

"You cannot help him. I like Mark too, but I cannot allow you to endanger yourself out of misplaced sympathy. What has happened is God's will."

"This is not God's will; this is cruel. I don't believe this is what God wants." My voice probably sounded desperate, but in this moment, my will strengthened. I had never been so determined in my life.

At first, she didn't say anything. She seemed to be weighing her next words. "Life can be cruel, Madge. You must leave court tomorrow. I don't want you involved in this."

"I want to see him . . . only that . . . just to see him. I will go to Cromwell myself if that is what it takes."

"You will not. This is madness." She closed her eyes, and her face showed her alarm and grief. "All the Boleyns are suspect. George may be arrested."

"Nothing you can say will change my mind. If all else fails, I will go to the king."

"Madge, I have paid a high price to protect you."

"What kind of price?"

She inhaled slowly before she spoke. "I have allied myself with Cromwell. In the Tower, I will report your cousin's words to him and read her letters. In return, he has promised me that you will be safe. I am not at peace with my deception of her. What I am doing is likely a sin."

After this, my mother continued her arguments as we packed our belongings. She was silent while we took a barge to Whitehall under the setting sun. We passed the Tower, looming and casting long shadows on the riverbank. For the first time, I knew someone inside the walls—my own Mark who dwelled inside my heart.

The next morning, I expected my mother to order me and Mary to go to Norfolk. She wasn't used to defiance—not from anyone—and I wasn't used to defying her. During the night, I had prepared myself, becoming single-minded and resolute. To leave London without seeing Mark was unthinkable. I had vowed to disobey my mother, and I had no idea what she would do.

As I dressed and rehearsed what I planned to say, my mother entered my room. She handed me a note addressed to Cromwell—asking him to see me and grant my plea. "I beg you not to use this," she said. "You cannot help Mark; you must not put yourself at risk."

"But I must give him what comfort I can. What would you do in my place?"

I saw her eyes moisten, and after a moment, she said. "I don't know, Madge. I have never been as you are . . . I only know that I fear for you." Then she kissed my cheek and added. "If you must do this, go to Cromwell at Austin Friars after the trial is over. He may be enough of a Christian to permit your visit, but I doubt it."

She left my room to go to the Tower where she would spy to save her family.

35

IN THE TOWER

May 1536
Mark Smeaton, The Tower of London

My first hours in the Tower seemed like a nightmare. Now, it is my life before my arrest that seems like a dream. Once I lived in a palace with windows reaching nearly to the ceiling. The sun lit up my room and warmed my hands as I practiced and composed. Outside, I saw a garden—the flowers changed in every season. One night, I sat on a stone wall and kissed a beautiful young woman. We made promises in the moonlight.

Now, I exist in near darkness, my hands shackled and chained. Someone has brought my lute into the cell—I can just make out its case leaning against the wall. Every so often, I persuade myself that its presence means Cromwell intends to keep his promise to send me far away. But mostly, I see it as another cruelty, a means to remind me of all I have lost.

My mind keeps returning to the Carthusian monks—how did they keep from going mad? They spent weeks chained to the walls of their prison cells, their bodies upright and pinned to columns by their hands and feet. But these were men of unwavering faith which gave them a considerable advantage over me. Did they pray and recite psalms to reduce their agony? Did their faith protect them from fear and rage? I am not a monk or a priest or even especially pious. I fear I will go insane.

Maybe Gilbert Cromwell believes his master will let me live, but logic dictates otherwise. They need my confession so the king can divorce the queen. If they allow me to leave the country, I might tell someone they tortured and threatened me to make me confess. Cromwell understands this. I will have to die so his case against Anne Boleyn is watertight. I have to die so Cromwell can please the king.

In my worst hours, fear coils inside me. I envision executioners slicing my body open while the crowd shouts and jeers. I imagine my head on a pike, but my mind is alive. I can see my corpse wriggling and squirming beneath me.

Then, there are hours of rage—it seeps into my veins and possesses me. I hate the queen whose stunning self-pity doomed me. I hate Cromwell and his filthy thugs. I hate the king and Lady Worcester and all the tattlers yet unknown to me. Why do I have to lose everything because the king is tired of Anne Boleyn and wants to marry the exquisitely stupid Seymour woman? I want to curse them all—to call on God to consign them to the eternal flames of Hell. But I strangle myself into silence. I don't want to give the guards the satisfaction of hearing their prisoner shrieking and sobbing. How is it possible to lose all you have worked for—everyone and everything you know and love—in the space of a single night and day?

I curse myself for my weakness and brood over what I said when Cromwell questioned me—as if my words would have made a difference. To end the pain, to avoid Gilbert Cromwell's slamming boots, to escape burning and mutilation, I signed a document that endangers others. Cromwell will probably use it against the men who have treated me best. Could even God forgive such cowardice?

Yet if I had let them break my body and disfigure me, what good would it have done? They would have killed me and moved on to the next man. Someone else would have supplied their "evidence."

⚜

The guards are pleased enough to share their tidbits of information. Rochford, Norris, Brereton, Weston, and the queen are all in the Tower, like me charged with treason and fornication. All except the queen and maybe Norris are likely to die. The king will decide whether the rest of us die slowly or quickly.

Some guards enjoy speculating about sex with the queen. "How was it?" they snicker. "Did she lick your cock?" Several asked me whether she really had sex with her brother: "I heard he likes boys better," they say. "Maybe you know the answer to that yourself?"

A few revel in the idea that rich men will die shameful deaths. One takes special pleasure in standing at the door to my cell and describing the executions he has seen at Tyburn. The men scream and cry for their mothers, he says. They lose control of their bodily functions. Some bite off their own tongues when they clench their teeth in pain.

The night guard, an older man, is kinder. He told me that Weston—"a young man like yourself"—has been crying in his cell. Well, Weston isn't the only one. When the guards aren't near enough to hear me, I cry too. I cry from loss and fear and rage.

Several days ago, the night guard said, "It's not fair. The others aren't in irons. They say you're not a gentleman. You look like the rest to me."

"My father was a carpenter. I played the lute for the king."

The past tense—I already think of myself in the past tense.

He paused, his pock-marked face filled with pity. "Are you guilty? Have you betrayed our sovereign king?"

"I am guilty of many things, but I am not guilty of this."

"Then my good wife and I will pray for you."

That night, he "forgot" to lock my wrists in irons after he took away my evening meal. Since then, he unfastens the clasps at night, but locks me up again in the morning before he leaves. He brings in water and soap, so I can wash up. He brought me a fresh shirt and undergarments—belonging to his son, he said. His wife then washed and cleaned what I was wearing. I was grateful for this charity.

I have considered asking him to bring me pen and paper so I can write to Madge. Perhaps he could bring the supplies from my palace room. I have money hidden there in a cabinet, and I would be glad to give it to him for his help. But having weighed this plan, I realize that any communication with Madge might endanger her, and I cannot take this risk. I have to assume that she has learned what has happened. I pray she guesses the truth.

When the night guard is on duty, I can walk to the window and see a glimmer of the moon and stars. I recall another night under the moonlight and tell myself to concentrate on it—that brief hour when my heart and mind soared into the sky. I can't let myself forget.

In ways that I don't completely understand, the guard's kindness has eased my fear and rage. This morning, I whispered my thanks to him.

"Do not forget, young sir, God is merciful."

"So I've been taught."

"Then, in these terrible days, you must believe it. Believe it with all your heart."

I said I would try to do this because I wanted to repay his charity. But my true thoughts are more cynical. God may be merciful, but His mercy must be for others. I doubt He will help me in the days to come—not if my death serves Thomas Cromwell.

36

THE TRIAL

May 12, 1536

Mark Smeaton, Westminster

orris, Weston, Brereton, and I stood trial today—a mockery of the rule of law. Rochford and the queen will be tried separately because of their higher rank—in the next three days, according to the guards.

Cromwell made sure I was ready. Yesterday, I heard footsteps outside my cell. "Smeaton, you have a visitor." The heavy door scraped against the floor.

"Don't bother getting up." Cromwell's owl-eyed brute laughed at me as I sat on the floor with my arms fastened to the wall.

"Go to hell."

"Well . . . the pretty boy has lost his famous manners. If I go to hell, you'll be there before me."

"What do you want?"

He bent over and put his face close to mine. His breath smelled of stale ale. "Just a reminder: Don't be stupid at trial." He knelt on one knee and placed his knuckles against my jaw. "Stupid . . . like denying your confession. Do that, and you'll get a traitor's death . . . slow . . . painful . . . your flesh sliced up like meat." He pushed his fist against my head, pressing it hard against the wall. The pain began, and he increased the pressure. I bit my lip, trying not to squirm. "With a skilled executioner, it can take hours; you'll scream and wet yourself. And my master has promised me a turn beforehand. When I'm done, no one will recognize you. I like playing with fire."

He let go and stood up. He had the eyes of a wolf eager to shred its prey.

"Do you expect a reply?" I had to smother my terror to pronounce the words.

"No, just say what my master wants . . . I'm sure you understand."

Later, the night guard unlocked my irons so I could move about freely for a while. But I was so panicked I could barely walk over to the window. All I could think of was the owl-eyed man bringing an orange-hot poker to my face.

꩜

"Let's go, Smeaton. Hurry up."

Early in the day—I'm not sure what time—guards took me from my cell and hustled me down hallways where men's skeletal faces loomed behind bars in the doors. One guard shoved my shoulder so hard I nearly lost my balance. He shouted, "Hurry it up, I said!"

We turned corners and climbed through a labyrinth of stairs and passageways. Smells of urine and excrement seeped into my nose and mouth. When we entered a courtyard near the river, I looked back at the Tower's turrets, completely shrouded in fog. For weeks, I had longed to see the sky, but there was no sky to be seen this morning. Norris, Weston, and Brereton stood some feet away, also surrounded by guards. Weston looked at me emptily, as if his soul had already left his body. Norris and Brereton held themselves stiffly, both immobile. We gathered passively—animals being led to slaughter.

The boatmen waited at the river to take us to Westminster Hall: I was directed to sit in a boat beside Norris while four guards positioned themselves in front and behind. Weston, Brereton, and their guards occupied another boat ahead of us. I had often envied and resented Norris—he was betrothed to the woman I love. He had wealth and privilege from the moment he was born. But his weeks in the Tower had made him a husk of a man. His hands shook, and when he saw that I had noticed this, he hid them beneath his cloak. Sir Henry Norris tried to conceal his fear, but I was the coward who had endangered everyone. All the world would know this when Cromwell read my confession at trial.

Without thinking, I turned to Norris. I doubted I would have another chance. "Sir, I beg your forgiveness."

"What for?"

"For signing the confession . . . I. . . ."

"Did you have a choice?"

"The prisoners will be silent."

Cromwell conducted his charade in one of London's most beautiful buildings. I knew Westminster Hall well, having played there many times. As I walked in, I recalled the wonder I felt the first time I saw it—rows of arches with polished wood tracery, beams carved into angels, their heads and praying hands flying up above us along both sides of the hall. But facing charges of high treason, I had no heart to admire the splendor. [23]

The four of us filed into the court surrounded by a new detail of guards. My eyes turned to the men sitting as a group ahead of us. The Dukes of Norfolk and Suffolk were in the center, the Earl of Northumberland and Sir Henry Pole nearby. This was no ordinary jury waiting to weigh evidence. They all understood what the king required.

Norris, Weston, and Brereton knew these men as equals. They had dined with them, sported with them, and visited their houses as guests. I had played for most of them at one time or another. A few had requested favorite songs and extended their compliments after my performances. Behind the jury, broad steps led to an immense arched window. If the sun came out this day, it would shine on the men who judged us.

The prosecutors, Cromwell among them, occupied a long table on one side of the room. Spectators filled rows of benches on the other. Witnesses waited behind the lawyers, some quite illustrious. William FitzWilliam, Earl of Southampton, held his body stiffly as he sat in a comfortable cushioned chair. A few people leaned against the walls, Nate Gage and Silas Bray among them.

We stood in the dock behind a waist-high wooden railing. The guards placed their hands on the hilts of their swords to discourage us from trying to flee—it would have been a futile act ending in a grisly death. Nearly everyone was whispering to his neighbor while the four of us waited silently. The king wasn't even there.

A bell sounded. The voice of one of Cromwell's clerks pierced the buzz of conversation. "I call this court into session."

After ringing his bell three times, the clerk finally settled the room. "Sir Henry Norris, Sir Francis Weston, Sir William Brereton, and Mark Smeaton are summoned here, this twelfth day of May in the year of Our Lord 1536, to answer charges of high treason. As the evidence will show, the accused have committed many treasonous acts against our sovereign king. These include having carnal knowledge of the king's wife, the Queen Anne Boleyn, and, in collaboration with her, plotting the king's death."

Brereton stood closest to me, and I sensed the anger he held inside. Weston, a little farther away, was ashen, his blond hair disheveled. He stared at nothing in particular. Norris had adopted a soldierly posture, shoulders pulled back, head held high. I tried to stand erect and appear calm, but my fingers trembled. Cromwell shuffled his papers.

In this moment, I was more conscious of my low rank than I had ever been. I had never seen a trial, and I could barely follow the legal phrases. I didn't know what rights I had—if I had any. At times, I imagined myself watching the proceedings from above, as if I were already dead and looking down on past events on Earth.

The words of the indictments floated in the air. The queen "despised her marriage." She entertained "malice" toward the king. She "uttered sweet words" and gave us gifts, motivating our crimes. We tempted and encouraged her "to act on her frail, female lust." Small snatches of truth twisted into a devious, murderous knot.

"Sir Henry Norris, the evidence will show that you traitorously yielded to the queen's procurements, to her kisses, touches, and vile provocations on the sixth and twelfth of October, in the year of Our Lord, 1533, and that you had illicit intercourse with her at other times, both before and after, sometimes by your own procurement and sometimes by the queen's. It is further charged that in Greenwich on the eighth day of April in the year of Our Lord, 1536, you conspired with the queen and others to cause the death of the king. How do you plead?"

"Not guilty. I deny all charges without reservation."

A quaking servant testified about whispered conversations overheard in the queen's inner chambers. A maid reported finding Sir Henry's clothing tossed on a chair near the queen's bed and hearing a man's voice behind the curtains. Cromwell read letters from several of the queen's ladies. Lady Worcester's statement offered a lengthy account of the day the queen talked about the king wearing "dead men's shoes" and suggesting that Norris wanted to marry her.

The lady's report was much as I remembered the conversation myself, but in her retelling, it was damning.

William FitzWilliam, Earl of Southampton, testified that he had questioned "the accused" after his arrest and that Norris had given him a letter addressed to the king. Southampton was notorious for "handling" any nobleman who stood in His Majesty's way—blackmail being his favored tool. In return for these services, the king had given him vast quantities of land and gold.

Southampton spoke smoothly and wore ornate medals of office. He was impressive—anyone would believe his words were true. He testified that Norris had written a letter admitting his lust for the queen and begging for mercy in the most abject way. The letter apparently described one "reckless conversation" in particular. Although Norris stood some feet away from me, I heard his quick intake of breath.

"This is contemptible, sir, utterly contemptible." Norris stumbled over the word "contemptible" the first time he said it, and his voice was hollow and thin. "I have never lusted after the queen. I had no illicit relations with her at all. I deny it at the peril of my soul."

The clerk held up the letter, displaying it for the court. "Sir Henry, do you withdraw your confession? Do you deny giving this letter to the Earl of Southampton during your interrogation?"

"I gave Sir William the letter to give to His Majesty, but it is not a confession. I wrote to the king to explain some words that had passed between the queen and myself, words that have been distorted and misjudged. You have it. Show it to the jury . . . let them decide."

The clerk looked at Cromwell, and Cromwell nodded. I assumed the letter explained the "dead men's shoes" conversation. If this was treason, it was the queen's treason. Norris wasn't the one who said it. In the jury box, the Duke of Norfolk took the letter from the clerk. He glanced at it before passing it to the others. Not one juror looked at it for more than a second or two. Some didn't look at it at all.

Norris was known for his calm demeanor. I had never heard him raise his voice to even the most disrespectful servant or annoying diplomat. Yet he shouted at Southampton, "You malicious, lying cur! You said you would give my letter to His Majesty! Did you give my letter to the king?"

Cromwell rose. "Sir Henry, a replica of your letter, copied word for word by one of my own clerks, was included in a sheaf of papers delivered to His Majesty last week."

By this time, Norris must have realized the king would never see his letter, hidden deep within a stack of tedious documents, just another sheet of paper in His Majesty's voluminous "official reading." Cromwell knew the king's habits—His Majesty never went through these official papers. They just sat there, collecting dust, until some- one took them away. For an instant, I was strangely relieved. I wasn't the only one who had been duped.

When Weston's turn came, he faced the jury, controlling his shaking hands by clasping them together behind his back. Richard Rich, Cromwell's oiliest deputy, read the charges which listed specific days of fornication with the queen. "Sir Francis Weston, how do you plead?"

"I plead not guilty. I was not even in Greenwich on those days."

"Are you denying you were in Greenwich in November and December 1534?"

"Yes, I deny it absolutely. I was in Surrey on family business . . . I was there for about two months."

Rich turned his back to Weston and took several documents from the prosecutors' table. He paused, appearing to read them carefully. Approaching Weston again, he held the documents out, but Weston didn't take them.

"I hold in my hand three letters of testimony stating that you were in Greenwich in November and December 1534 and that you were seen entering the queen's bedchamber at least six times. The Earl of Southampton has provided a sworn statement that he saw you and spoke to you on numerous occasions during the period in question. Are you suggesting His Lordship is lying?"

Even in these circumstances, Weston managed a smile and a clever reply. "I am suggesting Sir William is mistaken. My wife will swear I was in Surrey, and I believe she remembers it well. My second son was born nine months later."

Someone laughed, but the rest of the room was silent.

"I am afraid your wife's testimony would not be persuasive, Sir Francis." Rich walked toward the jury. "Who are we to believe? The Earl of Southampton, the king's counselor, a man known to you all? Or a traitor's wife, a woman who faces ruin if her husband is judged guilty? She has every reason to lie."

Weston said little after that. More servants testified, dutifully quoting from Weston's flirtatious conversations with the queen. Silas Bray described the conversation I had heard—when Weston called the queen "the goddess" who owned his heart and claimed to adore her above all others. But in Bray's fictitious ending, Weston and the queen then left the room together and disappeared into her chambers.

It was true that Weston's teasing often bordered on the erotic. He complimented the queen and danced and joked with her. I had seen him wink at her from across the room. But he had flirted openly with half the women in the king's palaces, women of every age and station.

Brereton's turn was next, and the charges against him were the least convincing. He was rough and thickset, an unlikely paramour for a refined queen. He played cards with her and gave her a dog and an expensive falcon, but to me, the idea that he was her lover was preposterous. I wondered how he had offended the king—or crossed the Seymours or Suffolk or Norfolk. Or maybe it was Thomas Cromwell.

I saw Nate Gage move forward, and he glanced at me contemptuously as he stepped up to testify. Before swearing the oath, he removed his hat to reveal his red-brown hair which hung in oily clumps around his neck. Rich asked him to describe a visit he made to Richmond the previous summer.

"Do you remember one day in particular?"

"It was a Sunday, shortly before the queen began her lying in."

"And what did you witness that day?"

"I saw Sir William Brereton and Her Majesty together. It was in the afternoon, and they were whispering and touching each other in sinful ways. The queen opened the front of her dress, so Brereton could stroke her breasts. She liked it and encouraged him to kiss and lick her skin."

"I see," Rich replied before he turned to jury to underscore the tale. "If Master Gage had not seen this wickedness with his own eyes, one could scarcely believe it. Sir William Brereton traitorously defiled the king's wife, and she encouraged him." Rich resumed his questioning.

"And where did this take place."

"It was in a little-used library. They thought they were alone."

"Master Gage, did you see anything else that afternoon?"

"After a while, another man entered and joined in their vile behavior. This one lifted the queen's skirts and ran his hands between her legs."

"Do you know who this second man was?" Rich asked.

"It was the musician, Mark Smeaton." An appreciative murmur rolled through the room as Gage delivered his outlandish lie. Most of those attending the trial enjoyed lewd stories about Anne Boleyn, whether they were true or not. They were a form of entertainment.

Then my turn came, such as it was.

I had vowed many times to deny my confession at trial. I had practiced what I would say—I had never lain with the queen. Cromwell tricked me. His men abused me and threatened to disfigure me. They forced me to sign a false confession. But my resolve died before I opened my mouth. After Gage's farcical invention, I knew the truth didn't matter. It wouldn't even help the queen.

Cromwell rose to question me himself, which set off a hum of whispered commentary. Then there was silence, and everyone watched him walk toward me, holding my confession in his hand. I tried to stand as I had seen the others do. I touched the wooden railing in front of me to occupy my mind and steady myself.

"Mark Smeaton, you have confessed and pled guilty to the offense of having illicit relations with the queen on the twelfth and thirteenth days of April and the nineteenth day of May in the year of Our Lord, 1534. These illicit relations continued, occurring as recently as the twenty-ninth day of April in our current year. Do you acknowledge you signed this document before me on the first of May in the year of Our Lord, 1536?" [24]

I had sung before kings and princes, but my voice left me as I started to speak. I saw them putting a noose around my neck and sharpening their blades to cut me apart. I could hear the crowd roaring in excitement, eager for the blood and screams to come. I looked at my hands, trying to snap myself back to the present. Cromwell walked closer, and my eyes locked onto the gold chain on his chest. I remembered meeting Cardinal Wolsey when I was seven years old. Cromwell's chain was nearly identical—heavy, repeating S shapes with a Tudor rose in the center.

Cromwell moved his powerful body in front of me and held my confession in his hand for me to see. I couldn't speak. I could barely breathe. He spoke louder. "You signed this document before me on the first of May, did you not?"

What a clever man he was. He knew I wanted to tell the truth.

"Yes, I signed it. It is my signature."

He turned to his clerk. "Please present Master Smeaton's confession to the jury."

Returning to the table, Cromwell selected several other documents. "We have additional evidence—statements from Master Silas Bray and Lady Worcester among others—confirming your lust for the queen and your carnal knowledge of her."

I was surprised Bray had gone this far: signing a letter that meant my death. But how many times had I underestimated his jealousy of me? I had underestimated him from the start.

Cromwell spoke again: "You are further charged with conspiring with the queen, George Boleyn, Lord Rochford, and Sir Henry Norris in April of our current year to cause the death of the king and enable the queen to rule in his place."

Suddenly, my wits came to me, and my words rang out. "I never plotted to kill the king."

"So, you plead not guilty to the charge of conspiring with the named accomplices to cause the death of the king."

"Never . . . I never did this. I never plotted against His Majesty."

Cromwell turned his back to me and spoke to his clerk. "Enter his plea as 'not guilty' to the second charge of conspiracy to cause the death of the king. Add that the accused, Mark Smeaton, humbly begs pardon for his offenses and beseeches His Majesty, our gracious sovereign and a man of Christ, for mercy."

It was over. Cromwell's dark, narrow eyes peered at me, and his lips contracted. Had he just saved me from a traitor's horrific death? Was this his way of helping me after conspiring to have me killed?

The jury's verdict came immediately: All four guilty, all four sentenced to be hanged, drawn, and quartered at Tyburn, subject to the king's mercy. I listened to the words, but my mind couldn't contend with them. Brereton, standing at my side, whispered: "Don't believe it. The king will never do it. We'll lose our heads, that's all."

His certainty calmed me. And, for some strange reason, I was relying on Cromwell to intercede for me.

⚜

We left the trial and Westminster Hall surrounded by a dozen armed men. They led us to the boats to return to the Tower. That's when I saw a man in a priest's cassock. Paul Markham was waiting beside the river. He approached the group, and two of the guards pulled their swords. Paul raised his hands to show he was un-armed.

"I have come back," he called out to me. The guards brandished their weapons, but apparently decided not to attack an unarmed man in clerical robes. Paul watched as we sat down in the boats, and the oarsmen pushed away from the riverbank. A glimpse of my friend, a few seconds only—it was an unexpected blessing. I hoped Paul wouldn't put himself in danger trying to help me. I was beyond the aid of any man.

This time, Weston was next to me, his fair skin colorless. He seemed resigned as he spoke to me. "You must hate me. I brought you into the group. You would still be playing concerts for the king if I hadn't."

I had to stifle my tears when he said this. Was he thinking he was to blame? "But you favored me . . . I profited." I looked back at Westminster Hall. Paul was still on the bank, his figure receding in the distance. I bent my head and spoke quietly, hoping to tell Weston all that I wanted him to understand. "The confession—I wasn't able to fight them."

"I know. I only hope it wasn't . . . too terrible."

The guards had decided to let us talk.

"Do you have any news of the queen and Rochford?" I asked.

"They say the queen will be sent to France so the king can marry the Seymour woman. I fear that George is lost."

We only had a little time, so I rushed to give him my most impor-tant information. "I spoke to Rafe Sadler about Prince and Flanders. He promised to care for them."

"Rafe? Good . . . I am glad of that. He will spoil them the way you have."

꒳

I don't know when I will die—or whether the king will grant me a merciful death. I had accepted that my life was over this morning when I stepped into Westminster Hall. The jury's verdict was never in doubt. Now, as I wait here, what matters most has become clearer to me. First, I pray to be allowed to die bravely and quickly, not like a gutted animal, naked and writhing before a roaring crowd. Second, I pray to God to forgive me for my cowardice. I am more hopeful about the first.

37

WHO WOULD YOU SAVE?

May 15, 1536
Madge Shelton, London

I was preoccupied when my serving woman told me that a man called "Paul Markham" wished to speak with me. I didn't recognize the name. That afternoon, I was to visit Cromwell. As my mother advised, I had waited the long, sorrowful days between Mark's arrest and his trial—I did little except go to the chapel to pray. Otherwise, I kept to my rooms where grief and fury overwhelmed me. My sister Mary kept me informed—more arrests, absurd charges, lurid stories, a trial with a predetermined end. Rumor had it that the king, too, paced and raged in his rooms alone.

But on this day, my wait was over. I spent the morning rehearsing all I would say to Cromwell and considering how to respond to questions he might ask. I needed to concentrate on the task before me. I didn't want to talk to some visitor. I didn't want to talk to anyone.

"Do you know why Master Markham is here?"

"He's a priest, ma'am. He said it was urgent."

I could imagine nothing more urgent than what I was about to do, but I relented just in case the visit was important. He was a young man, not much older than I was, and I remembered him when I saw him—one of the king's musicians, the one who walked with a limp. He bowed and said he had come to seek my help to see a friend in the Tower: "Mark Smeaton, ma'am, perhaps you remember him."

"Yes, of course." I hoped I sounded detached and unconcerned.

My visitor's face was earnest. "You must have heard about the charges and the trial."

I nodded and looked past him, searching for an object to gaze at in order to maintain my composure. His words ricocheted in my consciousness: *Mark Smeaton, ma'am, perhaps you remember him.*

"No one should die without some comfort and kindness," he went on. "I am afraid Mark is alone."

I pictured Mark imprisoned—no friends or family coming to reassure him of their love. I saw him mounting the scaffold to die. I tried to erase the images, but they had haunted me since his arrest. Long ago, I had memorized every detail of Mark's eyes and lips, every curve and shadow of his features. Once, I had recalled them in daydreams and happy recollections. During these terrible days, I saw him facing death, and my very soul sickened at the thought.

On the face of it, my visitor and I had a common purpose—to see and comfort someone dear to us. I wanted to believe this man was Mark's friend and my ally, but I barely knew him. Suppose Cromwell had sent him to trick me—to question me and test my loyalty. Anyone could put on a priest's robes and dangle a rosary from his belt. Whatever I said could be used against me and my family.

"Do you believe the charges against him?" Again, I attempted to appear disinterested.

"I do not know, ma'am. The Mark Smeaton they talk of is not the man I know. But this is not my purpose. I only wish to ease his anguish as he faces death and offer him the solace of God's love."

I wanted to weep when I heard this, but I couldn't take the risk. I asked, "But why have you come to me?"

He hesitated before answering, sometimes a sign of truthfulness. Spies generally invent their stories ahead of time.

"Those I might have approached have been arrested . . . Lord Rochford and the others. But you know powerful people, Mistress Shelton. I believe your mother is still trusted." He raised his eyes, and they seemed to darken with memory. "I saw your expression, ma'am, when you listened to Mark playing. I hoped you might be willing to help me. It would be an act of mercy."

I stood silent for several seconds. Paul Markham's body stiffened as he waited. I breathed in and knew that turning him away was impossible. I took the risk of trusting him.

"I am grateful you have come to me, good Father. I wish to see Mark too."

He bowed and then said quietly. "Yes, ma'am, I understand. God has answered my prayers."

⚜

When Cromwell was in London, he lived in a respectable dwelling at Austin Friars, but he had begun building a palace after his rise to power. He had purchased a string of neighboring inns and lodgings to clear the way for his grand plan. Some at court gossiped about how he had persuaded the nearby friary to sell him a large swath of its land at such a favorable price.

Although work on the buildings was still underway, the grounds were already magnificent. The broad, sweeping lawn of ornamental yews easily surpassed the one at Whitehall. The friars' old property was planted with apple and pear orchards that created a spring canopy of pink and white blooms. On this day in May, I couldn't help comparing the trees' pale, delicate beauty with the brutality of Cromwell's world.

Accompanied by my serving woman, I neared Cromwell's current house by walking through dust-filled paths where sweaty men unloaded carts of bricks. A few of them bowed, while most of them stared. More than once, I slipped my hand into my pocket and touched my mother's note to ensure I had it with me. During these minutes, I felt a resolve I had never felt before, forgetting all danger to myself. I thought only of Mark and my determination to see him once more. Surely God and Cromwell would grant me that.

First, I spoke to a servant. Then Gilbert Cromwell appeared, his rumpled doublet stretched unattractively across his bulky chest. He bowed to me and nodded to my serving woman. "Mistress Shelton, I apologize. My master is occupied."

He must have spent years lying on his kinsman's behalf, but he seemed unaccountably ill at ease. Maybe the scale and number of lies they were telling about those they were killing bothered even him.

"I have a message from my mother," I said. "I believe Sir Thomas will want to see it right away."

"If you will be seated, ma'am, I can give it to him."

I glanced at the chairs he offered to us and remained standing. "My instructions are to deliver the message to Sir Thomas in person."

He glanced at a closed door to the side. "All right . . . give me a moment." He placed his fingers on the door handle but turned back to speak to me. "Norris will die no matter what you and your mother say. The king is adamant, and your cousin Rochford was judged guilty an hour ago."

My stomach twisted, and I tasted vomit rising into my throat. "Please ask Sir Thomas to speak to me. I believe I deserve that courtesy."

"It will do no good."

"I will wait here until he sees me."

My only thought was to get inside the Tower to see Mark.

⚜

"Mistress Shelton, I can do nothing for Sir Henry, nor for Rochford. Your mother has been helpful, and I would grant clemency if I could."

Sir Thomas Cromwell greeted me formally and offered me a seat near his desk. I had entered alone, leaving my serving woman waiting outside, her face a web of fear. Leather-bound volumes, scrolls on tables, an astrolabe on a stack of books—Cromwell's work room suggested his respect for knowledge. The papers, maps, ink, and quills on his desk showed his appetite for work.

"Sir Thomas," I began. "I understand what is possible and what is not. I ask a small kindness only."

"I promised Lady Shelton that you and your sister could leave London—I am surprised you have waited this long. I advise you to return to Norfolk today. I have no wish to entangle you in this affair."

"My sister and I will leave tomorrow night. My visit does not concern my family or Sir Henry. I have come for a different reason."

"What is that?"

"Paul Markham, who was a court musician and has entered the priesthood, wishes to visit Mark Smeaton to comfort and pray with him."

"How do you know this?"

"The priest sought me out; he came from Devon when he heard about his friend's arrest. He wishes to offer the consolation of prayer to the condemned."

Cromwell stood up and placed his fingers on the astrolabe. "How do I know this priest is not a conspirator? Allowing any visit is risky."

"Perhaps . . . but denying a condemned man the grace of God's words would be a risk in the next world. Don't you agree, Sir Thomas?"

He twirled the astrolabe, apparently weighing the pros and cons. I could see how he used silence as a weapon, a way to unnerve others in the conversation. I continued speaking with as much con- fidence as I could muster. "The Tower is filled with guards, sir. Do you truly believe there is danger of escape?"

He lifted his hands and interlaced his fingers before delivering his decision, much as the king would do. "Yes, the risk is small. The priest will be searched before seeing the prisoner. He can bring a Bible and a rosary, but that is all."

"Thank you, sir. I am grateful for your help. But I also wish to visit Mark Smeaton. If anyone wishes to search me, it will be a humiliation I will endure."

"You want to go into the Tower to see Smeaton?"

He delivered these words with a surprised sarcastic grunt, and he elongated Mark's name with a sneer.

"This is my request, sir . . . nothing more than a visit."

"This is insanity." He walked closer to me. "Does your mother support you in this?"

"No, but she did write to you."

"But why . . . what is Smeaton to you?"

"You are wrong, sir, to assume no one cares if he dies. You know he is innocent."

"He signed a confession."

"And would you swear on a Bible that he did it of his own accord?"

Cromwell stood right in front of me, closer than would be considered polite. A squat man who disguised his ugliness with costly robes, he assessed me—not as a man assesses a woman, but as a spymaster assesses a hazard. I sat frozen, afraid I had gone too far.

He backed away a few inches and breathed heavily. "All right, Mistress Shelton, I will grant your request if you answer a single question honestly."

"I always prefer honesty, sir, whenever possible."

"I can save none of these men. The king's fury is too great. I have spared them from the most terrible punishment—they will all die by the axe."

He returned to his desk and leaned on the corner of it. His voice became less threatening, as if he were truly curious. "But let's say I could save one of them, based on your entreaty, which one would you choose?"

"I would save Mark Smeaton."

He responded with a mocking, triumphant laugh before adding, "Not your intended husband? Not your family? This is a curious morality."

"Sir Henry, my cousin George, the others—they played the games of politics, and they knew the risks. Mark only loved his music."

Cromwell stared at me without speaking.

"Sir Thomas, at the peril of my soul, I promise you, I only want to speak to him."

There was another long silence, and I thought I had failed. Then Cromwell said, "Gilbert will take you and the priest to the Tower tomorrow. The execution will be Sunday."

ℭ

My mother was waiting for me when I returned to our family quarters. "She has been judged guilty," she told me. "They read out a sentence of death, although I assume the king will send her away. I must return to her now, but I wanted to make sure you are safe."

"Cromwell said I could visit Mark tomorrow. I will go there with a priest."

While I was at Austin Friars, I had suspended my fear and grief to accomplish my mission. But once I was with my mother, my tears came in convulsive waves. I ran to her, and she held me like she had when I was a child.

"I don't understand why you are doing this, Madge, but it is a kindness worthy of Christ." She stroked and kissed my face. "But you must prepare yourself. Mark may have been badly mistreated. He is unlikely to be the same."

I pulled away—I didn't want to think of this.

"The queen blames him for signing the confession," my mother said. "I doubt he had any choice."

"Do you blame him?"

"No . . . your cousin's own words convicted her. But you must be ready. Your young friend has every right to be furious. He may be injured or incoherent."

When Paul Markham and Gilbert Cromwell arrived the next day, I pulled the priest aside to whisper about this possibility—that Mark might not be himself, that the man we both loved might have vanished already.

"I will talk with him first," the priest said. "If I believe that your visit will comfort him, I will bring you into the cell."

Though the thought of not seeing Mark was almost unbearable, I agreed to this. I would do whatever would help Mark most.

Gilbert Cromwell stood some feet away, listening. "He wasn't harmed," he said. "I saw him myself at my master's house in Stepney. He wasn't harmed at all."

28

WAITING FOR MERCY

May 16, 1536

Mark Smeaton, The Tower of London

few hours ago, I heard a clatter of keys and the shuffling of men outside my cell. I hoped the night guard had come to remove my shackles so I could see the stars and watch for the dawn on my last day of life.

There were other possibilities, of course, although I had deliberately closed my mind to them. I could be taken to Tyburn to face a barbarous death or to a boat headed to a foreign land. Utter terror or unending exile—I saw no point in contemplating either.

A guard I didn't know stepped inside the cell. "Smeaton, it's the priest come to take your confession."

"I don't want a priest."

He ignored my reply and stooped to unlock my hands. He dragged the shackles and chains aside while I remained seated on the floor. In the next moment, Paul appeared before me, dressed in brown confessor's robes. The door grated shut, and the key turned over. We were locked inside alone.

His face was drawn but as dear to me as ever. He knelt and clasped my shoulders, and I allowed him to embrace me. I felt his hand against my back and shuddered in my struggle to hold back tears. He held my shoulders even tighter. "I have come to see you, my friend. Let's sit and talk."

He positioned himself on the floor beside me. Like me, he leaned his head against the wall. "I am a month short of ordination, but the bishop has allowed me to hear your confession. God will forgive you, Mark, and welcome you into heaven." He turned his head to look at me—I could tell that he believed these words completely.

"Does God welcome cowards to paradise?"

"God loves and welcomes all sinners, and we are all sinners in some way."

"But what about cowards? What about someone so weak that he puts his friends in danger? Even the angels would revile a man like that."

"Saint Peter was a coward."

I pictured the saint as I had seen him in paintings. "I thought he was crucified upside down."

"Saint Peter died as a martyr beloved by Christ, but before that, he was a coward. Don't you remember?"

"No."

"It is one of the most important stories in the Bible—told in all four Gospels. In the hours after the Romans took Jesus away to be crucified, some townspeople asked Peter if he knew Jesus, but Peter said, 'I don't know the man.' Fearing for his own life, Peter lied and disowned God's only son three times that terrible night. Peter was a coward, and yet God forgave him . . . God will forgive you and help you."

Despite my lackadaisical faith, I was raised in the household of a cardinal. Part of me yearned to confess and find faith and forgiveness. This is the solace offered to even the most despicable. Paul knelt beside me and gave me the Bible he had brought with him. He placed his hand on my head, and I heard his words of prayer as he asked God to have mercy on his "unfortunate friend."

"Let me hear your confession, Mark, and bring you God's comfort."

"Comfort? What kind of comfort can I have now?"

"Let me pray with you."

"Do you think it will help?"

I turned my face away from him and put the Bible on the floor. "All over London, people are hoping I die a traitor's death. No mere beheading for a coward and lowborn villain like me." Then I looked at him directly, my closest friend: "Can I pray to die quickly? Is that allowed? Dear God, let me die quickly rather than screaming and writhing in agony."

"But haven't they told you? His Majesty has been compassionate. You and the others will die by the axe. The king has already signed the papers,"

I should have been grateful—I should gotten on my knees and praised God and His Majesty for their grace. But fury doesn't go away so quickly. In that moment, I hated everyone. I hated the world itself.

"Mark, let me help you prepare for death," Paul said. "You will have the forgiveness Christ brings to all of us, even the vilest sinner."

"But I did nothing. What kind of God lets this happen?"

I must have cried out loudly. I saw Paul's astonishment, but I continued, rage streaming out of me as if it would never end. "They forced me to sign the confession. None of it is true. You're a priest now. What happens to my eternal soul if I pray for forgiveness for crimes I never committed? Isn't that another lie?"

"Mark, I have never believed these charges." He spoke quietly, pressing his hands together. "But we all need forgiveness."

"Maybe I will tell the truth on the scaffold tomorrow. They couldn't stop me then. Maybe God will give me the courage to speak honestly."

"Mark, don't."

He spoke sharply, his eyes dark with appeal and desperation. "It could go very wrong for you—even at the end. They might change the manner of execution . . . You must say as little as possible." He grasped my forearm to plead his case. "It won't help the others. The truth is, I couldn't bear to see it. Please, Mark . . . don't take this risk."

And then, I cried openly for the first time. I placed my hands over my face and wept. I cried the tears of a man who has lost everything, the tears of a man who rose to unexpected heights and then found his carefully tended life obliterated in the space of weeks. Paul watched, sitting silently beside me. When my tears slowed and I uncovered my face, he picked up the Bible and gave it to me to hold again.

"Whatever you say is between you and me and God. Your death is near. Only God can help you meet it with courage and serenity."

I told him all of it—what happened with the queen, my dream of making love to her, what happened with Cromwell, my despair at my own weakness, my fears of damnation even though I had never lain with the queen or plotted against the king. The worst, I said, was that I had betrayed my friends. "I am a coward who doesn't deserve forgiveness."

"You faced unspeakable choices, Mark . . . and God forgave Saint Peter."

He began the prayers I had learned as a boy. I remembered every word. We spoke the holy verses together.

"O my God, I am heartily sorry for having offended you, and I detest all my sins."

"O loving and kind God, have mercy. Have pity upon me and take away the awful stain of my transgressions."

"Create in me a new, clean heart, O God. Don't toss me aside, banished forever from your presence. Don't take your holy spirit from me. Restore to me again the joy of your salvation."

Even as we prayed, I heard other prisoners crying out in fury and hopelessness. Slowly, the pain in my soul began to ease. Then Paul said the words I craved to hear: "I absolve you from your sins, in the name of the Father and of the Son and of the Holy Ghost." He covered my hands as I held the Bible. It was quiet, and I noticed his tears. He would soon have to leave.

I asked my final favor, confident that he would agree. "I have no pen or paper here. Could you visit someone for me and carry my message?"

"There is no need," he said. "I have proof of God's mercy and goodness. Stand up, wash your face; let's brush off your clothes. You have another visitor, but she cannot stay long."

⚜

It was a gift, the few minutes we had together. When I saw her, I bowed as I would have done at court.

"I wanted to visit . . . to be with you," she said. A single tear rolled down her cheek.

We sat down on the cold stone floor, our bodies close together as we leaned on one another. Her fingers gently wrapped around mine, and she whispered, "We won't have time to say all we want to say."

"It's enough that you are here. I've heard the condemned sometimes have visions."

"I am no vision. I wish our lives had been different." She rested her head against my arm and traced each of my fingers with her forefinger. I could barely believe I was close to her again. She removed her hood, and her soft, brown hair flowed over my shoulder. I touched the strands, smooth like silk, gleaming like the sun shining on a distant river.

"How many words have we ever spoken to each other?" I asked.

"Not many, but enough." She smiled, and for a small moment in time, I forgot my misfortune. An occasional whisper, our hands clasped and our bodies touching, unspoken phrases of love and loyalty, an unexpected blessing from God.

Half an hour later, maybe less, Paul came back. "She has to go. She is leaving London tonight."

"You will be safe?" I asked.

"I am going to Norfolk. My mother has arranged it. I believe she would have saved all of you if she could."

"No one has that power."

I prepared myself for my dream to end. Paul stepped into the hall, and I was alone with her one last time. We kissed and held each other, and then we kissed one final time.

"Be happy in life and remember me," I said.

She touched my face. "There is no chance I could forget."

⚜

Paul escorted her out of the cell and returned an hour later. "The carriage has pulled away. She is out of London by now and safe from harm."

"I didn't expect you back."

"A small negotiation and payment to the guards . . . I wanted to give you these."

He held out a rosary and a gold coin. I took the rosary with more gratitude than I would have thought. I wrapped my fingers around the wooden beads—the words of the prayers coming into my head, just as I had learned them as a child.

Paul waited and then extended his hand with the gold coin again.

"What's this for?"

"You have to give it to the executioner . . . it's customary." He slipped it into my pocket.

"I am afraid I may not die well."

"I believe you will."

He wrapped his hands around mine as I clasped the rosary. "Feeling the beads will give you strength," he said. "Tonight, think of what you will say before you die. God knows the truth, so don't say much. When you kneel at the block, think of a prayer or words or a memory that comforts you . . . and then you will be in the hands of God."

"Maybe I should practice . . . like I would for a concert."

"Maybe—it's not a bad idea. I will be near, as near to the scaffold as I can get. If you are confounded, look at me. You are dying in God's grace, remember that. Your soul is not in peril."

When he got up to leave, he saw my lute leaning against the wall, still in its traveling case. He took out the instrument and brought it over to me. "You may not feel like playing now," he said, "but perhaps later. The cardinal's gift . . . the music . . . it has sustained you throughout your life."

"Why don't you take it? Something to remember me by?"

"They would never let me leave with it. But I took your box of music from your room—your serving boy let me in."

"No one will play it with my name on it."

"No, but I gave the box to Mistress Shelton, who will send the sheets to important people. Your music will survive you, a beautiful gift to those who hear it. I put your father's carved horse in the box, so they wouldn't throw it out. I expect she will keep it."

"Yes, I expect she will."

We embraced, and he was gone. I was alone, but not as alone as before. The night guard looked in to ensure that no one had locked me in irons again. I would be free the last night of my life, at least to that extent. My prayer to see the two people I loved most in the world had been answered. It was far more than I had hoped for.

⚜

I held the lute and admired it. I enjoyed its beauty again. I played a few of the old songs I had learned as a child, strumming quietly so no one would hear. I thought of the gleam of Madge Shelton's hair and of the soft sound of her breath.

A guard came to the door, the pitiless one who had taunted me about Tyburn. I was afraid he might take the lute away or even smash it into pieces—he was that kind of man. But he said and did nothing. He stood near my cell and listened.

39

TOWER HILL

May 17, 1536

Mark Smeaton, The Tower of London

*L*ast night, I slept little, shifting in and out of wakeful-
ness. I thought of Madge and Paul and wondered why
God had allowed me to see them. Was it, as Paul said, proof
of God's goodness and mercy? More than once during the night, I
pressed the Bible to my chest and recited my friend's comforting
words: "You are dying in God's grace, remember that. Your soul is
not in peril."

Yet now that the time is hours away, I struggle to contain my
fear.

I have decided what my last words will be and which memory I
will summon as death is near. As Paul suggested, I try to prepare
myself with mental exercises like those I once used as a player. Back
then, I envisioned myself entering a stately room and bowing to my
audience. I saw the musical notes in my mind's eye and felt my fingers
on the lute, their movements agile and exact. Today I will climb the
stairs to a scaffold and stand before a jeering crowd. When my name

is called, I will step forward and give a coin to a masked man. Then I will kneel, place my head on the block, and hold still while he swings his axe. I will do this calmly and bravely—this is what I tell myself.

A few weeks ago, the queen read my fortune: "Most of your life will be fortunate," she had said as she fingered my palm. "When you die, you will die as a gentleman, on an equal footing with titled men." Rochford, Norris, Weston, Brereton—what Anne Boleyn predicted is true. Today, we all face the same executioner on the same scaffold on this same morning in the midst of an English spring. I pull Paul's rosary from my pocket and pray that the others will forgive me.

From what I can tell, standing at my prison window, the day is fine with glimmers of sun and the chirping sounds of birds. The door scrapes open—the night guard, with a cup of ale and bread in his gnarled hands. Another charity from this kind old man, but my stomach twists and coils.

"Thank you, but I am not hungry."

"You should take a bite, young sir. You will be the last to die. Some men grow weak—I have seen even the boldest falter. Eating some bread will help."

The ale is warm and the bread tasteless—my last breakfast is plain. But I try to show my gratitude. "You have been good to me, sir. I wish I could repay you."

He places his hand on my forearm, and I welcome the human touch. "Do not be afraid," he says. "It will be quick, and then you will be with God."

"Will you be on the scaffold?"

"No, that is work for harder, fiercer men. But my wife and I will pray for you. You must not doubt it."

"Yes . . . please pray for me."

☙

Footsteps, men's voices, bodies moving, keys jangling—I know these sounds well by now. This time, they signal the end.

A stout man I haven't seen before enters my cell along with four guards. One announces him: "Sir William Kingston, Constable of the Tower." The constable is darkly dressed, with emblems of high office hanging on his neck. I stand, as I have done throughout my life, and bow to a man of higher rank.

Kingston unrolls a document: "Mark Smeaton, having been judged guilty of high treason, you will now be taken to the place of execution."

The place of execution . . . the beginning of the end. . . .

Think that you are about to play the most difficult performance of your life, I instruct myself. I tug at my sleeves to neaten them and straighten my doublet by pulling at the waist. I run my hands through my hair and step forward to present myself. I don't want the guards holding my arms. I want to walk to the scaffold freely. I reach into my pocket for Paul's rosary. "May I take it?" I ask.

Kingston's voice is unexpectedly gentle. "Yes, this is allowed." He glances at the lute and Paul's Bible lying near it. "Shall I return these to the priest who visited you?"

"Yes, thank you, sir. I am most grateful."

I think of my time with Madge Shelton and God's grace in letting us meet.

I walk with the guards on either side of me—down hallways and through an interior courtyard—until we reach a large ground floor room. Outside, church bells are ringing—it is Sunday morning. I can hear the low rumbling and occasional shouts of a crowd.

The other men have arrived before me: Boleyn standing apart, Weston seated on a bench by the wall. Norris and Brereton are close together but seemingly oblivious to each other's presence. Without their lavish cloaks to broaden their shoulders, they look smaller than I remember them. Their rings, furs, and feathered hats have been taken from them. Since they have been judged traitors, their lands and titles will go to luckier men. Death for some while others celebrate. More nameless officials and guards fill the room.

Boleyn wears only a white silk shirt with the neck untied—no doublet or vest. He looks at me with an expression I can't interpret—maybe pity, maybe guilt. Norris, Weston, and Brereton appear exhausted and haunted. In effect, we are already dead. Kingston reads a document enumerating our crimes, justifying our execution, and ending with, "May God have mercy on your souls."

Positioned by title and rank—Boleyn first and me last—we take our places to walk to "the place of execution." Weston holds up his hand, suddenly as self-assured as he was in the past. "Sir William, I ask for a moment. Less than a minute. You have my word."

Kingston nods and motions the guards to stand aside.

Weston looks at each of us in turn and then says, "We should all die as friends. Let us shake hands and love and forgive one another as we leave this world."

When Weston's palm touches mine, I fight off tears. I am not sure, of course, but Weston is the only one of us who might have bedded the queen. He lived heedlessly, flirting and joking and relying on his charm to escape judgment. Yet, he is kind-hearted—his gift for companionship hasn't left him, even when he is about to die.

The five of us shake hands all round. When George Boleyn takes my hand, he places his free hand on my upper arm. It is the traditional gesture of comrades-in-arms and men going into battle. "Mark" is all he says.

Our goodbyes are a small clemency, but we quickly reassemble in line. The guards surround us, ready with their swords. We walk into another courtyard and cross to the other side where we climb the stairs to a sturdy wooden platform. A few plump clouds dot the deep blue sky. The crowd roars when Boleyn comes into view. Kingston directs us to stand at the back of the scaffold, all of us facing the block. He addresses George Boleyn, Lord Rochford as "my lord."

In the distance, I can see paths where I rode Flanders and

Prince into the countryside. I picture the hills in summer, fall, winter, and spring. I recall the fields and brooks, the copper beeches, the boys who approached to pet my horses. I suppose today is perfect for an open-air execution—five men beheaded on a sunny day, all lovers of the queen, they say. For most in the crowd, our deaths will become a story to tell at the tavern, a tale for sitting around the hearth: "I saw the traitors die that day. I was close enough to smell the blood." I slip my hand into my pocket to feel the beads of Paul's rosary. He said he would be close by, but I don't see him anywhere in the first few rows.

The block, with its neck-sized cutout, is a dozen feet away. Two muscular men carry a large wooden crate to the side of the scaffold. I expect this is where they will store our heads and bodies before they bury us—a nobleman, three gentlemen, and a commoner tossed in together. I grip the rosary and repeat my last speech in my head.

A beefy man holds a heavy axe, the sun glinting on its blade. I look up at the sky. Don't think about it. Just remember what you're going to say. Next to me, Brereton inclines his head. "Saw a lot of blood in my soldiering days. After Boleyn and Norris, you'll be used it."

His gruffness distracts me—this fighting man who shares my lot. I secretly recite my last plea to a merciful God. "Lord, give me the courage to die bravely—this is all I ask." Soldiers probably pray something similar.

Kingston reads another proclamation, and the crowd's hisses punctuate each mention of our names. I search for Paul's face—there are hundreds of people pushing forward, all maneuvering to get a better view. Peers of the realm, officials, townspeople, shopkeepers, tradesmen, peasants, children. Suppose Paul hasn't been able to find a spot where I can see him.

Some shout insults about the "whore," even though the queen is not here—perhaps she is on her way to France. Some point and boo at us, especially at Rochford. But others are quiet, holding Bibles to their chests. An older man in a stylish hat stands near the scaffold, his face sorrowful and gray. He has the same straw-colored hair as Weston. I heard that the father knelt before His Majesty pleading for mercy. His rank earned him a hearing, but his appeal could not move an angry king.

And then Paul is there in the second row, his face pale but serene. He must have wriggled and squirmed his way to the front. I thank God for this man's goodness and friendship. I think of Madge again and pray that she is safe at home. I let myself imagine the silken strands of her hair skimming my fingers. I am still amazed that I had been able to kiss her.

George Boleyn, Lord Rochford, of noble blood, goes first, as he has done most of his life. [25] He faces the crowd, and I watch him closely to learn what I should do. He bows to Kingston and the other officials and gives the executioner a golden coin. He begins to speak his last words, and silence falls over the crowd. Some of his phrases startle me. He describes himself as "the most evil man" of all of his acquaintance, "a wretched sinner" who deserves to die "twenty times." I don't believe he committed incest with his sister. He must be thinking of something else.

When the executioner picks up his axe, Rochford turns toward us, his back momentarily to the waiting crowd, his eyes shimmering with tears only we will see. Then, he steps up to the block, kneels, and places his head carefully on the wood. Whispering a prayer for God's forgiveness, he stretches his arms straight out to the side—the sign, I now assume, that he is ready for death. The executioner positions the axe above Boleyn's bare, pink neck and assesses his target before taking aim. He raises the blade high to the sky and uses his full force to bring it down.

The crowd murmurs in unison as Rochford's body convulses, and his head drops onto the scaffold next to the block. I stare at the buildings, the clouds, the trees in the distance—anything to avoid seeing what is in front of me.

But my attempts to distract myself are useless. I watch as the executioner picks up my elegant patron's severed head and presents it to the people—a dreadful proof of death.

I clutch the rosary so tightly the cross nearly punctures my palm. I look for Paul's face and watch him press his Bible to his chest as he moves his lips in prayer. The first killing is horrific, but it is over. George Boleyn, Lord Rochford, the gracious courtier who loved music and his sister, is a ruined, broken, bloodstained corpse.

Sir Henry Norris is next. After bowing to the constable and the executioner, he faces the crowd and asks for God's forgiveness—that is all he says. His right leg quivers but he shows no other sign of fear. The spectators roar as his head is cut from his body, but the crowd is getting smaller, I notice. Perhaps the rest of us aren't notorious enough to compete with the lure of a fine Sunday in May.

Weston is suddenly stronger and more impressive than he was while we were waiting. He gives the executioner a golden coin. His last words could have applied to me as much as to him. "I had thought to live in sin another twenty or thirty years and then to make amends. I never thought it would come to this."

No, me neither.

Weston looks at his father, kneels, and quickly dies. Brereton clasps my arm in friendship. We are comrades now. "See you on the other side," he says.

When his name is called, he approaches the block and stands motionless for a long minute, a shadow of defiance in his stance. He raises his chin and looks out over the crowd. His voice booms, but he says only that he has offended the king and asks for the prayers of all good people. His display of strength bolsters me. Nothing else matters now, only that I meet death calmly.

"Mark Smeaton, step forward. You have been sentenced to death for the crime of treason. Do you wish to speak?" I hear my own heart beating and leaves rustling on the nearby trees. I look out at the crowd, now a third of its original size.

After each execution, workmen scuttled forward to pick up each man's corpse and severed head. They have placed them in the crate with more care than I expected. But the scaffold is now drenched in blood, and the smell envelops me as I begin to move. I nearly lose my footing in the slippery liquid, but I quickly regain my equilibrium. I remind myself of the rule of performing: Do not let an early error steal your confidence. It's how you finish that matters. I glance backward to see my own footprints in someone's blood, or more likely, in the combined blood of all four men.

I hold the rosary and thank God for the grace he has shown me. "Masters, I pray you all pray for me, for I have deserved this death."

That much is true. I deserve to die for my cowardice, although not for treason or having sex with Anne Boleyn. But all of this is be-tween me and God now. I no longer care. I place the rosary in Kingston's open hand, and as the others had done, I remove Paul's coin from my pocket and give it to the executioner. I stand quietly for a few seconds before kneeling and positioning my neck on the block. I stretch my arms out wide.

And then the music pours over me, pulsating and alive.

I am back in Cardinal Wolsey's chapel, a young boy singing in the choir. Master Peter leads us, and our hymn fills the church and ascends to the highest rafters. The men's voices, which are deep and strong, alternate with the boys' voices, which are as light and clear as glass. Sounds echo and reverberate. Chains of notes separate and then coalesce. To me, the music is magnificent and astonishing. It escorts and shelters me.

40

ECHO PARK

Late May 1536

Madge Shelton, Norfolk

There's a wood near Shelton Hall where the trees block out the sun. When I was little, the darkness frightened me, but these days, I find it matches my mood. Then, as now, sounds echo in the shadows—the squawks of birds, an occasional call of a fox. Now I come to Echo Park to remember those who died, Mark most of all.

After I saw him, the priest accompanied me as we left the Tower and walked to a carriage waiting in an adjacent road. By unspoken agreement, we went far out of our way to avoid seeing the scaffold. "I am going back inside," the priest told me, "to give him what comfort I can." I must have looked doubtful because he added, "I have money to bribe the guards."

"Are you sure you have enough?" I asked, and then I gave him all the coins I had.

My sister, my serving woman, and my slumbering greyhound made up the traveling group—all of us silent, though Mary sobbed from time to time. Gilbert Cromwell rode on horseback beside the closed carriage until we reached the city outskirts. I wasn't sure whether he was protecting us or making sure we truly departed.

Once we pulled away, I leaned my head against the carriage back and reviewed every second of my time with Mark. I sealed it in my memory. His wooden box of music was on the seat beside me. Galahad shuffled and rearranged his paws several times before he rested his narrow head on my foot and went to sleep.

After we arrived at Shelton Hall, I stayed in bed for several days, my grief and anguish becoming a sickness that poisoned my body and soul. The servants tried to care for me, and my old nurse sat at my side. Mary brought Galahad into the room, hoping he would comfort me. She held and stroked my hand. When my mother arrived from London, she told them, "There is no consolation for events like these. We must leave her for a while."

Once I began to recover, my mother talked about the executions. "The men met death with courage—this is the report I have. All five died as gentlemen, and the people remarked on it." She looked at me directly. "Mark died quickly and without pain."

"He died because ambitious people lied to please the king."

She didn't deny it, saying only, "I haven't stopped praying for all of them . . . especially your Mark."

She witnessed my cousin's execution—it was her duty to be nearby. In Anne Boleyn's final speech, she described the king as a "merciful prince" and a "gentle and sovereign lord." I heard this story with some bitterness. [26] If my cousin had exercised equal caution during her last year as queen, the others would be alive. But she suffered reversals of fate that were not her fault. I try to remember this.

Sir Henry sent me a letter written in the Tower. It began with, "Perhaps our marriage was not meant to be." His words were kind and stoic, and he wished me well, asking only that I occasionally visit his children. Most people would be surprised to learn that Sir Henry's death pained me less than the deaths of the other men. He

had the solace of believing he would see his wife in the next world—
he always loved her more than me. Maybe in the future, I will be like
him. I will continue with life, as we all must do, but I, too, will have
given my heart to someone who has died before me.

George tried to do everything right, but his devotion to his sister
doomed him. Weston lived with careless charm until his luck ran
out—I doubt he intentionally harmed anyone in his life. Brereton was
a solid man of hunts and dogs and soldiering. He had helped the king
keep peace in the North—no one can explain why he was targeted.

And Mark? He asked me to remember him—as if I could forget.

Mary was with me when I opened the box of music. She gasped
at the sight of the small wooden horse carefully tucked inside. When
I brought it near my heart, she asked, "Do you think Mark hated me?"

"I don't think so—that was a long time ago, something you did
as a child."

"Did you love him?"

"Yes."

"And he loved you?"

"Yes."

"But it wasn't real . . . it had no future."

"It was real to us."

⚜

In the coming months, I will send copies of Mark's compositions to
all my friends and relations. Since no one would sing or play a traitor's songs, I will have the sheets copied without his name. He had
labeled them only as "a madrigal" or "a fantasia," but I recognize
most of the pieces by their verses. I've decided to add titles, to help
draw attention to them: "The Lovers Meet," "My Lady Greensleeves,"
"A Meditation in the Woods."

I will ask those I know to give the sheets to their players, who will pass them along to other players, who will pass them along to players not yet born. I will do all I can to ensure Mark's songs are heard, though he is no longer here to play and sing them. Perhaps one or two will endure.

Author's Note

The Queen's Musician is a work of fiction based on a handful of historical facts. In 1536, a young man named Mark Smeaton was executed for treason, accused of committing adultery with Anne Boleyn. Little is known about him or Madge Shelton, the book's two storytellers. Historians have floated multiple theories about both of them.

Mark Smeaton was a musician in Henry VIII's court, prominent enough to receive gifts and privileges from the king. He confessed to a treasonous affair with the queen, a confession that was almost certainly coerced. On May 17, 1536, he was beheaded along with four other men, all facing similar charges. Anne Boleyn died two days later. He was apparently "lowborn" and only twenty-three or twenty-four when he was executed. George Boleyn did give him a book, although not a volume of ancient poetry.

Most historians today doubt whether Anne Boleyn and the five men were guilty of any the charges against them. The indictments list alleged trysts on dates not long after the queen had given birth and/or when she was in a different location from the one named in the charging documents. Gareth Russell's *The Palace* gives a crisp and entertainingly skeptical summary of the evidence against the queen and the accused men.[27]. Claire Ridgway offers thoughtful and meticulous assessments of the indictments and trials in her books listed below.

Sixteenth-century observers often emphasized Mark Smeaton's "poor degree," as the poet, Sir Thomas Wyatt, phrased it. Some portrayed him as degenerate, the disgraced queen's "boy toy" lover. In other interpretations, he is painted as a pathetic young man, hopelessly infatuated with a woman who is, to use a modern expression, "completely out of his league." Anne Boleyn's partisans sometimes depict him as cowardly. He was, after all, the first to confess. But to me, that is a heartless viewpoint. His interrogation was likely brutal and terrifying.

In our own time, it seems fair to ask whether his lower social status prompted these negative judgments. He lived in an era of blatant, almost inconceivable, bias against the poor. Commoners could be tortured, but wellborn "gentlemen" could not. In our society, Mark Smeaton's "social climbing" would probably be seen as someone working hard to get ahead.

Today, no one knows what Mark Smeaton thought or feared or dreamed of during his lifetime. I have taken the liberty of reimagining a familiar tale from his perspective, blending fact, invention, and speculation. In telling his story, I have simplified and compressed historical events, often presenting them impressionistically, as someone far from power might have seen them. Cardinal Wolsey's surrender of Hampton Court, his political downfall, and his exile to York occurred over an extended period of time—not as the sudden collapse I describe. The resolution of the king's "Great Matter" was also far more complex than my rendition. I invented a number of characters for the purposes of this story, including Gilbert Cromwell and Silas Bray. I have omitted incidents such as the death of William Carey and the arrests of Sir Thomas Wyatt and Sir Richard Page. The accused men's trial was probably even more perfunctory than the one in this book. Hampton Court and the other palaces have been substantially renovated since the time of the novel, so the physical layouts and details are not exact. For readers interested in the factual backdrop to the novel, I have included reliable references throughout. And yes—*Greensleeves* is frequently attributed to Henry VIII, while I imply that Mark Smeaton wrote it. According to experts, the music is likely Elizabethan, composed after both men died.

So little is known about Madge Shelton that some believe that she and Mary Shelton were one person, not two sisters, Madge and Mary, as I have portrayed them. Madge Shelton was one of the queen's ladies and, according to some sources, she was betrothed to Sir Henry Norris. The king may have had a brief affair with one of the Shelton sisters. That's about all we have. There is no historical evidence of a romance between Mark Smeaton and Madge Shelton, and some experts would argue that a relationship between them is unthinkable, particularly on Madge's part. Yet, it also seems safe to assume that both young people were attractive and often in each other's company. I've imagined a relationship and made its illicit nature central to the story.

The Queen's Musician includes better-known historical figures such as Henry VIII, Anne Boleyn, Cardinal Wolsey, and Thomas Cromwell. Even here, there is significant uncertainty about basic facts such as Anne Boleyn's date of birth and the number of times she became pregnant. Experts offer starkly different theories about why the king fell out of love with Anne Boleyn and the exact reasons for her fall and execution [28]. Some five hundred years later, we are still debating the intentions and motivations of these powerful individuals. Were they admirable or vile? Who was guilty of what? I believe this lack of certainty explains why Anne Boleyn's story has spawned so many novels, plays, and films. What we do know is so dramatic and puzzling, but what we know is limited.

I am thankful to the skilled historians who have chronicled Anne Boleyn's life and times. Their expertise and hard work provided my starting point. I am deeply indebted to Claire Ridgway who created the online resource, *The Anne Boleyn Files.* For anyone seeking more detail on what historians know and don't know about Anne Boleyn, Mark Smeaton, and other characters in the novel, I recommend Ridgway's book, *The Fall of Anne Boleyn: A Countdown*, www.thefallo-fanneboleyn.com/. It's readable and compelling. Ridgway's YouTube videos covering all the Tudors can be positively addictive.

Other useful historical references include:

Clare Cherry & Claire Ridgway, *George Boleyn: Tudor Poet, Courtier & Diplomat*, 2014, https://claireridgway.com/books/george-boleyn/.

John Guy and Julia Fox, *Hunting the Falcon*, HarperCollins, 2023. This book delves into the historical record and highlights the international political rivalries that contributed to Anne Boleyn's downfall. It also contains information about the legal system at the time and the trials of this novel's central characters.

Eric Ives, *The Life and Death of Anne Boleyn*, Wiley-Blackwell Publishing, 2005.

Miranda Kaufmann, *Black Tudors*, Oneworld Publications, 2017, www.mirandakaufmann.com.

Suzannah Lipscomb, *1536: The Year that Changed Henry VIII*, Lion Hudson, 2012, https://suzannahlipscomb.com.

Claire Ridgway, *The Anne Boleyn Files*, www.theanneboleynfiles.com and *The Anne Boleyn Collection, Parts I, II, and III*, https://claireridgway.com. Ridgway's analysis of Mark Smeaton's life and his role in Anne Boleyn's downfall is thoughtful and well-reasoned. You can find it at www.theanneboleynfiles.com/bios/mark-smeaton/.

Alison Weir, *The Lady in the Tower: The Fall of Anne Boleyn*, Ballantine Books, 2010. Weir's book contains an extensive discussion of what is known about Mark Smeaton and how he was regarded at the time.

ENDNOTES

1. For more on the role of music in Henry VIII's life and court, see *Henry VIII: A Machiavellian Musical Monarch,* www.royaltymonarchy.com/opinion/papers/henry8.html

2. See Miranda Kaufmann's *Black Tudors* for more on John Blanke: www.mirandakaufmann.com/black-tudors.html

3. Key historians describe Anne Boleyn finding a similar drawing. See Alison Weir, *The Lady in the Tower*, Ballantine Books, page 37; Eric Ives, *The Life and Death of Anne Boleyn*, Blackwell Publishing, page 145–146.

4. Adapted from "Sugar in Tudor England," Renaissance English History Podcast, http://www.englandcast.com/2019/07/episode-126-sugar-in-tudor-england/.

5. There are conflicting theories about how and when Anne Boleyn initially attracted the king's attention, and my fictional version combines elements of several of them. For a historical account, see Claire Ridgway's "Anne Boleyn Plays Perseverance: March 1522," *The Anne Boleyn Files*, www.theanneboleynfiles.com/anne-boleyn-plays-perseverance/ and "Henry VIII Falls in Love with Anne Boleyn," *The Anne Boleyn Files*, https://www.theanneboleynfiles.com/henry-viii-falls-in-love-with-anne-boleyn/

6. See Eric Ives, *The Life and Death of Anne Boleyn*, Blackwell Publishing, for a historical analysis of the white falcon's symbolism.

7. This scene draws from Claire Ridgway's "Childbirth in Medieval and Tudor Times by Sarah Bryson," *The Tudor Society*, www.tudorsociety.com/childbirth-in-medieval-and-tudor-times-by-sarah-bryson/

8. For more, see "The Holbein Gate & the Secret Marriage of Anne Boleyn," *The Tudor Travel Guide,* https://thetudortravelguide.com/2020/01/25/the-holbein-gate-the-secret-marriage-of-anne-boleyn/

9. For historical depictions of Anne Boleyn's coronation, see Claire Ridgway's series of articles in *The Anne Boleyn Files*, www.theanneboleynfiles.com/anne/coronation/ and John Guy and Julia Fox, *Hunting the Falcon* (2023), Chapter 20, https://www.harpercollins.com/products/hunting-the-falcon-john-guyjulia-fox?variant=410062090073186

10. Miranda Kaufmann's *Black Tudors* contains more information about Blanke: www.mirandakaufmann.com/black-tudors.html.

11. Adapted from a poem by Rumi. The Persian poet's work was not translated into European languages until the late eighteenth century, but I believe his words capture Mark's thoughts: https://www.goodreads.com/quotes/5322592-1-one-went-to-the-door-of-the-beloved-and and https://rumiscircle.com/translating-rumi/

12. See Claire Ridgway, "The birth of Elizabeth I," *The Anne Boleyn Files*, https://www.theanneboleynfiles.com/the-birth-of-elizabeth-i/.

13. See Elizabethi.org, "Queen Elizabeth I: Christening, Contemporary Account," https://www.elizabethi.org/contents/earlyyears/christening.htm.

14. Claire Ridgway, "The Pregnancies of Anne Boleyn and Catherine of Aragon," *The Anne Boleyn Files*, https://www.theanneboleynfiles.com/the-pregnancies-of-anne-boleyn-and-catherine-of-aragon/ and Eric Ives, *The Life and Death of Anne Boleyn*, www.goodreads.com/book/show/31086.The_Life_and_Death_of_Anne_Boleyn.

15. The Tudor Enthusiast, "The Execution of Bishop John Fisher," https://thetudorenthusiast.weebly.com/blog/the-execution-of-bishop-john-fisher

16. For an interesting summary of Sir Thomas More's life and trial, see Douglas O. Linder, "The Trial of Sir Thomas More: An Account," *Famous Trials*, https://famous-trials.com/thomasmore/986-home

17. Claire Ridgway writes about the execution of the Carthusian Monks in *The Anne Boleyn Files* at https://www.theanneboleynfiles.com/19-june-1535-the-executions-of-three-carthusian-monks/

18. "Nonesuch", a traditional Irish folk song, www.traditionalmusic.co.uk/irish-songs-ballads-lyrics/nonesuch.htm

19. My re-creation of this conversation between Anne Boleyn and Sir Francis Weston is adapted from several historical accounts, notably Alison Weir, *The Lady in the Tower*, Ballantine Books, page 214 and Claire Ridgway's reporting in *The Anne Boleyn Files*. See for example: www.theanneboleynfiles.com/the-arrests-of-sir-francis-weston-and-sir-william-brereton/.

20. This chapter is based on a reported exchange between Anne Boleyn and Sir Henry Norris often called the "dead men's shoes" conversation. I have adapted my retelling from Claire Ridgway's summaries in *The Anne Boleyn Files*: "Was Anne Boleyn in love with Henry Norris?" at www.theanneboleynfiles.com/anne-boleyn-love-henry-norris/ and "29 April 1536: Anne Boleyn, the Marmalade Cupboard and Dead Men's Shoes" at www.theanneboleynfiles.com/29-april-1536-anne-boleyn-the-marmalade-cupboard-and-dead-mens-shoes/. Another scholarly source is John Guy and Julia Fox, *Hunting the Falcon* (2023) https://www.harpercollins.com/products/hunting-the-falcon-john-guyjulia-fox?variant=41006209073186

21. Anne Boleyn apparently spoke of this exchange with Mark Smeaton after her arrest, and I have reimagined it from his point of view. You can read differing interpretations of this conversation in Alison Weir, *The Lady in the Tower*, Ballantine Books, page 239; Susannah Lipscomb, *1536: The Year that Changed Henry VIII*, pages 75–77; John Guy and Julia Fox, *Hunting the Falcon* (2023) https://www.harpercollins.com/products/hunting-the-falcon-john-guyjulia-fox?variant=41006209073186, and in Claire Ridgway's reporting in *The Anne Boleyn Files*, for example, www.theanneboleynfiles.com/courtly-love-flirtation-and-the-fall-of-anne-boleyn-part-two/.

22. You can read historical accounts of Anne Boleyn's last days as Queen in John Guy and Julia Fox, *Hunting the Falcon* (2023) https://www.harpercollins.com/products/hunting-the-falcon-john-guyjulia-fox?variant=41006209073186, and Claire Ridgway, *The Fall of Anne Boleyn, A Countdown*, https://www.thefallofanneboleyn.com/. Another intriguing summary is Ridgway's review of the BBC2 program, *The Last Days of Anne Boleyn* which includes comments from Hilary Mantel, Philippa Gregory, and David Starkey among others, https://www.theanneboleynfiles.com/the-last-days-of-anne-boleyn-a-[review/.

23. This chapter is a fictional account of what is known about the trial and the evidence presented against all four men. For a historical view, see Claire Ridgway, *The Fall of Anne Boleyn: A Countdown*, www.thefallofanneboleyn.com/, and Alison Weir, *The Lady in the Tower: The Fall of Anne Boleyn*, pages 309–311.

24. See Claire Ridgway for a well-reasoned discussion of Mark Smeaton's confession in *Mark Smeaton—Part 2*, https://www.theanneboleynfiles.com/mark-smeaton-part-2/

25. The men's statements and other details about this historical event have been adapted from Claire Ridgway's *The Anne Boleyn Files*, https://www.theanneboleynfiles.com/17-may-1536-the-execution-of-george-boleyn-lord-rochford/. See her blog and video discussing the men's executions at www.theanneboleynfiles.com.

26. Most studies of Anne Boleyn's life provide detailed descriptions of her execution and last words. See for example, Claire Ridgway, *The Fall of Anne Boleyn: A Countdown*, www.thefallofanneboleyn.com/ and John Guy and Julia Fox, *Hunting the Falcon* (2023) https://www.harpercollins.com/products/hunting-the-falcon-john-guyjulia-fox?variant=41006209073186.

27. Gareth Russell, *The Palace: From the Tudors to the Windsors, 500 Year of British History at Hampton Court*, Atria Books, 2023. See pages 67–72. https://www.amazon.com/Palace-Windsors-British-History-Hampton/dp/1982169060

28. See Claire Ridgway, "The Last Days of Anne Boleyn—A Review and Rundown," at https://www.theanneboleynfiles.com/the-last-days-of-anne-boleyn-a-review/ and "Henry VIII and Anne Boleyn—How Did Love Turn to Hate?" at https://www.theanneboleynfiles.com/henry-viii-and-anne-boleyn-how-did-love-turn-to-hate/.

AFTER YOU FINISH

Questions for Book Clubs and Individual Readers

Please choose the questions that interest you most.

1. *The Queen's Musician* takes place during the Tudor era. How acquainted were you with the Tudors before you began this book?

2. Have you read other novels or seen movies or TV programs set in this era? Do you have a favorite? What did you enjoy about it?

3. How familiar were you with Anne Boleyn's story before you began? Had you heard of Mark Smeaton? How did your starting point affect your reactions as you read the novel?

4. This novel features two storytellers: Mark Smeaton and Madge Shelton. What are the key differences in their backgrounds and perspectives? Do you see any similarities in their personalities, beliefs, and values?

5. How would you describe Henry VIII as he appears in this novel? What about Anne Boleyn?

6. Historians, novelists, playwrights, and moviemakers have described Henry VIII and Anne Boleyn in diverse ways. Are the depictions in this book similar to or different from those you've encountered elsewhere?

7. Both Mark and Madge observe Anne Boleyn's astonishing rise and fall. Did the queen's character and personality contribute to her ruin, or do you think any woman in her circumstances would have met a similar end?

8. Cromwell accuses Mark of crimes he did not commit. Is there any way Mark could have avoided what happened to him? Did he make any mistakes, either large or small?

9. Do you have a favorite among the other four men convicted and executed along with Mark? Which one and why?

10. What about the other secondary characters? Did any of them draw your particular attention? Which ones?

11. Mark and Madge lived in a society with rigid class boundaries. How did these strict social rules affect each of them?

12. Gossip and rumor were commonplace in Henry VIII's court. What role did rumormongering play in the novel? Which characters suffered most from it?

13. Do you see any similarities between the politics of the Tudor court and our own politics today? If so, what are they? What are the clearest differences between then and now?

14. Do you think there is a moral or lesson to this story? If so, how would you describe it?

ACKNOWLEDGMENTS

So many brilliant and kind human beings offered advice and encouragement while I was working on *The Queen's Musician*. My dear and astonishing friends, John Immerwahr and Kathy Byrnes, reviewed multiple drafts and contributed wonderful ideas. Kathy persuaded her book club to read an early version, and the group's detailed insights were particularly helpful. John and Kathy's enthusiasm lifted my spirits throughout this project. John Doble, a gifted playwright and screenwriter, suggested several key plot tweaks and twists. Elizabeth Doble offered wise and generous counsel from her publishing career. I am grateful to Gail Weigl, an Anne Boleyn maven who once lived near Hampton Court. Gail gave me fascinating and useful historical guidance. My friend, the dazzling pianist and composer Josu Gallastegui, taught me so much about music. Much of what I learned from him is reflected in this book.

I have also benefited from the savvy and expertise of literary reviewers and editors, including Mark DeGasperi, Mark Spencer, Now Novel's Jordan Kantey, and Lisa Ferraro Parmelee. I am hugely indebted to Brooke Warner at SheWritesPress/SparkPress and my fabulous copy editor, Jennifer Caven, My amazing editing and production team included Lauren Wise, my savvy and reassuring associate publisher, Julie Metz who designed my stunning cover, and Stacey Aaronson who created the elegant interior design. I'd also like to give a round of applause to my terrific BookSparks team: Rylee Warner, Hanna Lindsley, and Crystal Patriarche.

Writing can be a solitary enterprise, but I have been supported by an extraordinary group of friends and colleagues. My deepest thanks to one and all.

ABOUT THE AUTHOR

Photo credit: Susan Teplinsky Photography

Martha Jean Johnson is a writer of fiction and non-fiction and the author of a series of books and articles on public opinion and public policy. *The Queen's Musician* is her debut novel. She also reviews trends in historical fiction and discusses her own love of reading and writing in her biweekly blog, *Historical Magic*. She recently worked with the National Issues Forums Institute, an organization that encourages civil discourse and nonpartisan deliberation on national and local issues.

During a long public policy career, she analyzed and reported on American public thinking, working with noted social analyst and public opinion pioneer, Daniel Yankelovich. She has published articles in *USA Today* and *The Huffington Post* and appeared on CNN, MSNBC, and PBS. She is the author of a series of nonfiction paperbacks on major political issues, co-authored with Scott Bittle and published by HarperCollins. She holds degrees from Mount Holyoke College, Brown University, and Simmons College. She lives in Jersey City, New Jersey.

Looking for your next great read?

We can help!

Visit www.gosparkpress.com/next-read or
scan the QR code below for a list
of our recommended titles.

SparkPress is an independent boutique publisher
delivering high-quality, entertaining, and engaging
content that enhances readers-lives, with a special
focus on commercial and genre fiction.